"THANK YOU, GREAT ONE, FOR ALLOWING ME TO CATCH YOU. THANK YOU FOR THE BLESSING OF . . ."

His voice trailed off when he saw the legs. *Legs?* He stared at a pair of boots, soggy pants, a jacket . . . a man. Lying on his stomach, a harpoon jutting from his back.

The hunter swore softly, stunned by what he was seeing. Had he fallen asleep? Was this a dream?

The pack suddenly rumbled and he flinched, losing his grip on the flashlight. It fell, bounced on the ice and went out with a glassy pop. Darkness. He was alone with a corpse. Or worse, a tupilak, one of the demons his great-uncle had told him stories about.

Fighting to remain calm, he stumbled back to his pack and found the smaller flashlight he kept in reserve. He shined the tiny beam at the body, then redirected the light at the hole in the ice. Still incapable of comprehending this reality, he stood transfixed by the rising and falling of the waves. Until he noticed another object in the hole. A chunk of ice, he assumed.

Leaning forward, he aimed the light at it.

There was a face wavering eerily just below the surface: purple skin, blackened lips, mouth agape in a silent scream, two wide, terrified eyes staring up at him . . .

Other Inupiat Eskimo Mysteries by
Christopher Lane
from Avon Books

ELEMENTS OF A KILL
SEASON OF DEATH
A SHROUD OF MIDNIGHT SUN
SILENT AS THE HUNTER

CHRISTOPHER LANE

A DEADLY QUIET

AN INUPIAT ESKIMO MYSTERY

AVON BOOKS
An Imprint of HarperCollins*Publishers*

This is a work of fiction. Names, characters, places, and incidents are products of the author's imagination or are used fictitiously and are not to be construed as real. Any resemblance to actual events, locales, organizations, or persons, living or dead, is entirely coincidental.

AVON BOOKS
An *Imprint of* HarperCollins*Publishers*
10 East 53rd Street
New York, New York 10022-5299

ISBN: 0-380-81626-1
www.avonbooks.com

First Avon Books paperback printing: December 2001

Printed in the U.S.A.

10 9 8 7 6 5 4 3 2 1

AUTHOR'S NOTE

WHILE MY NAME is on the cover of this book, it should be noted that it was a team effort. Without my support crew, *A Deadly Quiet*—the entire Inupiat Eskimo series, for that matter—would be gathering dust on a shelf in my office. Therefore, I would like to take this opportunity to thank those responsible for seeing the project through to completion.

First, a genuine *taiku* to Lyssa Keusch, my editor at Avon Books. She has suffered long in her attempts to keep me and the series on track. (No small thing, I assure you.) It is her hard work that fills these pages. Also, a big thank-you to her staff and the various departments at Avon who are responsible for the mechanics of producing these lovely books.

I would also like to express my appreciation to Karen Solem at Writers House. It was Karen who introduced me to Avon and saved the first manuscript from a slow death on my bookshelf.

My family deserves credit for many things, including putting up with my moods and sometimes unorthodox work habits. My wife, Melodie, has been especially patient, allowing me to accumulate great heaps of Alaskan research materials, spread them out until the carpet disappears, and dredge through them for weeks on end. Thanks to my children for giving me space and, occasionally, the peace and quiet necessary to think out plot lines, and to my parents for their ideas and encouragement.

Lastly, I would like to thank the Inupiat—the Real People! I have enjoyed learning more about their culture and have come to highly respect their pride, their unique heritage, as well as their ability to adapt in a world of radical and perpetual change.

Please note that the story inside these covers is fictional. The events, characters, and even some of the locations were manufactured by my imagination.

I now bid you *tutqiun* (peace). May this book be a window on the mysterious, hypnotically beautiful land and people of Alaska.

Christopher Lane
May 2001

GLOSSARY

aaka—mother; grandmother
aapa—father; grandfather
aarigaa—terrific
aimaagvIk—home
aiviQ—walrus
akkupak—immediately
anaaluk—uncle
anaiyyuliqsI—minister
anaqasaagiaq—afternoon
anun—man
ataata—grandfather; great-uncle
ilat—family, relatives
ilgugniq—frostbite of the face
imiq—an alcoholic beverage
inyusuq—a person's soul
ivrulik—sod house
kila—animal helping spirit
kinnaq tinmiaq—crazy bird
Manaqtaaq AnugI—Black Wind
manIk—money
manniliqun—egg beater
miqliqtuuraq—baby
nigrun—animal
naluaqmiu—white person
naluaqmiut—white people
nanuq—polar bear

niu—leg
nuna—earth
paglan—welcome
piksrun—shovel
putu—hole
qaummaq—light, brightness
savaaq—job
siku—ice
sikuqqat—ice flow
sikuliaq—thin ice
suannan—power
TaggaQ—shadow
taiku—thank you
tanik—white person
tarrak—a dark, angry spirit lingering near a burial site, refusing to enter the afterworld
timi—body
tupilak—(plural; *tupilek*) a dangerous, part man/part animal monster thought to be created by a shaman in order to get revenge on enemies; these demonic beings would lie in wait under the ice, crawl on the ground, even fly to attack their victims
tuttu—caribou
tuungak—spirits
ugruk—bearded seal
umiaqpak—ship
unnuamI—during the night
uumman—heart
uvlugiaq—star

ONE

Lying prostrate on the frozen surface of the Chukchi Sea, propped up on his elbows, rifle cradled in his arms, he waited for the ugruk to turn its suspicious gaze away. It couldn't see him, he knew. He was as motionless as the ice itself, clothed in white from his hooded parka to his backpack to his bunny boots, hidden behind a shooting screen. Yet somehow the animal seemed to sense his approach.

It had taken hours to gain this position. Hours of crawling, sliding, flattening himself against the pack, inching forward . . . And he still wasn't in range. Not quite.

He would have been if this ugruk hadn't been so restless. Instead of emerging from the sea and basking lazily in the sunlight as was the habit of the average bearded seal, it had remained unusually aware of its surroundings, as though conscious of the fact that it was being stalked. Every few minutes it would lift its head, scan the floes, and then wriggle to a new resting place.

A dozen yards more and the hunt would be over,

he told himself. He "walked" six feet on elbows and knees, hesitated, ate up another three yards. Almost there. He was scooting along again when the seal lifted its head and barked at him. He stopped and watched it from behind the shooting screen. How could it possibly know he was there? He was upwind, virtually invisible.

Unless this was no ordinary ugruk, he thought, examining it through the scope. Perhaps it was peculiar, its kila charmed.

He waited until the animal readjusted itself and rolled away from him before continuing his slow, steady advance. Ten minutes later he was finally within range. He fingered the amulet dangling around his neck and made a conscious effort to relax before putting his eye to the sight, his finger to the trigger.

"Aarigaa . . ." he whispered in admiration. Such a big, beautiful ugruk. Charmed or not, it would be a fortuitous catch.

In the scope, he saw it abruptly twist its head toward him, almost as if it knew what he was planning and was either resigned to its fate or so arrogant that it doubted his ability to make the kill. It emitted another raspy bark and glared at him, seemingly daring him to shoot. It was a dare he would accept . . . and win.

Lining the cross hairs up on the beast, he curled his finger around the trigger and gave it a soft tug. Instead of kicking him in the shoulder, the rifle merely clicked loudly.

The seal struggled up and bellowed at him.

Damn! He aimed, pulled the trigger again. *Click!* What the . . . ?! He examined the gun, checked the ammunition. It was loaded, ready to go. He fired a third time. *Click!* Something was jammed. He shook his head and swore. The weapon had never failed him. He had hardly missed a target with it in twenty seasons. And now, as he was about to bag the biggest seal of his life, it had suddenly and inexplicably jammed? Impossible!

The ugruk admonished him with a mocking bark, then waddled off into the floes.

"I still get you!" he vowed angrily. Rising, he trotted stiffly back to the snow machine and sled he had parked a half mile away. Packing his rifle away in its case, he extracted a harpoon and a scratcher, then stuffed a trap into his pack, just in case the animal took to water. No matter how smart this ugruk turned out to be, he would be smarter.

Hustling back, he found the seal's trail. A very intelligent animal, he admitted, following the marks with his eyes. It had not only detected his presence, but had realized the danger of sitting out in the open and chosen to take refuge in a series of topaz-blue ice hills. It would almost be a shame to defeat such a cunning adversary. Almost.

He ran after it, pack ice crunching under his boots, breath rising and hanging in the arctic air like puffs of steam. Rounding the first knoll, he lost the trail. He slowed to a walk and squinted at the ground. It couldn't have just disappeared. He turned around and was about to retrace his steps when he spied his quarry. Maybe it wasn't so crafty after all.

Instead of slithering farther into the hills, it had merely relocated to another expansive flat off to the left. Sprawled out, face to the sun, it appeared to be asleep.

He moved quickly, trotting to within a hundred yards before dropping to his knees. The seal remained motionless. Whatever luck it had accumulated was running out.

Back on his stomach, he used the scratcher to rake the ground before pulling himself a body length forward. The two-foot wooden tool had a bony claw on the end that, when scraped across the ice, simulated the sound of a seal working at its breathing hole. His movements from here on in would mimic those of a seal traversing the floes. He would slither along, through puddles if necessary, pretending to rest every now and then, until he was close enough to impale the ugruk with the harpoon. It was the "old way" of hunting. Not as quick or as easy as a rifle. But just as effective.

He was still half a football field away from the ugruk, doing his best to look and sound like a seal, when he heard the deep, familiar rumble of the pack shifting. He felt the ground beneath him quake and braced himself for a shift.

Roused from slumber, the seal abruptly stood up, layers of fat jiggling. There was another groan and a small lead opened just a few feet from the seal. An escape route. It was so convenient as to be spooky. Was this ugruk a magician?

He leapt to his feet and made a mad, stumbling dash at it, harpoon raised. But the seal casually pulled itself to the lead and slid into the water. By the time he arrived, the lead was already shrinking.

It was some sort of sorcery, he decided, watching the two plates of ice close ranks over the water. He had seen leads yawn and snap shut fast enough to trap a man. But this . . . ? An ugruk who discerned that trouble was in the wind and exhibited the ability to control the shape of the ice?

For a long moment he considered giving up. He wouldn't starve if he went home empty-handed. There was a grocery store just a few blocks from home. Still, he was a hunter and had been all his life. Letting an ugruk get the better of him rubbed him wrong. He was too stubborn to concede defeat.

Fueled by pride, as well as a tinge of annoyance at the animal's ability to escape, he began investigating the area. There had to be a breathing hole nearby, otherwise the ugruk had sealed its own fate and would die under the pack. A half hour later he found it: a gap the size of a golf ball through which he could see the dark waters of the Arctic Ocean splashing back and forth.

He took out his trap and hurriedly set it up over the hole. It was a crude device, nothing more than a feather suspended by sticks, yet it would alert him to the seal's presence. When the animal came up for air, its arrival would cause a rush of wind. The feather indicator would quiver and he would thrust the harpoon into the hole. The ugruk wouldn't have time to be afraid, much less evade the attack.

Kneeling over the trap, gripping his weapon, he looked from the feather to the western sky and back again in a split second. The already faint glow of day was fading. He guessed that it was around one P.M. It would be pitch-dark in another hour and remain so until ten tomorrow morning, when the sun made another brief visit, hovering just beneath the rim of the horizon. Hopefully, he wouldn't be here for that. But if he was . . . so be it. He had a flashlight in his pack, a small stove, enough food and water to see him through until dawn. He could use his sub-zero-rated sleeping bag to weather the night in the open. If he got cold, he would simply retrace his footprints back to the snow machine and either try to head back home or, more likely, pitch his tent and wait for first light.

Hunched over the breathing hole, he shook his head, amazed at how radically things had changed yet, in many ways, stayed the same. He was engaged in an activity that had been carried out by his ancestors for hundreds of years, using basically the same technology they had employed. And yet his own father had never owned a down sleeping bag. His grandfather had never even heard of a snow machine. Extracting a granola bar from the pocket of his REI expedition jacket, he tried to recall the old days when, as a child, he had gone along on hunts, exploring the floes by dog sled, dressed in caribou-lined clothing and mukluks, eating dried whale meat and whatever they managed to catch. He missed the camaraderie, the laughter, the good feelings.

Eyes on the feather, he began to hum a song that

his granduncle had taught him, something the men had sung on nearly every outing.

The great sea
Has set me adrift
It moves me
As the weeds in a great river,
Earth and great weather,
Move me,
Have carried me away
And move my inward parts with joy.

Joy. That was the intangible element. It had accompanied their hunts like a familiar spirit, a friend. Whether they were tracking caribou, out at a whaling camp, or fishing for salmon . . . Joy. A deep-seated contentment. A sense of anticipation. Glad to be part of the circle of life. Thankful for the gifts of the tuungak and the gifts of God.

He laughed. It was an odd mix, this striving to appease the ruling spirits and, simultaneously, to obey the white man's all-powerful God. It didn't make sense. Either the spirits of wind, sun, snow, fertility, and the animals were in control of the world, or God was. It couldn't be both. Yet strangely, he believed in both. He had been taught to keep the traditions, to observe the taboos *and* to go to church each Sunday. It amounted to covering your bases, he decided with amusement. Since no one was quite sure who was in charge, you had to do your best to keep all the deities satisfied.

He offered a silent shotgun prayer to any and all ears that might be listening, asking that his efforts be blessed, that the elusive ugruk would return and that he would be given a steady hand with which to kill it.

These words were still echoing in his mind when the feather began to flutter wildly. Reacting with a speed and precision honed from a lifetime of practice, he thrust the harpoon in the hole and felt it hit home.

"Aarigaa!" He let out a victory whoop. The fight was over! He was the champion!

Smiling at this, he stood up and took the shovel from his pack. As he folded the metal handle out, he noted that this too was a modern invention. A welcome one. Just a generation ago, instead of collapsible shovels, the People had used bone-tipped clubs to land seals.

This was the reason he hunted, he told himself as he began to chip away at the hole. The thrill of the chase, the breathless moment when the capture was made, and the lingering triumph of the kill. Joy. Pure, distilled.

He sang the song again, boisterously this time, stabbing at the ice. The goal now was to widen the hole until the seal could be extracted through it. Unfortunately, the pack here was thick and hard. He could tell that the process would be long and exhausting, but he didn't mind. He had made the catch! Someone had heard his prayer and the enchanted ugruk had come back. He could hardly wait to tell his friends the story: a jammed gun, the seal's odd behavior, a failed scratcher approach, the successful breathing hole stab. It had the makings of a folktale. If he told it enough, it might become one.

He was still clanking away, making progress by increments, when night fell. According to his watch, it was just after two. He paused to set up his flashlight and unzipped his parka. The job was making him sweat. His arms were sore, his back aching. Yet he felt young and alive.

When the hole was two yards across, he reached for the bobbing harpoon. After he landed the ugruk, he would bless it, give thanks to its kila for sharing the meat with him, then dress the carcass out. If he worked quickly, he would be home in time for dinner. But the trick was landing it. There was an element of risk in this, even for a seasoned hunter. If he yanked too severely on the harpoon, it might come out and the animal would be lost. If he lost his grip on it, the weapon and the catch might drift under the pack. Worse, if he wasn't careful, he could slip and fall in. And there was always the chance that the ice around the hole, weakened by his digging, might collapse beneath him. Going into the water meant death.

He kicked the snow-covered ice at hole's edge until he had established a firm foothold, then adopted a wide stance that would enable him to keep his weight low. Balance was the key here. This was a large ugruk. To land it without a prolonged and possibly dangerous struggle would require both skill and luck.

He took a deep breath, gripped the handle of the

harpoon fiercely, and with a quick twisting motion, propelled the catch to land. The harpoon and the animal slopped into the shadows beyond the beam of his light. He chuckled at this, pleased with his technique. It had been textbook perfect, making the seal seem light as a feather. It all came down to leverage, he told himself.

"Aarigaa!" he shouted again, lifting his head to the stars. The gods were truly with him today. He would have to cajole his nephew into accompanying him next time. This was not to be missed: a test of physical endurance and a mystical experience. No television program could rival it.

He went to the pack and found his knife. Removing it from the sheath, he picked up his flashlight and approached the ugruk.

"Thank you, great one, for allowing me to catch you. Thank you for the blessing of . . ."

His voice trailed off when he saw the legs. Legs? He stared at a pair of boots, soggy pants, a jacket . . . A man. Lying on his stomach, a harpoon jutting from his back.

He swore softly, stunned by what he was seeing. Had he fallen asleep? Was this a dream?

He shuddered as an outlandish but wholly terrifying idea hit him: the ugruk had transformed itself into a man. He had hunted and killed a man!

The pack suddenly rumbled and he flinched, losing his grip on the flashlight. It fell, bounced on the ice and went out with a glassy pop. Darkness. He was alone with a corpse. Or worse: a tupilak. One of the demons his great-uncle had told stories about.

The tupilek were monsters—part animal, part human—the creations of powerful shamans that hid beneath the ice and attacked hunters.

Fighting to remain calm, he stumbled back to his pack and found the smaller flashlight he kept in reserve. He shined the tiny beam at the body, examined it suspiciously, as though it might rise up and attack him at any moment, then redirected the light at the hole in the ice. He blinked at the black water. A tupilak?! Still incapable of comprehending this reality, he stood transfixed by the rising and falling of the waves. Until he noticed another object in the hole. A chunk of ice, he assumed.

Leaning forward, he aimed the light at it.

"Aiyaa!"

There was a face wavering eerily just below the surface: purple skin, blackened lips, mouth agape in a silent scream, two wide, terrified eyes staring up at him.

He swore and slowly backed away. Moving the narrow beam back and forth from the floating face to the beached body, as though light was somehow capable of warding off evil, he grabbed his pack.

The ugruk hadn't been charmed, he realized, turning to run in what he hoped was the direction of his snow machine. It had been cursed.

TWO

"GO-HEAD, RAY. Give it shot."

"I don't know . . ."

"What? You 'fraidy cat?"

"I thought you told me you were the champ, back a few years."

"I was."

"Then get after it."

Ray looked at Billy Bob, who was grinning wildly, then at Lewis, who was giving him a cold stare, daring him to do it.

"He a big chicken," Lewis said disgustedly.

"I don't see you out there," Ray argued.

"Come on, partner," Billy Bob said in his sweetest drawl. "Let's see ya do it."

Ray sighed and shot a look at the bleachers. They were already more than half full and large groups of people were milling around the edges of the basketball court. It would be sort of neat, he decided, to prove that he still had it, especially in front of his family, friends, his peers. But if he blew it . . .

Billy Bob began limbering up, as if he were about

to do something athletic. "Come on, Ray. Stretch out." The cowboy was holding his hat with one hand, trying to touch the tips of his boots with the other.

Taking a deep breath, Ray rolled his shoulders and began to swing his arms.

"Aarigaa . . ." Lewis muttered happily. "That more like it."

"Just once," Ray said. "I do the high kick and that's it. Whether I hit the target or not."

Billy Bob stopped stretching. "I'm betting you can hit it."

"How much?" Lewis asked.

"You'd bet against me?" Ray glared at him.

Lewis shrugged. "Depends on odds."

As Billy Bob and Lewis discussed terms, Ray tried to relax. He had been the champion at this at one time, setting a record in the high kick—a record that had stood for nearly a decade and a half before being shattered just last year by Tommy Reed. Reed, a lanky high school senior, was expected to sweep the events this year.

"He not going do it," Lewis said, purposefully sinking into pigeon English. He did that whenever he really wanted to get under Ray's skin.

"Shore he is," Billy Bob shot back.

"I love being talked about in the third person, when I'm standing right here," Ray murmured.

"Da third what?" Lewis asked.

"He's the third person," Billy Bob explained. "I'm one, yer two, he's three."

Ray hopped up and down for a second, convinced

that no amount of stretching would prepare him for this, then walked to the center of the court. A stuffed ball about the size of a grapefruit was dangling from an adjustable hanger that resembled a portable gallows. The ball was suspended about six feet above the floor, high enough to keep the kids from kicking it, but not as high as it would go for some of the competitors.

Ray blinked at the ball, amazed that he had once been proficient at this skill. It was tricky even at the lower levels. You didn't just jump like mad and try to hit the thing. You had to take off, strike the ball, and land all on the same foot. It was quite a trick.

He noticed that the crowd had grown quiet. They were watching him. He could feel it. He wanted to turn around and walk off the floor, maybe pretend that he was just checking to see if the device was ready to go.

"Give it a kick, Ray-mond!" someone yelled.

"Yeah. Let's see that kick!" someone else shouted.

The crowd began to clap and hoot their encouragement.

Ray stepped back and focused on the ball. This was a bad idea, he decided, something he never would have attempted had it not been for Lewis. What was he trying to prove? That he was still seventeen? That he wasn't a chicken? That he was a crazy thirty-something Inupiat who didn't know when to hang it up?

Unable to decide which, if any of these, might be his motivation, he started forward, crouched slightly, and propelled himself up. If felt smooth, and as he rose into the air he could tell that he would have no problem hitting the ball. He watched his foot kick out, saw it strike the ball, saw the ball fly away on the rope, then felt himself falling.

The trip down was fast. Somehow, he managed to get the kicking foot back under him, thus satisfying the rules. He lost his balance, however, as his ankle gave way, and he landed hard on his back, the air rushing from his lungs in a loud "huff."

The onlookers started to applaud, then changed their minds and issued a series of gasps and "ohs." A terrible silence followed. It was broken, finally, by a cackling laugh.

"Dat was great!" Lewis roared, as if seeing his longtime friend and colleague hit the deck had been the most hilarious experience of his life.

"You okay?" Billy Bob asked, rushing over to help him.

"I'm fine," Ray hissed, raising up. Actually, he was far less than fine. For a long moment he couldn't breathe. Fire raced from his waist to his neck. This subsided quickly and he was able to stand. It was when he got to his feet that he realized he had injured his ankle. He winced and bent to examine it. Lifting the cuff of his Levi's, he saw that it was already swelling, tender to the touch.

"You break it?" Lewis asked.

"I'm gonna break you," Ray muttered.

The crowd, now apparently satisfied that Ray had survived, began to cheer. He raised a hand and waved at them, trying his best to smile. Billy Bob and Lewis tried to assist him off the court, but he refused their offer. It hurt like heck to walk, but it was better than being carried. Even has-been athletes had a modicum of pride.

The three of them went to the locker room, where a dozen or so teenagers and young men were changing for the competition. Ray laid down on a bench and Billy Bob took off in search of ice.

"You got it," Lewis said.

"Got what?"

"Da ball. You hitted it."

"Hitted . . . ?"

"Ya. I lost da bet."

"I feel so sorry for you," Ray said sarcastically. His head was now pounding in time with the pulse in his ankle.

"I drop ten dollars."

"That's what you get for betting against me."

"Wonder if da cowboy go two outta three?"

"Doesn't matter."

"I wanna shot to get my ten back."

"Tough. I'm not going to risk breaking my neck again."

"You didn't break neck."

"I almost did. Then I would have had to break yours."

Lewis laughed. "You have to catch me first."

"I'd catch you," Ray vowed. "Eventually." He reached down and pressed on the skin above the ankle. Pain shot into his foot and he grimaced.

"It hurt?"

"No, Lewis," Ray said angrily, "it feels wonderful. Put your ankle up here and let me show you how it feels. Just let me get a two-by-four first and—"

Lewis laughed again. He seemed quite amused by all of this.

"Good thing Margaret isn't here yet."

"Oh, she here. I saw her in da bleachers."

"With the kids, I suppose," Ray grumbled.

"Ya. And Grandfadda."

"Oh, well, perfect. I can't wait to hear what he has to say. I'll never live this down."

"You hit da ball," Lewis reminded.

"Big deal."

"It is big deal for old guy, like you."

"*Old?* We're the same age!"

"No. You three monts older. Makes big diff-rence."

"Are you saying you could beat me at the high kick?"

Lewis shrugged. "I still got da dunk."

Ray shook his head. Lewis was a full foot shorter than he was, and the only dunking the little twerp had ever done was over at the elementary school where the baskets had been lowered to about five feet. He had plenty of verbal and physical energy, but not much in the way of vertical leap.

Ray was about to say something to this effect when Billy Bob showed up with an Ace bandage and a pair of Pepsis.

"Where's the ice?" Ray asked.

"Right here." The cowboy poured the colas off into a sink and then held the two paper cups against Ray's swollen ankle.

"Couldn't you find a bag of ice?"

Billy Bob shook his head. "I had to shell out almost six dollars just to get these." He lifted one of the cups away and squinted at the injury. "You need a doctor?"

"No."

"It might be broke."

"I doubt it."

"Looks perty bad."

Ray hoped the cowboy was wrong. It would be the worst form of humiliation to break a bone in an exhibition in front of most of the town. Anyone who hadn't actually witnessed it would hear about it by evening.

"Maybe I oughta call a doctor," Billy Bob said.

"I'm fine!" Ray insisted, gingerly wrapping the bandage around his ankle.

"That's good to hear," a voice said.

He looked over and saw the captain approaching.

"So . . . Attla," the captain said, unable to hide a grin, "I hear you did a neat little acrobatic trick for the crowd."

"Who told you?"

"I got a full rundown from about five people as soon as I came through the front door. Sounds like it was really something."

"Yeah, too bad you missed it, sir," Ray said.

"Seriously, you okay?"

"He got da ball," Lewis explained. "He just have trouble on da landing."

"He mighta broke somethin'," Billy Bob said.

"I'm fine. I just sprained my ankle."

"So you're good to go?" the captain asked.

Ray could tell that the question had to do with more than just his health. "Why, what's up?"

"Got a call from TaggaQ."

"Yeah. And . . . ?"

The captain glanced around. "Let's talk outside." He led them out of the locker room and through the exit. Ray hobbled along, fighting to keep up. Each step was monumentally painful, and if it hadn't been for his pride, he would have asked to be taken to the E.R. The guys were probably right. It was most likely broken.

Outside it was already quite dark. Columns of steam stood over the surrounding buildings, professing to the subzero temperature as well as the absence of wind. It was perfectly still and also perfectly clear, the stars gleaming through a thin band of Northern Lights.

"Lookie there," Billy Bob gushed. He pointed at the sky. "Ain't that perty?"

The captain, all business now, never even looked up. "Got a call from TaggaQ," he repeated. "They turned up a couple of popsicles out there."

"Anybody we know?" Ray asked. TaggaQ was fifty miles up the coast to the west, within the scope of the North Slope Borough, but not on the beaten path of the Barrow Police Department.

"No ID yet."

"What happen?" Lewis asked. "A-nudder nanuq get some-body?"

"Another what?" Billy Bob wanted to know.

"No. It wasn't a polar bear this time. They were found under the pack ice."

"By whom?" Ray asked.

"Whom?" Lewis said, squinting.

"Some local guy was out hunting and found the bodies when he dug out a seal hole."

Ray shrugged. "Probably an accident. They were probably out there hunting too." Every so often someone was lost to the ice floes. If they weren't attacked by a polar bear, a true threat, they could easily get lost or injured, succumb to hypothermia, or simply fall into the water and not make it out. Ray had experience along all those lines.

"Probably," the captain agreed. "But we need to look into it."

"Why can't Kuleak handle it?" Ray asked. Charlie Kuleak was the law enforcement officer at TaggaQ.

"No one seems to know where Kuleak is," the captain explained.

"Day try da hooch factory?" Lewis asked jokingly. Though TaggaQ, like Barrow, was officially dry, liquor somehow managed to find its way into the village. Kuleak had a history of drinking, and had actually been found intoxicated on the job more than once. He had retained his position for the simple reason that the borough had been unable to find a replacement. You couldn't pay a city cop, or even a Barrow cop, for that matter, enough to live in tiny TaggaQ. There was virtually no crime and the only thing to do was sit on your duff, drink coffee, and try to stay awake. It was worse than being a bank security guard.

"Very funny," the captain said in a stern, professional tone. "Anyway, I need somebody to head over there and check things out."

Lewis, Billy Bob, and Ray just stood there.

"No volunteers, huh?"

"I gotta be at da games," Lewis said. "I'm da head judge for da seal hop race."

Ray rolled his eyes at this.

"Uh . . ." Billy Bob said, "uh . . . I was kinda hopin' to . . . I mean, I was supposed to . . ." His voice trailed off as he failed to come up with an excuse.

"Okay. Ray and Billy Bob," the captain said. "You're on it."

Ray winced as his ankle shot pain up his leg.

"Is that gonna be a problem?" the captain asked, nodding at the taped ankle.

"It's pretty sore," Ray tried. He truly did not want to go all the way out to TaggaQ, miss the first afternoon of games, get home late . . . Or worse: have to lay over up at the village. But neither did he want to wimp out and be taken to the doctor.

"Too sore to get around on?" the captain pressed.

Ray sighed. "No, sir."

The captain produced a set of keys and let them dangle from his handle.

"Too sore to drive, though, huh?" Billy Bob asked. The department had just acquired a new Ford Explorer, and Billy Bob had been itching for a chance to drive it.

"It's automatic, isn't it?" Ray countered. He hated being a passenger. If there was driving to do, he wanted to do it.

"You betcha," the cowboy said. "Got shift on the fly four-wheel-drive. I bet she'll do the century mark when we get her out in the open."

"I'll drive," Ray said. He took the keys from the captain.

Fifteen minutes later, after having explained his assignment to Margaret and endured a short but enthusiastic razzing about his high kick blunder from Grandfather, Ray was in the Explorer, his gimp foot on the dashboard, a sack of ice balanced on it. Billy Bob was at the wheel.

THREE

"I AIN'T NEVER been to Tag-gack," the cowboy said as they were passing through the outskirts of Barrow.

"You haven't missed much," Ray said. He had leaned the seat back as far as it would go. If Billy Bob ever stopped talking, he might just be able to get in a short—

"Thing is, most places ain't much to look at. I mean . . ." He paused to sniff and to adjust the pinch of snuff he had stuck between his cheek and gum. Whenever he "chewed," Billy Bob had an annoying habit of making wet, sloppy, cow noises with his lips. "Believer it er not, there are some towns in Texas that are nothin' to crow about."

"Imagine that," Ray mumbled, his eyes now closed. He had taken some aspirin and was now waiting for it to kick in. Surely his ankle wasn't broken. Was it?

". . . Hope and Re-al . . ." the cowboy was saying. "It's not sa-much what a place looks likes as what's there fer ya. I'm talking 'bout friends and family, a-course."

"A-*course*," Ray said, trying to duplicate the patented drawl. Despite several years in Barrow, it had not lost any of its twang.

"Yer not makin' fun of me, are you, partner?"

"Would I do that?"

Billy Bob laughed. "Only if you got half a chance."

Ray reached over and slugged Billy Bob gently on the shoulder. "You're a good sport."

"Now, are you being serious er—"

"Seriously."

"Okay, then . . ."

Even with his eyes closed, Ray could tell when they left town by the amount of action in the shocks. The road to TaggaQ was not so much a road as a trail. In summer it was an often impassable bog. In winter, thanks to the ice, it was nice and hard—hard enough to make your teeth chatter. The challenge at this time of year was to keep from veering off course and sliding into a ditch or, as one vehicle had somehow managed a year earlier, into the floes of the Chukchi Sea.

"Be nice if they put up some streetlights out here," Billy Bob said. "I mean, it's darker than a skunk's tail."

Ray considered this before noting, "Isn't a skunk's tail striped with white?"

"Huh?"

"Never mind."

"You know, it's a good thing I'm driving."

"Why's that?"

" 'Cause you know how car sick I get." Billy Bob

had once gotten nauseous at a stoplight after driving only a couple of blocks. "Long trips is worse," he continued. "My stomach just don't like being confined, I suppose. It's like it's got a mind of its own."

Ray laid there, not really listening, wishing he hadn't let Lewis talk him into doing that high kick. He wasn't sure which hurt more, his ankle or his pride. And Grandfather . . . the old man seemed to have gotten a real kick out of it—and had even tried to make that very pun.

Getting old, even when you were just thirty-something, stunk, Ray decided. After fuming over this for a moment, he thought about Grandfather. The man was ancient. In his nineties. And his body was wearing out. His mind too. How did that feel? It must be frustrating. Depressing. All the virile, vital years of youth behind you, nothing to look forward to except degenerating toward the grave. Ugh!

"That foot botherin' you?" Billy Bob asked.

"What? No. It's fine."

"Probably be the size of a melon by the time we get on up to TaggaQ."

"Better not be." He made a mental note to be nice to Grandfather when he got back. Nicer, at least. It was tough treating him kindly when he was so antagonistic and bitter. He hadn't always been that way, of course. Despite the fact that Ray hadn't gotten along with the old man at every turn, Grandfather had at least carried himself with a sense of pride. Not anymore though. He'd been having so many health problems. He was on oxygen now, had been diagnosed with Parkinson's. The man was fading fast. Another good reason to tell him how he felt about him, to thank him, to set things right—before it was too late.

"Are your grandparents still alive?" Ray asked.

"Mine? Well, some of 'em. I lost my grandpappy on my daddy's side along about ten years back. I still have my grandmother, though she had a stroke last summer. Luckily, it was a mild one, and she's back to being fit as a fiddle. You cain't tell nothin' even happened."

"The reason I ask is—" Ray tried to interject.

"Then on my mother's side, now that's another story altogether because her folks got divorced when I was . . . oh . . . just a little feller . . . maybe eight or ten. Right in there." Billy Bob went on to describe the divorce in great detail, the motives for it, whose side he had taken, the transition to a stepgrandfather when his grandmother remarried, the various ailments of all three of the individuals . . .

Ray lost interest and became dreadfully sleepy. He managed to throw in a "mmhm" and nod every so often, but was actually only half conscious. There was no firm demarcation line between the drone of Billy Bob's voice and the onset of a dream:

He was walking along on a huge expanse of ice. It was perfectly flat, perfectly white. He could feel the cold seeping up into his boots, up his legs, into his torso. There were no mountains, not even any changes of grade as far as the horizon. Had he been awake, he would have realized that such a place does not exist, except maybe in Antarctica. In the North, the ice was always marred by the jumble of floes. But he was not awake, so it made good sense—he was on the frozen Arctic Ocean, walking west. Behind him, he could tell where the land left off. Even though there was no alteration in the ice, he could somehow tell. In front of him, perhaps a hundred yards, was another finger of land. It too was covered in ice. He stopped and was thinking to himself that behind him was Alaska, before him Russia, and that he had never realized how close they were to one another, when there was a loud popping sound. The smooth surface of the ice cracked, shifted dramatically, then began to part. He fell to his knees, clinging to a large plate of ice that was angling up toward the sky.

Suddenly a head jutted up from the sea. It was grotesque-looking, with wide hollow eyes and an open mouth, more animal than human. It climbed out of the lead, using the claws of its front paws for traction. One of its rear legs had a seal-like flipper for a foot, the other a bird's talon. As it stood up, Ray saw that the bones of its back and ribs were exposed. Its neck was long and the head at the end of it was seated crookedly.

Ray let go of the plate of ice and slid backward, landing on the flat ice with a thud that knocked the wind out of him. He fought for breath and watched as the "monster" somehow grew. It stretched and expanded until it towered over him like a giant.

He tried to move, but couldn't. He was paralyzed, his clothing stuck to the ice. The thing looked down at him, showing what few teeth it had in a malicious grin, and began to laugh maniacally.

"What . . . what . . . are you . . . ?" Ray stuttered.

As it bent toward him, short, bearlike front limbs and huge claws reaching forward, it cackled, "Manaqtaaq AnugI."

The words were still echoing across the frozen sea when the claws took hold of him, lifting him skyward. The monster opened its mouth until it was as large as the sky and proceeded to swallow Ray. He felt himself disappearing into darkness.

"You all right, partner?"

The Explorer was bouncing and jolting over a section of rough ice. Billy Bob, instead of watching the road, was watching Ray.

"You all right?"

Ray nodded, unable to tell exactly what he was. He felt groggy, his chest tight with fear. The pain in his ankle reasserted itself and he was suddenly nauseous.

"You want me to pull over?"

Ray shook his head.

"Ya got yerself a little nap," Billy Bob announced happily.

Closing his eyes, Ray tried to calm himself. He was panting and felt like he had been holding his breath.

"What's man-a-tack ana-gee?"

"Huh?"

"What's man-a-tack ana-gee?" the cowboy repeated, mangling the Inupiaq words.

Ray blinked at him and the dream suddenly returned in all of its vivid imagery: the sea of ice, the way it had heaved and broken open, the hideous creature that had emerged.

"It was a tupilak."

"A what?" Billy Bob asked, still paying more attention to Ray than to the road.

Gesturing for him to focus on driving, Ray tried to explain, "A tupilak is a . . . it's a . . . a monster." He shook his head, trying to shake away the vision. "It's from mythology. Originally from the Greenlanders, I think." When Billy Bob shot him a look of confusion, Ray said, "The Inuits of Greenland. They used to believe that there were demonic creatures that would wait under the ice to attack people."

"That don't sound too good."

"The idea was that powerful shamans would assemble tupilek out of parts from dead animals and humans, sing a charm over them, and send them out to get revenge on their enemies. Some were so evil that they returned to terrorize their makers."

"Kinda like Frankenstein."

"A little, I guess." Actually, the whole concept was much more gruesome than Frankenstein. The intent was purely violent.

"What's that got to do with man-a-tack ana-gee? That's what you said right before you woke up."

"I did?"

"Yeah. You said it about three times, real worried like."

Ray could almost hear the beast hissing the words at him. It was a name, he realized now. The creature's name. "It means 'black wind.' "

"Black wind . . . ?" Billy Bob said. He was making that face again, the one that conveyed confusion. "Now who ever heard of such a thing? Wind cain't be a color, unless it's part of a dust storm, like the ones we used to get back in West Texas. Now that wind was brown, I tell you. Brown and hot and not something you wanted any part of."

"It was just a dream," Ray said dismissively, as much to himself as to Billy Bob. He had dreams all the time, some good, some bad, and every so often a disturbing one. This particular dream was undoubtedly the result of his ankle injury, the stress of having to leave town on short notice, being assigned the duty of investigating two popsicles. When he was anxious, Ray's subconscious tended to go into overdrive to work things out.

"Is tup-ee-lack a tale yer grandpappy used to tell?"

"No."

"Shore would make fer a good campfire story: the black wind monster roamin' around, lookin' for his next victim."

"Let's talk about something else."

"Shore thing." There was a long pause. Finally, Billy Bob said, "What should we talk about?"

Ray got comfortable and closed his eyes again. The road was in pretty bad shape, making for slow, shaky going. It would be a little while before they reached TaggaQ. He decided that he would try to sleep some. It would probably do his ankle good and might even relax his mind. The chances of having another "daymare" were slim.

"Why don't you tell me about your family," Ray suggested.

"My family?" Billy Bob asked. "Why, I done told you about them."

"Tell me again," Ray said, already sinking.

"Well . . . let's see. I suppose it all starts back with my great grandpappy. He was born and raised in Mills County and, believe it or not, knew Billy the Kid."

Ray nodded. He had heard Billy Bob's ancestral recitation several times before and it was always sleep-inducing, better than any over-the-counter sedative.

The cowboy's voice continued on, the words blending together into a hum that was almost pleasant. Ray could still hear Billy Bob, though he had no idea what he was saying, when the ice field reappeared. There was a lead at the center and, before he could draw back, up came the tupilak: the same ugly, disgusting tupilak with the same awful expression on its accursed head.

"Manaqtaaq AnugI," the thing growled at him.

"Black Wind," Ray muttered, feeling the dread and panic rush back into his chest.

The ice shook, the entire landscape quaking. Ray began to slide toward the monster.

"What in the world is that?!" he heard Billy Bob exclaim.

Opening his eyes, Ray realized that the Explorer was bumping and jolting over a particularly rough section of road.

"Lookie there!" Billy Bob said, pointing out the front windshield. "What do you suppose that is?"

Ray squinted out the windshield at an array of lights hovering in the distance.

"Ain't that the ocean?"

Glancing down at the compass on the dashboard, Ray noted that the cowboy was right. They were facing due north. The lights were out over the frozen sea.

"Suppose it's a rig?"

Ray blinked and shook his head. There were no rigs off the coast of TaggaQ. Besides that, the splay of lights was too elongated to be a rig. They had to span fifty, maybe a hundred yards.

"Kinda spooky."

"Yeah . . ." Ray rubbed his eyes and for a long moment couldn't decide if he was awake and seeing some strange phenomenon that qualified for an episode of *X-Files* or still asleep and having another weird dream.

FOUR

"You don't suppose that's one of them there flyin' saucers, do ya?" Billy Bob had stopped the Explorer in the middle of the road and was looking at the lights, slack-jawed.

"I don't know what it is," Ray admitted.

"I wish I'da brought my camera. You always hear-tell of folks seein' things, but they can't show ya no proof."

"I'm seeing it too, if it's any consolation."

"What do you wanna bet it's fulla E.T.'s," the cowboy said.

"You're as bad as Grandfather."

"How's that?"

"He's always trying to find a supernatural cause for natural occurrences."

"Are you sayin' it ain't fulla E.T.'s?"

"I'm saying there's a logical explanation for it."

"Such as?"

"I don't know . . . maybe it *is* a rig."

"Don't look like no rig I ever seen."

"Let's keep going," Ray urged.

The cowboy shifted the Explorer into gear and they began bumping over the ice again. Five minutes later the road turned and, with the "UFO" hovering eerily off to their right, they caught their first glimpse of TaggaQ: a few dozen pinpricks of light arranged in a crooked rectangle.

"That's it," Ray announced without enthusiasm.

"Not much to it, is there?" Billy Bob commented.

"The scary thing is, it's bigger than my home village."

"Nik-suit, right?"

"Nuiqsut," Ray corrected.

"That's what I said."

They rolled into TaggaQ to the sound of ice crackling beneath the studded snow tires. Most of the homes and businesses looked deserted. Ray directed Billy Bob down the main street to the office of the sole law enforcement officer. It was a small converted house with a tiny fenced yard and a weathered shingle that read: TAGGAQ POLICE HEADQUARTERS. The windows were dark.

"Don't look like nobody's home," Billy Bob said as he parked next to the gate.

"Let's go see." Ray zipped his parka and pulled on his mittens before popping the door open. He hoisted his leg from the dash to the snow, stood up and managed one step before collapsing against the hood of the Explorer, his vision obscured by stars. He heard Billy Bob's boots scuffing the ground as the cowboy hurried to his rescue.

"I shoulda taken you to the doctor."

"I'm fine," Ray claimed, still unable to see anything but a field of fire.

"The heck you are. You pro'ly busted somethin'."

Ray shook his head. "I think it's a sprain."

"Well now, sometimes a sprain can be worse than a break."

"Is that right?" He clung to Billy Bob until he got back his sense of balance and the stars had cleared, then began shuffling toward the gate of the police station.

"Same thing happened to Terrell Davis."

"The football player?" Ray asked, only remotely interested. He had reached the fence and was leaning against the post, summoning strength for the walk to the front door.

"Yep. Sprung his ankle in the first game of the 2000 season. He was the same way as you: tried to keep going, acted like it was nothin'. But it wound up sidelinin' him for the season. Turned out to be a stress fracture."

"That's rough." As they went up the ice-glazed walk, Ray decided that the ankle had just gotten stiff from the trip. Given enough walking, it would eventually loosen up. Actually, he didn't so much believe this as he hoped it to be the case.

Billy Bob blathered on about Davis and the Broncos and was in the process of segueing to the recent woes of the Dallas Cowboys, one of his favorite subjects, when they reached the door.

Ray tried the knob, but it was locked. There was a doorbell, so he pressed the button. They heard the bell echo back from inside.

Breaking from his review of the pantheon of great Cowboy quarterbacks, Billy Bob said, "Told ya. Nobody home."

"There has to be somebody around." Ray rapped on the door and it clicked open a crack. He pushed it back. "Hello . . . ?" Stepping in, he found the light switch. A bare bulb hanging from the center of the ceiling flicked on.

The "office" consisted of a collapsible table and a half-dozen metal folding chairs that had been set up in what had once been a living room. The table was functioning as Kuleak's desk. It had been erected in front of the dilapidated hearth, and held a coffee can full of pencils and pens and several leaning piles of newspapers and magazines. A square of butcher paper had been taped to the center of the tabletop like a blotter. A tall, hand-carved wooden plaque sat at the near edge of the table: POLICE CHIEF KULEAK.

"Hello . . . ? *Chief* Kuleak," Ray tried again. When there was no answer, he went to the table and glanced at the blotter. It was covered with doodles, most of which involved words with letters scratched out and rearranged. Ray noticed that the newspapers were all folded back, the crossword puzzles exposed. He picked up the top puzzle. It was from the *Anchorage Times*. So was the next one. And the next. A little ways down he found the *Washington Post*. Near the bottom was the *New York Times*.

He walked stiffly around behind the table and found a calendar taped to the back edge: the *Sports Illustrated* swimsuit edition. On the hearth were three small boxes. One contained office supplies:

more pencils, staples, paper clips, paper. Another held more newspapers and several crossword puzzle books. The last had a cell phone, a coffee mug, and a tall thermos. Ray placed his hand on the thermos out of habit, then asked himself what he was doing.

"What are you doing?" Billy Bob wondered.

"I don't know. Something's . . . funny."

"What? I like a good joke as much as the next fella," the cowboy said.

"I don't mean ha-ha funny."

"What kinda funny do you mean?"

"Strange." Ray looked around. "I mean, I know this is a podunk village and there's not much for a cop to do here. Plus Kuleak is less than dependable."

"What'dya mean?"

"He has been known to tip a bottle."

"Oh . . ." the cowboy said, lifting his eyebrows. "So you're thinkin' he's off on a binge, 'stead-a doing his duty?"

"Well, that's a possibility. But . . ."

"But what?"

Ray picked up the thermos. It was cool to the touch. He screwed off the top and sniffed the contents: booze. "Whiskey," Ray guessed. Full strength. Kuleak didn't even bother watering it down with coffee.

He picked up the cell phone, flipped it open, got a dial tone, flipped it shut. Billy Bob was watching him, asking with his eyes what was going on.

Ray shrugged. "I'm just sniffing around. You know me."

"Yeah. Yer always tryin' to figure somethin' out."

"Why don't you call the captain and tell him we're here and that Kuleak isn't around."

"Shorely." The cowboy got out his own cell phone and dialed.

Ray wandered into the kitchen area. There were dirty dishes in the sink, several dirty mugs on the cabinet. He sniffed one of the mugs and found the same pungent aroma that had been in the thermos. He glanced into the refrigerator and saw a small collection of condiments, a half-empty carton of eggs, a carton of milk. In the freezer was a large slab of what appeared to be caribou meat.

It struck him for the first time that Kuleak must not only work in the "headquarters" building, but live there too.

He went down the hall and found two tiny bedrooms and a bathroom. The latter was filthy and had a still-damp towel hanging over the free-standing metal tub. There was no toilet. That, he realized, would be out back. Many of the buildings in TaggaQ had yet to see indoor plumbing. At least Kuleak's place had running water. Ray reached and twisted the hot water valve. The pipes groaned and a thin stream of rust-colored water came belching out of the faucet.

Switching the water off, he moved on to the first bedroom. It had a door of steel bars. Steel bars were over the window too. There was no furniture, only a blanket and a pillow. This was the TaggaQ jail, he realized. Very quaint. And not all that secure. But it would work for the local troublemakers, most of whom were probably sloshed upon arrest.

The second bedroom was a mess: clothing scattered all over the floor, crossword puzzles stacked next to the bed, another couple of coffee mugs. The mattress was on the floor without a frame, the sheets and blanket unmade. Ray tipped back the single pillow and found a handgun. He left it there and returned to the living room. On his way, he looked in the coat closet. It held two coats, one a traditional fur parka, the other a Seattle Seahawks windbreaker. There were boots on the floor and a small carpet sample. Ray peeled the sample back and saw what he had been searching for: a small door. He lifted it out by the ring and was rewarded with a bird's-eye view of a full case of Jack Daniel's. So that was where Kuleak kept his stash.

Ray had nothing against a guy doing crossword puzzles while on duty or amusing himself with centerfold calendars. The winters were long, cold, and very dark up here, and you had to have some sort of hobby. But this village, like the others, was dry. Furthermore, a law enforcement officer, charged with protecting and serving the public, could do neither if he was sloshed. Ray had a problem with alcohol in general and zero tolerance when it came to his fellow officers. When they finished up with the popsicles, he planned to charge Kuleak with possession of a controlled substance, dereliction of duty, inebriation during work hours—though he had no evidence of this other than circumstantial—and move to have his badge stripped, his pension cut off. If Ray got his way, Kuleak would see some jail time too.

He replaced the "secret" door, which Kuleak hadn't bothered to conceal very well, put the boots back, and returned to the living room.

"The captain says he hasn't heard from Kuleak," Billy Bob reported.

Ray looked around again. Something was nagging at him, but he couldn't identify it.

"What's the matter?"

"Probably nothing. I just . . ." He went back behind the table. "It seems weird that Kuleak would be gone so long."

"We don't know how long he's been gone," Billy Bob said. "Maybe he just stepped out."

"No. Somebody reported two bodies out on the ice."

"*Under* the ice," Billy Bob corrected.

"Whatever."

"And according to the captain, Kuleak hasn't been heard from."

"I'll betcha he's off with his buddy, Mr. Beam."

"He's a Jack Daniel's man," Ray said.

Billy Bob nodded, then shook his head in disgust. "Many a man been knocked to his knees by old Jack."

"Many a Native," Ray muttered, his anger swelling. His father's drink of choice had been vodka, something introduced to the People by the Russians. Ray still held a grudge against Russians in general, for the very reason that without their influence, his father might not have become addicted and might have been able to . . .

"Maybe he's sleepin' it off somewhere," Billy Bob said.

"That's the problem," Ray said. "He lives here. Sleeps here. Drinks here. Works here, if you can call it work."

Billy Bob sniffed, waiting for more.

"He left home and the office, didn't take his phone or his thermos."

"Coulda had him a bottle," Billy Bob suggested. "Didn't wanna be bothered, so he left the phone. And . . . who's to say? He coulda got him a woman somewhere abouts."

"Yeah . . . that's possible, I guess."

"But you don't think that's what's goin' on, do you?"

"I don't know what's going on," Ray replied. He blew air at the table and the makeshift "headquarters" before limping for the door.

"Where to?" Billy Bob asked as they closed the door and started down the steps.

"I don't know that either," Ray admitted, taking each step gingerly. "I'm sure the whole town knows about the bodies by now. We get someone to tell us where they are, have a look. Then we head back home."

"You don't think we need a coroner?"

"It didn't sound like we would. I mean, the bodies either froze in the Chukchi or they didn't."

"And you think you can tell that, without a doc?"

Ray shrugged. "If they have bullet wounds or

gaping holes in their skulls, we'll have someone sent over. Otherwise . . ."

They reached the Explorer and surveyed the street.

"Shore looks dead around here."

Billy Bob was right. The village was quiet. Too quiet. It was still early, yet the few stores lining the main strip of road appeared to be closed. It looked more like midnight than mid-afternoon, the heavy darkness adding to the effect.

"Maybe . . . maybe they all went over to the games," Ray thought aloud. He knew that many of the residents would have driven to Barrow to watch, but also knew that not all of them would have. Then it occurred to him: "It's possible that they shut things down out of respect to the accident victims."

"I reckon that must be it."

"They have a medical center . . . somewhere," Ray said. "That's probably where the bodies are."

They both got back into the truck. Billy Bob started the engine and checked his mirrors before pulling away from the curb. This was a useless gesture, Ray thought, doing a head check himself. There was no traffic. No movement. Nothing. It was as though the entire place had been abandoned.

"Kinda gives me the creeps," Billy Bob said.

"What's that?"

"It's like . . . like a ghost town."

They drove for another block, rolling slowly along, checking windows and signs.

"Right up there," Ray said, spotting a red cross.

Billy Bob pulled up to what was designated simply as MEDICAL CENTER. There was a dull glow in the windows, testifying to the fact that while the other residents might have bugged out, the docs and nurses had hung around. Or at least, had forgotten to turn out the lights on their way out of town.

Ray popped the door open and was about to get out when he noticed something up the street: a pulsing of light. He watched it for few seconds before recognizing it. When he did, he snapped the door shut. "Go," he told Billy Bob.

"Where?" the cowboy asked.

"There," Ray directed vaguely.

"Okay." The cowboy shifted into gear and started up the street.

"Faster."

"If I go much faster, we'll be visiting one of these here buildings, up close and personal. The road is a regular ice skatin' rink. Looks like it's been hot-mopped er somethin'."

"Faster!" Ray insisted.

The cowboy complied and the back tires spun as they accelerated. "What, exactly, is it we're hurrying for?"

"Right up there." Ray pointed through the windshield. "It's a fire."

FIVE

As they approached the light, it became a flashing that reflected against the buildings, bathing the glossy ice of the road in a brilliant orange.

"Well, it shorely is a fire," Billy Bob said.

They could see the actual flames now: eight points burning against the black sky, creating a nearly perfect rectangle.

"Now, what in blazes . . . ?" Billy Bob wondered.

"It's the cemetery," Ray said. He pointed at the half-buried, snow-encrusted crosses that were reaching up from the white, frozen earth behind the flames. "They're digging a grave."

Billy Bob stopped the Explorer a short distance from a whalebone fence that bordered the cemetery. The torches had been erected on the crest of a low rise, and their shadows danced frantically across the graves.

"They use the fire to heat the ground," Ray explained.

"Must taken 'em a while to dig, seein' as how it's so cold and hard."

"It can take days," Ray told him. He zipped his parka again, pulled up the hood and pulled on his mittens.

"What're you gonna do?"

"See who it is they're burying."

"Oh . . . ! I get it. You're thinking that maybe . . ."

"Maybe." Actually, he was thinking there was no maybe about it. Unless some old timer had coincidentally died at the same time that two bodies had been found in the sea . . . But that was the strange part, he thought. Surely the local authorities had been directed not to do anything with the corpses until the Barrow Police Department had a chance to look them over. Of course, the local authorities amounted to Kuleak, and he was most likely off somewhere, sleeping one off.

"But it looks like there's only one grave," Billy Bob observed, getting out. He left the truck running, the heater on.

"So far. Like I said, it can take days and several shifts digging around the clock to manage a grave in this weather."

"Why don't they just wait till spring?"

"The same reason white people don't keep their dead in the back bedroom until a convenient time for a funeral. Because it's creepy. You can't find a culture on the planet that isn't at least a little shaky when it comes to the subject of death."

Ray watched his breath drift and felt a sting as the wind carried it away. With the departure of the sun earlier in the afternoon and now a rising wind, it would be a wickedly cold night. He didn't envy the gravediggers.

As they walked up the incline and into the cemetery, Ray was careful to walk around rather than over the plots of pristine, wind-sculpted snow in front of each cross and headstone. Ahead of them, the shadows in the torch area became dark, featureless figures as they climbed out of the pit. One of them whistled, and in a moment, the door to a shed at the back edge of the cemetery opened. Out came the next crew: three men in RefrigiWear outfits, bunny boots, hoods and face masks, gauntlet mittens. Relatives and friends of the deceased, Ray assumed, again pitying them their task.

He and Billy Bob reached the grave site and peered in. It was about three feet deep. A good start, but far from being finished, especially considering the condition of the ground. Jackhammers would have a hard time penetrating the concretelike layer of permafrost. Ray raised a hand to one of the torches, but could feel no heat. The wind was stealing it away. It was also beginning to move the snow, which was light on the top layer and was pelting their pant legs like sand. This would only make the digging more difficult—a race to get the pit finished before it filled up again with drifting snow.

The two crews passed each other on a trail beaten into the snow, and the off-shift men disappeared into the shed. A short, metal stack stuck up at an angle from the roof of the shed, Ray noticed, and was giving off either steam or white smoke.

The fresh crew arrived at the grave and got into the pit without speaking to or even glancing at Ray and Billy Bob. They took up the shovel and picks left by their predecessors and began hacking with the slow, deliberate strokes of men who knew they would be at it for quite a while and needed to conserve energy.

Ray waited until one of the men paused to adjust his mittens. "Hello . . . ?"

The hood twisted and two dark eyes glared at him out of a lined, weathered face. The man sighed, his whole upper body rising, then falling, a long stream of breath reaching up out of the pit. He put the shovel down and climbed up, then started for the shed, gesturing for them to follow.

Ray limped along, noticing that the cold was effecting his ankle. It didn't hurt as much, but was getting very stiff.

At the shed, the man held the door open for them and ushered them inside. Hot air hit them in a stifling wave. Ray unzipped his parka and threw back his hood. The interior of the structure was even more cramped that it appeared from outside. Four freestanding heaters had been pushed into the corners and were blowing toward the center. A Coleman stove was set up near the door. It held a coffeepot and a burbling pan of soup. A box of supplies sat next to the stove: potato chips, a coffee can, and a dozen or so cans of Campbell's soup. The only furniture in the room consisted of two chairs and a cot. The latter was occupied by one of the diggers, who, still wearing his gear, was already fast asleep. The other men had scooted the chairs in front of two of the heaters and were defrosting themselves.

Ray was about to introduce himself when the man who had invited them inside handed him a snow beater. Ray thanked him, used the swordlike instrument to pat the snow from his pants, and handed it to Billy Bob.

"To brush the snow off," he explained to the cowboy.

"Twenty bucks a shift," the man said wearily. "With yer own piksrun."

"What? Oh . . . we're not here to—" Ray tried to say.

"Gonna need masks," the man continued, digging two ratty ones from a box beneath the stove. "Udderwise, you get ilgugniq. It's cold as a mudder out dare." As he handed them to Ray, he added, "Coffee's free. Soup: a buck."

Ray smiled, not only because the man had mistaken them for workers, but also because he was charging a buck a bowl for canned soup. "Actually, we're with the Barrow police."

"Police . . . ?" the man said with a mixture of disdain and suspicion.

Billy Bob dutifully dug his ID out of his parka and displayed it, but the man turned away without examining it.

"Whatd'ya want?"

"We're here to look at the pop—" Billy Bob started.

"We're looking for Police Chief Kuleak," Ray interrupted. The subject of the newly dead was touchy, if not taboo among the People, and was not an appropriate topic with which to open a conversation with a stranger. As for the term "popsicle," it was not for use outside the department, for obvious reasons.

"Good luck." The man zipped his parka again, put up his hood, and started for the door.

"You have no idea where he might be?"

The man glanced back at Ray and wrinkled up his nose, the nonverbal Inupiat cue for no.

"We got a report of an accident," Ray ventured, choosing his words carefully. "I figured the police chief would be on top of it."

"You figured wrong," the man said. He threw back his hood and looked at Ray with angry eyes. "He's never on top-a nothin', except a bottle-a imiq." He went on to denounce Kuleak with curses.

It suddenly hit Ray. "Are you one of the . . . survivors?"

"One of da what?"

"Did you . . . I mean, were you related to one of the . . . accident victims?"

The man's face shifted subtly from anger to what Ray took to be resignation, possibly even sadness. "I lost my boy."

Ray waited a beat, to show respect to the man and the deceased. "So that's who the grave is for?"

The brows rose over the man's melancholy eyes, the cue for yes.

"I know this is difficult, sir," Ray continued, "but we need to ask a few questions." They also needed to examine the body, but he would bring that up later, hopefully after establishing something of a rapport.

"Whatcha wanna know?"

"Well, for starters, your name and the name of your son."

The man swallowed at this and began to breathe unevenly. He stood, holding their gaze until he regained some of his composure. "Eddie Reed."

Eddie Reed? Ray squinted at the man. An Eddie Reed had lived in Barrow until maybe two years back, when he and his wife had gone through a nasty divorce. This had to be a different Eddie Reed. The Eddie Reed of Barrow was only about ten years older than he was. This guy—gray, receding hairline, a face that had been around—was at least sixty, maybe older.

"What's your son's name?" Ray asked, convinced that it couldn't be the same man, but also somehow certain that it was.

Reed swallowed again, teared up, and breathed deeply before managing, "Tom."

"Tommy? Tommy Reed?" Ray asked. "The basketball player?"

"Ain't that the high kick champion you was talkin' about?" Billy Bob wondered.

Reed began to cry, but without shame, without turning away. Tears streamed down his otherwise stoic face.

Ray waited for what he deemed the right amount of time before consoling, "We are very sorry for your loss, Mr. Reed."

He watched the man weep, and slowly found glimpses of the Eddie Reed from Barrow. Ray really did feel sorry for him. First the divorce, which had obviously taken its toll on the man, now this.

Reed wiped his face on his parka before asking, "Sure you don't want soup?"

"No, thanks," Ray said.

Reed frowned at the pan on the stove. "Only reason I charge is to help pay for da anaiyyuliqsI."

This was one of the most pathetic things Ray had ever heard: selling canned soup to pay for the minister for his son's funeral. "Actually, uh . . . sure, I'll take some."

Reed looked to Billy Bob.

"I ain't all that hun—"

Ray caught him with an elbow. "He will too." Ray produced two dollars and handed them to Reed.

As he filled tin cups with soup, Reed explained, "All da diggers is working for free. They're ilat—nephews and bruddas and brudda-in-laws. But if somebody comes needing work, I gonna pay 'em. Somehow. I'll figure a way."

They stood there and ate the soup without speaking. Outside, the wind was beginning to howl, and in the shed the hiss of the burners on the Coleman stove seemed outrageously loud.

A couple of minutes passed before Ray asked, "Can you tell us what happened? To Tommy, I mean."

Reed shifted his weight and sighed, looking older and more tired than ever. "He was hunting."

Ray nodded. This was not nearly enough information, but he had to proceed slowly. “AiviQ?”

Reed’s nose crinkled.

“Ugruk?”

The eyes widened, somehow maintaining their sadness.

“So he was out hunting seal,” Ray reviewed, mostly for Billy Bob’s benefit, but also to give Reed space and time. “It’s been a good year for ugruk in Barrow.”

“Here too,” Reed said.

“We had a couple of boys get lost out there though,” Ray segued, hoping to draw Reed out.

“Tom never gets lost,” Reed said. Then he teared up again, probably from the realization that he had just used the wrong tense.

“He knew the ice, huh?”

“You bet. I took him hunting with me since he was just miqliqtuuraq.” Reed held out his hand to show just how little Tommy had been. “He was a good boy. Always quiet and real patient. Sometimes more patient than me.” Reed almost laughed, but it didn’t make it out of his throat. “He’s real good with a gun. And a knife. Tommy can clean just about anything. Even a tuttu. All by hisself. Since he was . . . six or seven. Dat’s why it don’t make no sense.”

“What doesn’t?”

“Him gettin’ froze like dat.”

Ray waited again. This was no time to remind the man that the Arctic did not play favorites and could take a life no matter how skilled the owner happened to be in survival.

"Death doesn't ever seem to make a whole lotta sense," Billy Bob threw in.

Ray warned him with his eyes. Though they were now discussing the tragedy and fishing for details, using the word "death" was still anathema. Bad luck, according to the elders. Thankfully, the gaffe didn't seem to offend Reed.

"I heared from him in da anaqasaagiaq."

"Which afternoon was that?"

"Yesterday." Reed shivered slightly and rubbed his hands together. "He was doing aarigaa."

"How did he contact you?" Ray thought to ask. "I mean, if he was out on the ice . . ."

"I give 'im walkie-talkie fer festival."

"You mean Christmas?"

The eyes widened. "Dat way, he can call, tell me where he's at." Reed bit his lip. "I spend big manIk. Got da best: Moter-olla. Top of da line."

Ray nodded. He had seen the walkie-talkies offered in a catalog. They were quite expensive. He wondered how the man could afford them.

As if reading his mind, Reed said, "I worked in Prudhoe fer-a couple tatqIq last summer. Make enough fer Moter-ollas and fer a new Po-lar-ees." Reed shook his head at the memory. "Dat was good savaaq. Real good job."

"So," Ray said, trying to get Reed back on track, "you talked to Tommy yesterday afternoon and then . . . what?"

Reed shrugged. "The next thing I know, I'm being woke up by Kuleak."

"The police chief," Billy Bob said, trying to keep up with the account.

"When was that?" Ray asked.

"UnnuamI sometime. Real early."

Reed fell silent again and Ray had to prompt, "Kuleak woke you up in the middle of the night and . . . ?"

"He tell me dat Old William found Tommy under da ice."

Ray waited as Reed fought off another bout of tears. Then, "Who's Old William?"

"One of da elders. He's a old guy. Maybe . . . sixty. More even."

Ray nodded, thinking that sixty wasn't all that old. What would Reed call Grandfather, who was in his nineties? Ancient?

"What was this Old William fella doing out on the ice?" Billy Bob asked.

"He was hunting too. He's always hunting. Never got married. So he can do like that. Very lucky."

Sidestepping this slam on marriage, Ray said, "Who was Tommy with?" This was a cagey way of asking who the other victim was, without mentioning the words body, corpse, dead man . . .

"Yeah," Billy Bob said. "There was supposed to be two pop—"

Ray nailed him with another elbow before he could finish.

"Da udder guy was naluaqmiu."

"A friend of Tommy's?" Ray inquired.

"No. He was, uh . . . a visitor . . . Tommy took him out to show 'im how to hunt. Tommy was like that. He was a real good boy. A real good boy . . ."

Reed's voice trailed off.

"What do you think might have happened?" Ray asked.

Reed looked at him soberly. "I dunno. It coulda been a accident. But . . ." He shook his head. "Tommy was smart with da sikuqqat. It was like he was born for da ice. Never had a problem with it."

Until now, Ray thought.

"So . . . I dunno. Maybe Old William is right."

"About what?"

Reed looked at them and for the first time appeared frightened. "He swears it was a tupilak."

Billy Bob made a face at Ray. "Now ain't that the dinkdums. You was just talkin' 'bout them monsters."

"Nigrun and anun mix together," Reed said, still looking disturbed. "Sent out to kill."

"It's just an old legend," Ray said.

"But the People remember," Reed said.

"It's superstitious baloney," Ray countered. "Some insecure shaman made the whole thing up to try and get folks to pay attention to him."

"Maybe," Reed said. "Maybe not."

SIX

"YOU DON'T REALLY believe that, do you?" Ray asked. "You don't believe a tupilak is responsible for what happened to Tommy?"

Reed shrugged. "I dunno what to believe right now."

Ray decided not to push the issue any further. Reed had just experienced a tragic loss. Right now he was in shock, reeling from the whole thing, trying to figure out how to deal with it. If blaming a mythological creature for his son's death helped him get through it, then who was he to argue?

Ray finished his soup and tried to think of something else to ask that didn't involve examining the bodies. Unable to, he told Reed, "We'll need to see him."

"I know," Reed said through a clenched jaw. He zipped his parka, pulled his hood up, fastened his mask, and waited for Ray and Billy Bob to do the same. When they were ready, Reed led them back out into the elements.

The wind was alive now, the darkness somehow

deeper and more all-encompassing. It was quickly turning into the kind of night that Grandfather liked to worry over, Ray realized. The old man would have said that the tuungak—the spirits—were upset, agitated about something, and he would have advised against being out in it. Though Ray didn't buy into this sort of animistic mumbo-jumbo, he had to admit that something didn't feel right. If he'd had the choice, he would have gone home and holed up for the evening with his family.

But he didn't have the choice, so he limped along behind Billy Bob, who was following Reed down the single track in the snow, toward another shed situated on the other side of the cemetery. It was smaller and leaned sadly to one side. The corrugated steel roof gleamed with ice-covered rust in the spots where snow chunks had slid off.

Reed stopped at the door and began working a padlock. After struggling with it for a moment, he swore and fished something out of his pocket: a bottle of deicing solution. Reed sprayed the lock and then clumsily spun the dial with his mitten-clad fingers. When he finally opened it, he cursed again and muttered, "Shoulda got a key lock."

He pushed the door open with some effort and then stood there.

"Aren't you going in?" Ray asked.

Reed shook his head.

Ray recognized the look in the man's eyes: subdued terror. According to Inupiat tradition, it was taboo to be in the presence of the deceased, much less handle a body. To that end, the terminally sick and the very old had often been taken far from the village and abandoned, left to die in isolation, their spirits released to the tuungak. Though that practice had fallen away in modern times, there was still concern over tarrak, dark angry spirits that lingered at the grave and could steal your soul. It was ridiculous and silly, Ray knew, but not all that unusual. White people were similarly uncomfortable with their dead.

Billy Bob was standing in the doorway, peering into the darkness. Ray nudged him, but the cowboy didn't move.

"What's the matter?" Ray asked.

"It's awful dark," Billy Bob said.

Ray produced a flashlight from his parka and handed it to him. Billy Bob shined it around erratically, casting an eerie, fleeting light on the interior: bare walls, a collection of gardening implements, including rusted shovels and pickaxes, a partially dismantled snow machine up on cinder blocks, a long wooden box . . . the coffin. It looked more like a shipping crate than anything else, the wood a B-grade knotted pine held together by nails.

"What if . . . ?" Billy Bob asked, aiming the flashlight at the corners, as if they might be home to bats or ghouls. "What if that too-pel-ik is still around?"

"It couldn't be because there's no such thing," Ray said, getting irritated. The wind was sharp, and he was in no mood to stand out in it. He gave Billy Bob a shove. The cowboy stumbled in, stopping just beyond the door.

Ray took the flashlight from him and went to the coffin. He tried the lid, but it was already nailed down. "I need to open this," he told Reed.

Without looking in, Reed said, "I know. But we're going to bury him akkupak."

It wouldn't be akkupak—immediately—Ray knew. Not with the ground frozen and nearly impenetrable. But Reed was speaking so that Tommy could hear him. Or rather, Tommy's inyusuq—his spirit. To be left unburied would be an offense that might bring wrath upon the responsible party, in this case Reed.

Ray turned around and found a toolbox next to the shovels. He extracted a clawhammer. "Hold the light for me," he told Billy Bob. When Billy Bob failed to move, Ray insisted, "Hold the light for me!"

The cowboy begrudgingly stepped forward and took the flashlight. At that moment the wind rose in a gust that shook the shed and, finding a crack in the wall, made a sound that rivaled the stereotypical ghost's call: *wooooooo . . .*

Billy Bob dropped the flashlight and it popped as it went out.

"Great . . ." Ray muttered.

"Hang on," Billy Bob said, his voice shaky. He produced a smaller penlight. "Here you go."

"Hold it for me!" Ray said.

"Oh . . . yeah . . . okay."

Ray began working on the lid of the coffin, trying to loosen the nails without totally ruining the wood.

Though he didn't believe all that stuff about the dead, there was no reason to push things. You might not reap bad luck from damaging an occupied coffin, but neither did you reap good luck.

"I don't mind telling you," Billy Bob confessed in a whisper, "this here is giving me the creeps."

Ray was about to chide him for being childish, but he was feeling a little of the same thing: in the dark, in the cold, the wind, their breath hanging in the air, out here in the middle of nowhere, prying open a coffin by the tiny, meager glow of a penlight. Several horror movies came to mind. Ray tried to ignore this as he took out one nail and started on another.

"You ever see the *Blair Witch Project*?"

"Yeah . . . Hold the light still."

"That was some show, I tell you. Scared the tar out of me, I don't mind sayin'."

"Me too," Ray admitted. He got the second nail and moved down the long pine box. "Point it over here."

"This reminds me of that, you know it?"

"Why's that?" Ray asked absentmindedly, his attention focused on the lid.

"They were all by their lonesomes . . . way out in the wilderness. Kinda like this."

Ray caught this part and also heard the wind rise again, the "ghost" singing, *wooooooo*. He shivered. "This is nothing like that."

"Well, it kinda is. Especially with that tupilak fella running around out there somewhere."

Ray stood up and faced him. "Okay, listen. There's no such thing as tupilek. It's a made-up thing. Just like the Blair witch."

"Now see," the cowboy said, "that's just the thing. Some people say that there witch is real and that the movie was actually based on—"

"Make-believe," Ray said, returning to the coffin.

"No. I was gonna say—"

"Listen to what I'm saying," Ray said. "Tupilek are make-believe creatures. Not real. They are fictional. Imaginary. A tall tale. How many ways do I have to say it?"

"I recall a 'tall tale' about a bog monster down in Arkansas. They made that into a movie, and as it turns out, there really is a 'thing' living in a bog . . . somewheres outside of Texarkana, I think."

Ray pulled another nail. Half of the top was free now. He had one more on the bottom and then they could probably push it open. "What does a bog monster in Arkansas have to do with a boy freezing to death in the Chukchi Sea?"

"Well—" Billy Bob began.

"Hold the light steady!"

"In the movie about the bog monster, they thought at first that he was just a legend too. You know, that he didn't really exist. Until—"

"Tupilek don't exist," Ray said. He was sweating under his parka now from the effort of pulling the nails.

"You know that fer sure, do ya?"

"Yes."

"Absolutely? Positively?"

"Yes. And that's my final answer."

Billy Bob missed this attempt at humor.

"Haven't you ever watched *Who Wants to Be a Millionaire*?"

"Shore! I even called in once to try and become a millionaire myself. Did they have a question on there about the bog monster?"

"Never mind." Ray finally got the last nail. "I think if we both pull, we can pry the lid back." He took another hammer from the tool kit and handed it to Billy Bob. The cowboy put the penlight into his mouth and positioned the hammer under the edge of the plywood lid.

"Ready . . . ?" Ray jammed the claw into the seam. "One, two, three . . ." The lid creaked and groaned, then lifted open, the remaining nails acting as a hinge along the other side.

For an instant the penlight lit up the contents: a body covered in a thick sheen of ice. The only exposed flesh, the boy's face, was as blue as a glacier. The eyes were open, the mouth also open, the tongue blue.

"Oh, my lands . . ." Billy Bob said, dropping first his hammer, then the penlight. The thin ray was extinguished.

"Did it break?" Ray asked as his eyes fought to adjust to the darkness.

"I don't think so, but . . ." Billy Bob was on hands and knees. "I found the hammer."

"Good . . ."

"Here's the light." There was a clicking sound.

"Doesn't work?"

"Nope. Maybe the batteries gave out."

"Yeah . . . maybe." Ray stared straight ahead. He couldn't see anything, not a contrast of shadows, not depth, nothing. Out of the corner of his eye he could just make out the door and, beyond it, the gray of the snow outside. He could also see Reed standing out there. Now Ray was the one with the creepy feeling. It was like a dream. A bad one.

"I got another flashlight back in the truck," Billy Bob said, fumbling to get up. "You want me to fetch it?"

"You could. Or we could do the blind men and the elephant routine."

"Is that a yes er a no?"

"Yes. Please get the flashlight," Ray said, fully annoyed now. He was tired, about ready to head for home. If he hadn't been such a stickler for details, he would have written Tommy's death off as the result of exposure. The kid was truly a popsicle. It didn't take Sherlock Holmes to deduce a cause of death: exposure. He had fallen into the sea and frozen solid. No mystery there.

But he had to make at least a superficial examination of the body. Just to be sure. To be thorough. Then they could go home. Except . . .

As Billy Bob trudged out of the shed and across the graveyard, Ray felt his way to the door. "Mr. Reed. . . . ?"

"Yah . . . ?" Reed answered, facing away from the shed, as though this would protect him from any supernatural curses that might be floating around.

The torch flames were trembling in the wind, the shadows from the pit trembling with them. Shovel blades and pick heads clinked and thumped against the frozen ground.

"Where's the other man?" Ray asked.

"Out dere." Reed nodded slightly.

Ray looked past him, at the ice floes. "Still in the water?" He sagged, thinking of the effort involved in launching a recovery operation.

"No. They took him to da *Uvlugiaq*."

"The star? What star?"

Reed lifted his arm, pointing.

Squinting, Ray could just make out the lights of the "UFO" he and Billy Bob had seen earlier. "Is it a rig?"

Reed shook his head once. "Umiaqpak."

Ray squinted at the "star" again. "A ship?"

"Day call it da *Uvlugiaq*," Reed said.

"Who?"

"Da taniks."

Tanik was another name for white people. But that still didn't explain the lights. "Is it something to do with oil? A tanker or something?"

Reed grunted, "No. Rooshin taniks."

Rooshin? "Russian?"

Reed sighed, and Ray took this as an affirmation.

"It's a Russian ship, then?"

Another sigh.

"What's it doing out there?" Ray wondered. The ice was far too thick at this time of year to navigate.

"Da *Uvlugiaq* is a siku breaker."

"An icebreaker. A Russian icebreaker . . ." This still didn't make sense to Ray. Since when did the Russians bring their ships in this close to shore?

"All part of da big putu."

Big hole? Ray was completely lost now. "The other—" He caught himself before saying *body*. "The other man . . . he's Russian?"

Reed shrugged.

"But he's out on that ship?"

A single nod.

Ray tried to make sense of this, but was unsuccessful. Tommy had been out on the ice, hunting with a Russian from an icebreaker anchored or maybe stuck off the coast of TaggaQ. Both had somehow fallen into the sea, both had apparently frozen to death. And all Reed could say about why the Russians were "in town" was that they were part of a "big hole." What was that supposed to mean?

"Are the Russians drilling for oil out there?" he asked, thinking that maybe it was an exploratory operation, a joint venture between the Americans and the Russians.

Another shrug.

They stood there, Ray staring at the distant lights, Reed examining the ground in front of his boots, until Billy Bob returned with the flashlight.

"Them fellas er havin' a heck of time makin' a dent in that ice," he said, gesturing at the pit. "It might be spring before they ever get it—"

Ray put a finger to his lips.

"What?" the cowboy wondered aloud.

"It'll be ready real soon," Reed vowed. "I gonna

go help. We gotta let his inyusuq rest. Gotta do dis akkupka."

"Gotta do what?" Billy Bob asked as Reed made his way back to the first shack.

"Immediately. He wants to bury his son as soon as possible."

"I guess I don't blame him none."

The two police officers went back into the dark shack. Billy Bob flicked on the light, and there was Tommy, lying in the crude pine box: eyes and mouth open in an expression of perpetual wonder.

SEVEN

"WHAT ER WE LOOKIN' FOR?"

Ray shrugged, aiming the beam of the light at the frost-encrusted forehead, then the eyes. "Anything that might suggest it wasn't an accident."

"Such as?"

"A gunshot wound would qualify."

"You think somebody shot 'im?"

"I was kidding."

"Oh."

He pointed the beam at Tommy's nose, his mouth, ears . . . Ray was no coroner, and without the layer of ice and the knowledge that the body had been recovered from under the floes, wouldn't have been able to give a sure cause of death. But he could recognize the work of a knife or a blunt object. Or at least he thought he could. Poison was beyond him, as were diseases and other ailments.

What he did know was that if you fell into the Chukchi Sea and didn't get out within a matter of moments, you would die. Which is what probably happened to Tommy. Why he had fallen in was a mystery. So was that whole bit about the Russian ship and the Russian man who had been hunting with him. But no matter how complicated things got in terms of international relations—he fully expected to have trouble gaining the approval necessary to examine the Russian body—death in the elements was still death in the elements. The northern coast of Alaska was not a friendly environment at this time of year, and even an experienced outdoorsman, like Tommy, could get into serious trouble in the blink of an eye.

As he worked his way down the body with the flashlight, Ray went over various scenarios in his mind. The two men had caught a seal and were digging out the hole when the ice collapsed and they both fell in. Or one of them fell in and the other perished in the attempted rescue. Or they had been fleeing some sort of danger and blundered onto thin ice. There were polar bears out there. And if you got in their way, you could become dinner. Except . . . surely they'd taken weapons with them. Only an idiot, a tourist, or someone with a death wish would go out there unarmed. Even if you were hunting the old way, you'd have a rifle in your pack.

"We'll need to talk to this Old William character," Ray thought aloud. "He found the bodies, so maybe he can fill us in on what happened."

"That's sayin' we can find him," Billy Bob said. "This here place is like a ghost town."

"We'll find him." Ray was running the light down the side of Tommy's parka. A real autopsy would require thawing the body and looking under the clothing. But unless there was some glaring anomaly, that would be unnecessary. Hopefully, they could avoid anything that might be perceived as "desecration," and Reed would be allowed to bury his son akkupak.

"That'd be an awful thing, wouldn't it?"

"What's that?" Ray tried to open one of the pockets on the parka, but it was frozen shut.

"Dying like that."

Ray nodded. Having succumbed to hypothermia on more than one occasion, he knew from experience just how brutal it could be. Given the choice, he would rather drown or bleed out. Given the choice, he would pick dying of natural causes.

"I can hardly stand it when my fangers get numb. I cain't imagine what it must be like when yer whole body is frostbitten."

"You don't usually die of frostbite. That's only a problem if you survive."

"I seen a guy on TV once with black fingers and toes from climbing Mount Everest."

"Did he lose them?"

"I don't think so. But they did have to take off part of his nose and part of an ear." The cowboy made a face. "Which was all the more a shame since the fella was handsome."

Ray examined the insulated pants as Billy Bob continued talking, jumping from frostbite to the subject of plastic surgery to the subject of products that promised to keep a balding man from going bald. There were no rips or tears in the fabric, Ray noticed. He moved the light up the other leg, checked out the parka again, returned to Tommy's face.

". . . but if Mother Nature wants you to lose yer hair, who are you to go changin' things around?" Billy Bob was blathering.

"We need to turn him over," Ray told him.

They each took an end and lifted, but the body didn't move. Tommy was not only frozen stiff, he was frozen into the coffin.

Ray handed the flashlight to Billy Bob. "Look around and see if you can find something to get him loose with."

Billy Bob went toward the back wall, taking the light with him. As the cowboy clanked around, Ray stood there with a gloved hand absently touching the corpse. It was like touching a block of ice. He could feel the cold seeping into his fingers.

It was a miserable time of year to die, he thought, an even worse time to have to bury someone.

"What about this?" Billy Bob lifted a crowbar into the beam of the flashlight.

"That'll work." Ray took the bar and began chipping along the sides of the coffin, careful not to touch the clothing or the body itself. It was tough work, the ice having spread to the edges of the coffin. He swung the crowbar hard, sending chips of ice into the air. The body had probably been placed in the box while still wet, he deduced. He jammed the crowbar down along the crevasse between the body and the wood.

"Aiiyaa!"

Billy Bob turned the light on the door where Reed was standing, eyes wide, an expression of horror on his face.

"What are you doing?!"

"Mr. Reed—" Ray started, holding up a hand.

"Why do you disrespect my family?!" Reed bellowed.

"We're examining the body," Ray said, immediately regretting his choice of words.

"*Body?* Dat's my son! He deserves honor!"

"We were just trying to turn him over, Mr. Reed," Ray explained. "It's our job to take a look and see what might have caused . . ." Ray's voice trailed off when he saw the gun. A handgun. A very large handgun. Either a .357 or a .44 magnum; it was difficult to tell in the shaky beam of the flashlight. Whichever, it would put a sizable hole in whatever it was aimed at.

"Get away from my son!" Reed ordered.

"You shouldn't do this," Billy Bob said. "We're police officers, sir, and—"

Reed pointed the barrel of the gun at Billy Bob's head.

"Take it easy, Mr. Reed," Ray told him.

"You get out! Get out of here!"

"Okay. Fine. We'll do that." Ray set the crowbar on the floor. "But how about if you put the gun away."

Reed didn't move.

"We're just trying to find out what happened to your son," Ray said in what he hoped was a consoling voice. He didn't want to anger Reed further, but out of a sense of duty added, "You know that if we have to, we can get a court order."

Reed sniffed at them, the gun now leveled at Ray. "He be buried by then."

"Exactly. So we would have to exhume him. Now I know that's not what you want, sir."

Engaging Ray's eyes, Reed told him, "You touch my son again, I kill you."

There was a long, tense silence. Ray believed the man. But he also believed that Reed was speaking out of pain and grief. After the shock wore off, he would change his mind and regret this standoff. "Taiku for allowing us to examine him," Ray finally said.

"Thank you . . . ?" Billy Bob wondered aloud. "But he—"

Ray warned the cowboy with his eyes. "Please allow us to express our sympathy."

Reed blinked at them, the gun drooped, and he finally put it away.

"Let's go," Ray told Billy Bob, nodding at the door.

"But we ain't done."

"We are for now," Ray returned quietly.

When they had exited the shack, Reed padlocked the door again, then left to join the diggers over in the pit.

"We gonna get us a court order?" Billy Bob asked.

Ray watched as Reed made his way to the grave site, walking like an old man: stiff, bent over, tired . . . When he reached the pit, he climbed in and became a shadow like the others.

"Are we?"

"What? Oh . . . uh . . . probably not."

"But you said—"

"I know what I said. But he'll come around. It'll be another day or two before they finish the grave. We'll come back."

"What if he don't come around?"

Ray shrugged. "From all outward appearances, I'd say Tommy fell into the water and froze to death. It's that simple. So unless something changes . . ."

"We could arrest him fer assaulting police officers," Billy Bob suggested. "Then we wouldn't need no court order."

Ray began walking toward the truck, taking a path in the snow that led around the edge of the cemetery. "You got any kids?"

"A-course not. You know I ain't never been married."

"Ever lose a child?"

"What? Well, how could I if—"

"Have you heard the expression: walk a mile in someone else's shoes?"

"Uh . . . I guess so."

Ray stopped and faced Billy Bob, their dull shadows dappled in flickering cross and tombstone patterns generated by the pit torches. "The man just lost his son. Unless I'm mistaken, Tommy was his only son, the last vestige of the family he had before the divorce."

"Divorce?"

"Right. He lives in TaggaQ, minus his wife and son. Anyway, right at this moment, his life sucks. Know what I mean?"

"Sorta."

"Good answer. Sort of. Neither of us can identify with what he's going through. Therefore it's a little presumptuous to judge him when he's right in the middle of a crisis, wouldn't you say?"

"I suppose."

"So let's cut him a little slack, give him some space. Like I said, there's no sign of foul play on the body. It looks like Tommy had an accident, plain and simple. Let's not turn it into a federal case."

Billy Bob nodded.

As they made their way to the truck, the cowboy said, "You sure got a good understanding of people."

"I don't know about that," Ray said, sidestepping this compliment. His wife, Margaret, had accused him of failing to understand her on numerous occasions. And she had been dead-on accurate.

"I'm serious. I'd-a never figured all of that out."

This was a prime opening, an opportunity to blast Billy Bob for being dense. Which he definitely was from time to time. But Ray let it slide by. He liked the cowboy. Despite Billy Bob's naiveté, his occasional inability to put two and two together, Billy Bob was his friend and, surprisingly enough, a good cop: dedicated, hardworking, incredibly honest. You couldn't ask for a better, more loyal public servant.

"Maybe if I'da gone to college, like you—" Billy Bob was saying.

"You don't learn human nature in college."

"Then how do you learn it?"

Ray aimed a thumb over his shoulder. "Just like that. You observe, experience, try to keep an open mind . . ."

Billy Bob was nodding, his face tight and serious. "I'm gonna try harder to do that."

Patting him on the shoulder, Ray limped around to his side of the truck. He opened the passenger door and was met by a suffocating wave of hot air. The interior of the cab was like a sauna. They both climbed in and began taking off layers of clothing—mittens, hoods, parkas . . .

"Now see, this here vee-hickle has what I call a heater." The cowboy shifted into drive. "Where to, partner?"

Ray gazed out the wet windshield at the torches and the diggers, their long black shadows stretched out across the snow. He then looked out at the ship. The *Star*, Reed had called it. Now that he knew it to be a vessel, it took on that shape: an oblong series of lights with a trio of spotlights hovering over it. The three spots were the tower of the bridge, Ray guessed. Or maybe the communications gear.

"We gonna have a talk with that Old Will fella?"

Ray nodded.

"Wonder where he lives?" The question hung in the air. "I supposed we could ask Mr. Reed."

"I don't think he's in the talking mood at the moment," Ray said. He could just imagine Reed reacting to the pair of them interrupting the excavation of his son's grave a second time. He might not stop at simply threatening them with the gun. "Let's go back to the police station."

"What fer?"

Thankfully, Billy Bob didn't wait for an answer. He turned the truck around and drove back up the street. It was just as deserted as before: no traffic, no pedestrians, only a few dim lights in the short row of storefronts. When they reached the station and he had parked by the curb, the cowboy looked at Ray expectantly.

"I'll be right back," Ray said. He got out and limped up to the office. They had left the door unlocked and the place was still unoccupied. He went to Kuleak's desk. There was a thin phone book on the floor behind it. According to the cover, it contained the numbers for residents of Point Franklin and TaggaQ. He sat down in Kuleak's chair, put the book on his lap, and was in the process of opening it when he realized he didn't know Old William's last name.

He paged to the W's. There was a Fred and a Richard Williams. He used Kuleak's Post-It pad to jot the numbers down, thinking that neither of them were likely to be Old William. A guy with a name like that probably didn't even have a phone.

Picking up the receiver of Kuleak's phone, he dialed the number for Fred Williams. It rang and rang. No one picked up and there was no answering machine. He dialed the second number and got a recorded message: this number is no longer in service.

Ray hung up and then dialed Barrow. The line

rang twice before a happy voice answered, "Barrow police."

"Hey, Betty. This is Ray."

"Raymond. The captain has been wondering about you two. What's the story? Did you get an ID on the bodies?"

"One of them."

"And . . . ?"

"Tommy Reed."

"Aiiya . . ." Betty muttered, suddenly sober. Though she was Athabascan, she spoke the language of The People and, after years in Barrow, even had an Inupiaq accent.

"Yeah . . ." Ray agreed.

"You want me to notify his aaka?"

"I don't think that's necessary. His father is up here overseeing things." Overseeing things was slightly misleading, but he didn't want to get into the whole business of the men chipping a grave out of the ice and Reed shooing them away with a handgun.

"He was such a good kid."

"I know. But . . . bad things happen," Ray said. "Even to good kids."

"Was it an accident?"

"Looks that way. We have some more checking to do. Which brings me to a question. You ever hear of a local up here in TaggaQ named Old William?"

"Old William . . . ?" She paused, then, "Not that I remember. I know they have a Rusty Bill over at Wainwright."

Ray was familiar with Rusty as well. The guy was

a very "colorful" character. "I figured if anyone had heard of Old William, it would be you."

"I appreciate your confidence, Raymond, but I'll have to disappoint you on this one."

"Okay . . . Well, thanks anyway."

"When are you boys planning on coming back in?"

"Not for a little while. I don't suppose you'd call . . ."

"Your wife? Sure. On one condition."

"What's that?"

"You bring the whole family over next weekend for dinner."

"You got it."

"Talk to you later."

As Ray hung up the phone, he spotted a small plastic box on Kuleak's desk. He pulled it over and opened the top. Bingo! An index card file. He went to the W's. And there were Fred and Richard. The numbers were the same.

He was thinking that they would have to pay Fred and Richard a visit—maybe one of them went by the name Old William or was related to the guy—when the cards fell open to E. There was Eddie Reed. Kuleak had filed him under E for Eddie.

Ray shook his head at this and, on a hunch, flipped to the O's. Surely Kuleak wouldn't file Old William by the first letter of his nickname. But the second O was in fact, Old William. Kuleak had even emphasized the O by underlining it.

Ray copied down the address, which involved no

numbers, only a road name and vague, hand-scribbled directions. There was no phone number.

He left the office, hobbled back to the running truck and got in.

"Well . . . ?" the cowboy asked.

"Let's go see Old William."

EIGHT

THEY DROVE PAST the graveyard again, where the flickering orange torches were sending fingers of steam into the darkness.

"How much farther?" Billy Bob asked as they left the town proper and continued into the expansive black void of night.

"It says a half mile. We're supposed to turn at the tree."

"The tree . . ." Billy Bob repeated skeptically. "I ain't seen a tree since Texas."

"It said turn at the tree."

"We might have to drive clean to Russia."

A couple of minutes later they saw something in the headlights: a tall, flat object. As they approached, Ray laughed. Someone had cut a piece of plywood into the shape of a Christmas pine and anchored it to a fifty-five gallon drum. The structure had been spray-painted green with red blobs that Ray assumed were supposed to be ornaments. On the trunk, running vertically up the tree, was the misspelled greeting: HAPY CHRISMAS.

"Now ain't that nice," Billy Bob said. "Somebody's got the holiday spirit."

"I don't think they ever lose it," Ray commented. The weathered tree obviously hadn't been taken down in years.

"Turn here?"

"Unless you think there might be more trees up ahead."

"Naw. I doubt that." Billy Bob turned the wheel and they started down a poorly graded section of ice. There were no tire tracks in evidence, only the occasional belt mark of a snow machine. In the distance, the lights from the ship hung low on the horizon, like evening stars.

They passed a tiny, abandoned Russian Orthodox church. Though the steeple was still intact, both of the horizontal pieces of the cross were dangling sadly. There was no glass in the windows and the front door was missing.

Billy Bob slowed the truck. "You think that's where this Old Will fella lives?"

"The directions said a quarter mile past the church."

They drove on a quarter mile, a half mile . . . The odometer turned over, marking a mile.

"Maybe we missed it."

Ray was thinking the same thing and was about to say so when a squat structure materialized in the headlights. It was encrusted in snow and ice and would have been invisible except for its square corners. The building wasn't much bigger then the shacks at the cemetery, and seemed to be partially dug into the earth around it. It reminded Ray a little of Grandfather's old ivrulik back in Nuiqsut. Except this was even more primitive.

A crooked smokestack stuck up from the roof. As they approached, Ray realized that the stack was fashioned of coffee cans connected with wire. Smoke escaped from the cracks between the cans and drifted sideways.

Billy Bob parked directly in front of the door, which was the only opening in the front of the house. There were no windows on this side.

They zipped up and pulled on hoods and got out. As Ray limped his way around the hood of the truck toward the door, he noticed two pairs of snow machine skis protruding from a snowdrift on the north side of the house. Apparently Old William hadn't ridden them in a while. Ray wondered how the old guy had managed to go seal hunting without a machine.

"You want me to take the back?" Billy Bob asked.

Ray almost laughed. "You think this guy's gonna run out on us?"

The cowboy shrugged.

"Where's he going to go?"

Billy Bob glanced into the darkness where the sea and the floes were. "I guess you're right."

Ray knocked on the door. It creaked and gave a little, but a chain on the inside kept it from opening.

"William?!" Ray said loudly. He didn't want to

startle the man, but if he was old, he might be hard of hearing. When there was no response, Ray knocked again. "William?"

Ray heard an engine turn over. "Snow machine!" he said, trying to run. "Take the other side!" He stumbled to the corner of the building and fumbled for his gun. It was in there somewhere, under his parka and RefrigiWear.

"William?" he called, finally extracting his service revolver. The snow machine engine coughed, sputtered, then revved to a shrill whine.

Ray hobbled to the back and saw a hooded figure astride a Polaris. "Barrow Police!" he shouted, his gun pointed skyward.

The man twisted the throttle and the snow machine performed a tight 180. But Billy Bob stepped out, his gun drawn also. The man veered away, turning north. He gunned the engine again but it coughed and died.

Ray and Billy Bob converged on the machine, guns now aimed at the ground at the man's feet. "Off!" Ray ordered.

The response was a noise that made Ray shiver. It was like a wolf howl or the yelp of a dog that had been hit by a car. The man rolled off the back of the machine and fell to the ground, pulling his legs up until he had assumed a fetal position. They could hear him crying.

Billy Bob looked at Ray. "Drugs?"

"Up!" Ray ordered, but the man just lay there, shaking, shivering, weeping. "Watch him," Ray told

Billy Bob. Holstering his gun, Ray reached down and pulled the man up by his arm.

"Don't hurt me!" the man began to wail in a piercing tenor voice.

Ray threw back the man's hood.

"Why, it's only a boy," Billy Bob said.

It was indeed only a boy: a tall, lanky kid of no more than thirteen or fourteen. Ray motioned for Billy Bob to put his gun away. While the cowboy complied, Ray pulled his own hood back. He then produced his ID.

"We're from Barrow Police," he told the kid.

The boy was visibly relieved. "Oh . . ."

"We're looking for Old William," Ray said.

"He's my anaaluk," the boy said.

Billy Bob looked to Ray for a translation.

"His uncle."

"He told me to run away if I heard something coming. That's what I was trying to do."

"Is your uncle here?"

"No."

"Do you know where he is?"

"No. He left and said if he didn't come back that I should go stay with my ataata."

"Great-grandfather," Ray explained for Billy Bob's benefit. "You have no idea where he went?"

"I don't know where, but I know why."

"Okay, why?"

"To warn the people about the tupilak."

"The half-man, half-animal thingamajig," Billy Bob said authoritatively.

"We got us one haunting the village," the boy said.

Ray sighed at this. It wasn't enough that the tupilak lore had been imported from Greenland. Now the locals were adding bits and pieces of white culture to it as well. *Haunting* the village? That sounded like something out of an old ghost story, or maybe a B-level horror flick. Next the kid would tell them that the tupilak could only be expelled by a Catholic priest or killed with a stake to the heart.

"Let's get in out of the wind," Ray suggested. His ears were already numb from the exposure.

The boy trotted to a half door at the rear of the tiny house. It had a knob and hinges, but even the kid couldn't go through without bending. It was either used for throwing out dirty water and waste—the snow around it was certainly dingy enough to support this theory—or served as an oversized doggie door.

The inside of the house was dark, cold, and smelled of both heating fuel and body odor. The dirt floor had been covered with flattened cardboard boxes. The kid produced a flashlight and led them to a card table with three folding chairs. As they sat down, he extinguished the light and they were enveloped in compete darkness.

"Your uncle doesn't have electricity?" Ray asked, zipping his parka higher. It seemed even colder in here than outside.

"He's got a generator."

"Maybe we should start it up."

"We can't."

"Why not? Is he out of fuel?"

"No. We got lots of fuel. But he said not to run anything, especially the lights, while he was gone, because qaummaq brings the tupilak."

It suddenly hit Ray that this might also account for the deserted look of the village. Maybe the other residents had bought into the tupilak business.

"If we keep the lights off, then the monster will only go to the graveyard. And he can't hurt people that are already dead."

The wind rose in a terrible gust, the walls shook, and Ray could feel a cold breeze on his face. The poorly constructed, drafty old shack was no place for a boy to live.

"What's your name?"

"Willy. I'm named for my anaaluk."

"How old are you?"

"Thirteen."

"You go to school?"

"Not anymore."

"Why not?"

"I don't know. After third grade my anaaluk say I don't need no more learning."

"He did, huh?" This amounted to child neglect in Ray's mind. "Did your uncle go with the police chief?" he thought to ask.

"I don't know. He just said he had to warn everyone."

This Old William was turning out to be a real character. He not only lived in a hovel and was apparently unconcerned about his nephew's education, but he believed in old wives' tales and had quite possibly spooked the entire village into a superstition-induced blackout.

"How's he gettin' around?" Billy Bob asked.

"He's on the Snow Cat," Willy said. "We don't got no car. But we got three good snow machines."

Ray briefly considered using a flashlight to search Old William's house. But there wasn't much reason for that. Old William wasn't a suspect. And light might upset Willy.

"Did your uncle say anything about . . ." Ray paused, trying to decide how to phrase the question. ". . . Did he tell you about finding . . . ?"

"The men that the tupilak killed?" Willy asked. "Yeah."

"What did he say?"

"Just that they were under the ice, where they couldn'ta got without being chased and attacked by a tupilak."

Ray nodded. That wasn't much help.

"Maybe we oughta stop talking about the tupilak, just in case."

"Okay." That was fine with Ray. The whole business was ridiculous: blaming a hunting accident on a mythical beast. A thought occurred to Ray. "What was your uncle doing out there on the ice?"

"Hunting ugruk."

"We done already figured that," Billy Bob pointed out, from somewhere off to Ray's right. It was strange sitting there in the dark, not being able to see each other.

"I know, I'm just . . . trying to think it through."

Was it possible that this Old William had accidentally shot Tommy and his companion and conjured up this crazy tale to cover his tracks? Or maybe he had killed them on purpose. That would require a motive, however, and at present they didn't have one.

"We need to have a talk with your anaaluk," Ray said.

Willy didn't say anything, and Ray wondered if the boy was scared. Maybe he didn't want to be left alone again, especially with a monster roaming his imagination, if not the village.

"We'll need you to go with us," he told Willy.

"We will?" Billy Bob asked out of the darkness.

"How come?" Willy wanted to know.

"Well, for starters, we wouldn't recognize him if we saw him."

"I could try and find a picture."

"That would be helpful," Ray said. "But it would be even more helpful if you'd go with us." He could tell that Willy was reluctant. "If you're worried about the tupilak, don't be. They never attack cars."

"They don't?" Billy Bob asked.

"And we're both armed. So if it's a smart tupilak, it'll stay out of our way."

"It's smart, all right."

"Why do you say that?"

"Uncle said it was wise and very clever. Which makes it even more dangerous."

Either this Old William was a master storyteller, Ray thought, or he had seen something to kick-start this monster imagery.

"Will you go with us?" Ray asked. Though they probably could have found the boy's uncle on their own, Ray wanted to get the kid out of the shack, to someplace warm. Later, he would see about getting him placed with other relatives or into the hands of social services. Even a foster home had to be better than this.

"I guess," Willy finally said.

The three of them got up and felt their way to the front door. When Willy opened it, the night seemed less dark, the cloud cover reflecting the meager scattering of lights in the village. The torches of the graveyard were like beacons, the lights of the offshore ship a twinkling of distant stars.

NINE

As they climbed into the warmth of the truck, its heater blasting out hot air, Ray noticed that Willy was wearing a fetish around his neck: an ivory likeness of a bear that dangled down the outside of his parka. According to tradition, this was supposed to keep evil at bay, not unlike a wreath of garlic warding off vampires. Inside the cab, Willy pulled down his hood and Ray saw a crude tattoo on the boy's neck. It was freshly engraved, still crusted with blood. Ray couldn't tell whether it was another bear or maybe a whale.

"Did your uncle do that?" Ray asked.

"Yes," the boy answered.

It had to have been painful, Ray thought. And it was, in some respects, a form of child abuse. What it conveyed, however, in Native tradition, was that Old William was worried about the boy and had taken steps he deemed necessary to ensure the kid's safety. Apparently Old William really was convinced he'd seen something supernatural out on the floes. That didn't mean there wasn't a logical explanation for it, just that the man had been genuinely frightened and had chosen to take defensive action.

"Analuuk says that the tuungak are pissed off."

Ray glanced at the boy. What a mix of old and new. "Did your uncle say why the spirits are 'pissed off'?"

"He says it's 'cause the naluaqmiut are making wounds in nuna."

"Wounds in the earth?"

"And it loosed a bad tupilak."

Ray nodded. This was a total distortion of the tupilak story. They weren't born of the earth. They were born of man. The whole thing was moot, of course, since they were baloney to start with.

"What's it take to catch one of these here tupilaks?" Billy Bob asked.

Ray admonished him with his eyes. There was no reason to egg the kid on.

"You gotta shoot 'em with a silver bullet. That's what Analuuk says."

It was all Ray could do to keep from laughing. At least before the arrival of television, the superstitions had been consistent. Now . . . they were all mixed up. The silver bullet thing, he thought, was for either a vampire or a werewolf.

"I seen a movie once where they done that," Billy Bob said. The cowboy went on to describe the film in excruciating detail.

While Billy Bob held Willy's interest, Ray tried to sort through things. Two men had died. The man who had discovered the bodies was out warning the village to beware the wrath of a rogue tupilak. The so-called police chief was off doing who knew what.

He glanced out the windshield as they came back into town. The torches in the cemetery were surreal looking in the almost total darkness surrounding them. One body was in the shed. The other was out on an icebreaker.

He turned and looked past Billy Bob, who was now regaling Willy with a blow by blow account of *Abbott and Costello Meet the Invisible Man.* Ray could see the ship. The highest of the lights had to be on the bridge or antenna tower, the others spread out along the bow and stern. She was sitting with her side facing shore. The question, he thought, was why she was there at all. At this time of year, even a high-tech icebreaker wouldn't be able to make any headway.

The other body was on the ship, he repeated to himself. So unless they found Old William or Kuleak, or Eddie suddenly did an about-face concerning the examination of his son, they would have to go out there. Ray wasn't looking forward to that. They would need snow machines. And it would take a while to pick their way through the floes.

There was a helicopter back in Barrow. He toyed with the idea of going home and setting up a flight. It would be a lot of trouble, but better than machining across the ice in the dark.

Ray lifted the radio mike. "Barrow, this is Attla, come back."

The radio popped with static.

"Barrow, this is Attla, do you read?"

After more popping, a voice asked, "What you talkin' 'bout reading?" It was Lewis.

"Lewis, I need to talk to Betty."

"Can't."

"Why not?"

"She . . . pre-sapposed."

"She's what?"

"Pre-supposed. In da ladies' room."

"Oh . . . *predisposed*."

"Dat what I said."

"Listen, I need a favor."

"What kinda favor?" the voice asked skeptically.

"We need a chopper down here—up here—wherever it is we are."

"Where are you?" Lewis asked.

"TaggaQ."

"Oh, yeah. What you need da chopper for?"

Ray explained briefly.

"So you really need it?"

"Yes."

"Dat's too bad."

"Why?"

"It left 'bout a hour ago. Got a-mer-ja-see out on a offshore."

"Great . . ."

"You could machine."

"I was trying to avoid that."

"Wouldn't be bad. It's not dat cold. Just a little under zee-ro."

"Not counting the wind."

"Yah. On da back of a Polaris, itta be chilly."

"Thanks, Lewis."

"No, prol-em."

Ray hung up the radio.

"That's a bummer," Willy said.

"What's that?" Ray asked.

"That we don't get to ride on a chopper."

"Yeah. It's a bummer." Ray caught the "we" in the boy's statement. If he thought he was going with them out to the ship, he had another think coming.

"I never been in a chopper," Willy said. "But I can still show you how to get there."

"Get where?"

"To that ship." He pointed. "You just said you needed to go out there."

"*We* do," Ray said, gesturing at himself and Billy Bob. "Not you."

"But I know the floes. I can be like a guide."

"No," Ray said flatly.

"It'll take twice as long without me."

"Why's that?" Ray asked. He knew the answer, but hoped the kid didn't.

"You don't know where there's sikuliaq and where it's not."

"There's no thin ice at this time of year," Ray shot back.

"Uh-huh. Because of what naluaqmiut been doing. It's all cracked up."

Ray wondered if this were true. Had the ice-breaker made the ice unstable?

"There's plenty of sikuliaq," Willy promised. "You gotta know where it is."

"We can figure it out," Ray said.

"Not until tomorrow, you can't. You gotta see it.

And the light don't come till like ten-thirty in the morning. You'll have to wait a long time."

The boy was right about that. If the ice was "iffy," it would be virtually impossible to traverse in the dark. And yet, they needed to visit the ship tonight, before Eddie and his crew got any further along with Tommy's grave. Before the ship did anything with the body they had. It truly was a "bummer" they didn't have a helicopter. It would take forever on a snow machine, always stopping to check the thickness of the ice.

"Pull up to the station," Ray said, flipping his hand at Kuleak's office. It was becoming a second home for them. When Billy Bob had pulled over, Ray said, "Even if we did let you tag along—which I'm not saying we'll do—we don't have machines."

"No problem," Willy shot back. "I know where we can borrow some."

Ray frowned at the kid, wondering why he wasn't surprised by this. Willy didn't attend school, probably couldn't add worth beans, but knew where to "borrow" snow machines.

"I'll be right back." Ray got out and limped into the office. The ship had probably been out there for some time. Surely, Kuleak had been in communication with it.

He went to Kuleak's desk and rifled through papers. When this yielded nothing, Ray tried the card file. No good. There was no radio frequency, no cell number, nothing. He stepped over to the radio. There was a notepad next to it, but it was filled with word puzzle doodlings: letters arranged in various combinations, terms underlined, crossed out, letters circled . . . Ray wondered if Kuleak ever did any police work.

He flipped on the radio and the unit gave out a high-pitched squeal of feedback. Ray hurriedly adjusted the volume and squelch knobs. It was an older model that was probably powerful enough to pick up signals from great distances at night. His grandfather had a similar one, though his was not reliable anymore.

Ray was about to twist the frequency dial when a voice came through. It was male, strong, clear, and speaking another language. Russian, he guessed. Maybe it was a signal from Siberia. He listened for a moment and then was about to scan the other frequencies when he recognized one of the words: *zvyezda*. Had it not been at the end of a phrase, he would have missed it entirely. Ray knew almost no Russian. But, having dealt with a few Russian tourists, he was familiar with a half-dozen terms: hello, please, food, rest room, thank you . . . He couldn't say them properly, but he could pick them out if the speaker went slowly enough. The word he had caught here—*zvyezda*—meant star. He knew this because the summer before, he had encountered a Siberian seeking asylum in Barrow. Though the man had eventually been sent back by the State Department, Ray had learned that his name was Zvyezda, which translated as "star." This was a pen name that the man hoped would become a self-fulfilling prophecy: he had dreams of becoming a Hollywood actor . . . a film star.

Ray was wondering if he had heard wrong or if it had been something else that sounded like *zvyezda* when it come over the radio again. There was no mistaking it this time. Star. Which is what Eddie had called the ship. Maybe Kuleak had left the radio set to the appropriate frequency. Wouldn't that be handy?

Ray lifted the mike. "Hello, uh . . . *strast-veecha.* This is Officer Attla of the Barrow Police Department."

"Shto?" the voice asked.

Ray assumed that meant "What"? He repeated his salutation.

The voice responded with a paragraph of Russian.

"I don't speak Russian," Ray told the man.

The voice continued, then there was a pause. Ray thought he had lost the signal. He tried hailing them again. Nothing. He was about to give up when another voice, this one female, came on. "This is the icebreaker *Arctic Star,*" the woman announced with a Slavic accent. "Who am I speaking with?"

Ray repeated his introduction yet again, following it with, "My partner and I request permission to come aboard this evening."

"This is highly unorthodox," the woman said coldly.

"We are engaged in an investigation and need to speak with the captain and possibly the crew."

"What is the nature of your inquiry?"

"I'd rather not discuss it until we get out there."

"Could this inquiry be conducted over the radio?"

"No. We need to come out," Ray said.

There was a pause. Ray could sense her reluctance.

"You are currently in American waters, are you not?" he asked.

"Da."

"Then the ship is under the jurisdiction of the United States government. If we are not allowed to board, I will have to inform the FBI," Ray said. He was bluffing. He would inform the FBI, eventually. But by the time they got someone up here . . . "So in order to avoid an international incident," Ray said, choosing his words carefully, "my partner and I request permission to board."

There was another long pause, then a bit of static that contained Russian. "Very well. The captain has granted permission. You may come aboard at your convenience." The woman sounded perturbed.

"Thank you." Ray started to give her an ETA, then thought better of it. Why let them know when they would arrive? That would only give them more time to prepare, cover up, hide . . . That was saying, of course, there was anything to prepare, cover up, or hide. "We'll be out in a while," he finally told her. "Unless you happen to have a helicopter on board."

"Shto?" It was the male voice again. The woman had already relinquished the radio.

"TaggaQ out," he said.

"Shto?" the man asked.

Ray flipped off the radio and left the office.

"Well . . . ?" Billy Bob asked when he got back to the truck.

"We're cleared to board the ship." He glanced at the empty seat. "Where's Willy?"

"He went to see about them snow machines. He said when we was ready, to come on over to the machine shop. It's right over there." Billy Bob point up the main street to a cardboard sign that was visible only because of the light of the truck. Someone had handwritten in magic marker the words: MACHINE SHOP.

Ray and Billy Bob got out and began gathering gear into day packs.

"How long you suppose we'll wind up being out there?" the cowboy asked. He was holding a thermos.

"Just long enough to examine that body. Unless they're storing it on deck, it should be thawed. We can look it over and turn right around and go home."

"Sounds just as simple as anything."

Ray nodded. That was the bad part. Things that sounded simple seldom were. He shoved a box of ammo into the pack. It already contained a space blanket, energy bars, waterproof matches, an extra set of gauntlet mittens, and a global positioning system device the size of a large watch. He hoped none of these items would be necessary, especially the extra bullets. But being a cop above the Arctic Circle was kind of like being a Boy Scout: you always had to be prepared.

"You got any of them chocolate candy bars left?"

"They're not candy bars."

"They taste like candy bars."

Ray withdrew one of the three energy bars and

handed it to the cowboy. "What happened to the ones I already gave you?"

"I ate 'em. They're about as good as a Snickers."

"They're also three or four times more expensive. Hold onto that one, okay?"

"You bet."

They zipped the bags shut, and after Billy Bob had turned the truck off and plugged the engine heater into a street outlet designed specifically for that purpose, they walked up the street to the machine shop.

"You know how to ride a snow machine, right?" Ray asked. It had just hit him that he had never seen the cowboy pilot anything but an American-made truck.

"Oh, sure."

"You've never been on one, have you?"

"Well . . . no."

"How about a motorcycle? You ever ride a dirt bike or maybe a Harley or something back in Texas?"

"I had me a horse once."

"A horse . . ." Ray muttered.

"He was as gentle as you could imagine."

"A gentle horse . . ."

"Used to eat right out of my hand. I called her Lassie."

"Like the dog?"

"Yes, sir. My pa wouldn't have no dogs. Didn't like 'em much. So . . . I had me a horse. That Lassie was some horse."

"Well, this will be a little different than riding Lassie."

"Oh, I didn't never ride 'er. She was a pony. Just fer show. Won a blue ribbon at the county fair one year."

"That's swell." They had reached the door to the shop, so Ray tried the knob. It was locked. He looked through the window but could only make out the dim shadow of what he assumed to be snow machines. "You sure he said this place?"

"Yep. We're s'posed to meet him around back."

"This is not the back," Ray said, failing to mask his irritation. He was getting tired, which made being around Billy Bob more difficult.

"No, it sure ain't."

"How about if we go around to the back?"

"Good idea."

They walked half a block, turned down an alley, then another. Using their flashlights to find their way, they moved slowly forward, through a narrow gauntlet of overflowing trash receptacles.

"Over here!" Willy called.

And there he was: astride a shiny new Polaris, two exact duplicates on each side of him. Behind him, the backdoor of the machine shop was standing open, the chain that had barred entry lying in the snow. It had been neatly cut.

"What did you do?" Ray asked.

"I got us some machines."

"I thought you knew the owner or something."

"I do. He's my uncle."

"Then why did you break in?"

" 'Cause he's not here now."

Ray squatted and examined the chain. "How'd you manage this?"

Willy leaned down and picked up a pair of hefty wire cutters.

"And where did those come from?"

"I got another anaaluk owns the hardware store."

Ray started to ask Willy if he'd broken into that store too, but didn't really want to know. "Your uncle's okay with this? He won't mind a little breaking and entering and borrowing of his three best machines?" Ray had already noticed that the models were top of the line and brand new.

"No. Especially if we're taking 'em to help get rid of the tupilak."

TEN

"I GUESS THE department will cover us on this," Ray reasoned, not at all certain that the captain would back him up. "We just need gas."

"Already got gas. My uncle keeps 'em gassed up so people can try 'em out." Willy started his and revved the throttle.

Ray helped Billy Bob fasten his mask, then led him to one of the machines. The cowboy looked it over, then glanced at Ray.

"Sit down on it," Ray instructed.

When Billy Bob was straddling it, Ray ran him through the basic controls, the gauges, knobs, brakes, and also gave him a brief lesson in shifting gears.

"It's really not that complicated."

Billy Bob nodded but didn't seem convinced. His eyes had a panicked look.

"You don't have to go," Ray said. "You can stay here. Stake out Kuleak's office. Wait for him to show up."

Billy Bob shook his head and tripped the ignition.

The machine growled, and when the cowboy revved the throttle, it shot forward, nearly taking Ray out before slamming into a Dumpster.

"You had it in gear!" Ray admonished. "Remember what I said?"

Billy Bob nodded.

"Don't put it in gear until we're ready to go. Got it?"

The cowboy nodded.

Ray checked his own machine, made sure it really did have gas, started it up. It sounded nice, the rumble of the engine smooth and deep. It was a couple years newer than his machine at home, had more horsepower and one of the upgraded luxury seats. A guy could get used to driving something like this, he thought.

Ray signaled for Willy to lead the way, and they started up the alley. Ray took up the rear, braking as Billy Bob weaved back and forth, sideswiping trash cans and discarded boxes. When they emerged into the open, the cowboy performed a 360.

Ray used hand signals to ask over the roar of the engines, "You okay?"

Billy Bob gave a thumbs-up, revved the machine, and nearly flew off the back as it shot forward.

Willy took them straight out of town, cutting across vacant lots and down unplowed streets until they descended onto the floes. At that point the darkness became absolute. They could see the lights of the ship winking at them at intervals, but otherwise they were traveling blind. The headlight beams from the machines seemed to be consumed by the night, inhaled by a black void.

Ray found himself hoping Willy was as good at this as he boasted. The ice was probably pretty solid all that way out to the ship. But if they did come onto any sikuliaq—thin ice—it would be handy to have someone along who could recognize it before it gave way beneath them.

Though he had been taught the art of hunting ugruk by Grandfather, Ray hadn't been out for seal in years. His ability to spot breathing holes and seal tracks, and to judge ice conditions, had deteriorated with lack of practice. He did remember, however, that color was the key to staying out of the water. Light blue meant the ice was thick enough to cross. Dark blue meant it was too thin. Of course, discerning that out here in the dark would be nearly impossible.

They went along, single file, with Willy in the lead, never veering to either side more than a few degrees, for about fifteen minutes. Then Willy slowed.

Billy Bob braked, slid, and then bumped Willy from behind. Though Willy's mouth was hidden by the mask, Ray could tell that the kid found this hilarious.

Willy got off his machine and crouched in the headlight beam. Ray walked over to him, crouched, but didn't say anything. He knew the kid was trying to read the ice.

It didn't appear to have color, Ray thought. It was black beyond the beam, gray at the edges of it, and white right in front of the machine. Being the week after Christmas was a plus. It hadn't been an especially cold year, but neither had it been unusually warm. Most of the time, by this point, the floes were solid and could be machined over without problem. Most of the time.

"See that?" Willy said, aiming his mitten.

Ray nodded. It was a deep, glassy crack that ran off in the general direction of the ship.

"That's from the naluaqmiut," Willy explained. "If it wasn't for them, we'd have good siku."

Ray nodded again, not sure this was true, that the ship could somehow have screwed up all the ice out here, but also unwilling to argue with their "guide."

"We gotta be careful," Willy said. "Make sure we don't fall into nuna."

"Okay," Ray agreed. He didn't want to fall into the earth any more than the next guy.

As he went back to his machine, Billy Bob shouted, "What'd he say?" He was sitting on his Polaris, the engine running, hands fixed to the handlebars.

"He said we need to be careful."

"Oh. Well, I think he's right as rain there."

Willy led again, and the miniature snow machine convoy continued, at a more cautious pace now, snaking along, turning at regular intervals, as if avoiding invisible obstacles.

The ship gained height and length. Instead of just a collection of lights, it became a shadow: a long bow, a con tower, even steam drifting against the night sky.

Seemingly oblivious to the ship, Willy kept up the circuitous route, sometimes leading them almost 180 degrees from their destination. It reminded Ray of a game he had played on the floes as a child: follow the leader. The difference being, they had played it with dog sleds.

As they slowly came closer to the ship, Ray could see more of the cracks Willy was so concerned about. Some of them had obviously been created by the icebreaker doing what it had been designed for—breaking ice. Others were more significant, almost like glacial fissures. Ray had never seen anything like that out on the floes.

Willy finally led them to the stern of the ship. Why he did this, Ray had no idea. He also had no idea how they were going to board. The ship would have to let down a gangway or something.

Willy brought his machine to a stop at the corner where the stern and the port side met. They were about twenty yards from the ship, within the glare of the halogen lights illuminating the back end and the letters: ARKETCHYESKI ZVYEZDA. The "Something" *Star*. The *Arctic Star*, Ray recalled the woman saying.

They got off of their machines and stood admiring the ship. It seemed grotesquely large and out of place, like something from a dream: too tall, too wide; the dangerous, grayish-white color of ice-encrusted steel. It reminded Ray of a warship.

"That there's a big boat," Billy Bob said.

There was a crackling sound and a new light hit them from the port side. Raising a hand against it,

Ray was able to make out a web of rope being unfurled. So much for the gangplank, he thought, starting for it. They would have to climb aboard.

As they neared the side of the ship, Ray watched for cracks in the ice. Strangely, there didn't seem to be any. That didn't make sense. The area surrounding it should have been the least stable. Unless . . . Ray's eyes went from the layers of frost on the side of the ship to the thick band of ice "connecting" sea and vessel, back up to the lines on deck far above, which were heavy with ice. The ship had been there awhile and was, it seemed, frozen in. That made sense. Even a modern, nuclear icebreaker could only navigate these waters until early fall. Maybe the *Arctic Star* had gotten trapped out here and now had to wait until the spring thaw to escape.

"What're we sposed to do?" Billy Bob asked. He had one mitten on the webbing, his head back, peering up the side of the ship, as though he expected an elevator to magically appear.

"I climbed these before," Willy said, starting up. "They got 'em over at the park." He made it look easy, ascending with the agility of a monkey.

Ray and Billy Bob took more time and care. It was tricky, Ray realized, trying to hang on to the ropes with thick mittens on, and equally difficult to keep your footing while wearing bunny boots and sporting a bad ankle. Though he hadn't anticipated this little obstacle course, it was exactly the kind of thing he had hoped to avoid tonight. Going up meant coming back down. Then they would have to do the floes again. It looked like it was going to be a very long night.

When they reached the deck, there were two men in parkas, masks, and hoods, waiting to help them aboard. They didn't say welcome, hello, or kiss my foot. They simply made sure that each of the visitors had both feet on the deck before reeling in the rope.

"We're with the Barrow Police Department," Ray informed them.

The men exchanged glances and kept reeling.

"Here on official business."

Billy Bob fought to extract his badge, then displayed it for them. They squinted at it, then him, before returning to their work.

"I don't suppose you could direct us to the captain or the bridge or . . ." He paused. Not only did the men probably not understand a word he was saying, but they weren't even paying attention.

"Thank you," he told them.

"*Indeerka,*" one of them muttered.

The other grinned at this.

The deck, like the rest of the ship, was covered in a thick layer of ice. A jungle of pipes and bulwarks gleamed bright white, and stalactitelike icicles dangled from everything.

To their left was the bow and more pipes. To the right was the tall bridge with the radar towers and antennas and thousands more icicles. It was like a ghost ship that had been frozen in time.

Ray led the way to the bridge and went in the first door he could find: a hatch that was standing open.

The narrow corridor inside was bathed in a bleak, yellow light and smelled of fish. The tile floor was lumpy with a covering of frozen, mucky boot marks. The hallway turned right, then left, before dead-ending into what amounted to a mudroom. Boots were lined up against the wall in pairs, and parkas hung from corresponding hooks. There were two doors, both marked in Russian.

Ray opened one and the odor of fried meat hit them. There was noise too, utensils clanking and men talking. The mess hall? He let that door close and tried the other: quiet, the faint aroma of pipe tobacco.

"Where do you reckon we're s'posed to go?" Billy Bob wondered.

"Your guess is as good as mine," Ray admitted. He went through the door. Maybe this led to the bridge, he thought. Pipe tobacco translated to officers, didn't it? Either that or the mechanical man smoked a pipe and they were headed for the generator or something.

They reached a set of metal stairs and started up.

"This is cool," Willy whispered. "I never been on a boat this big."

"Me neither," Billy Bob said, his voice similarly subdued.

Their squeaking footsteps sounded unnaturally loud in the stairwell. At the next landing, they reached a door, but it was locked. Ray continued up the stairs.

"Kinda weird they didn't send nobody to meet us," Billy Bob said. "Don't you think?"

"Maybe they're not used to having guests," Ray

tried. It was a little strange that there hadn't been an officer or someone to show them where to go. The two goons manning the rope ladder certainly hadn't been any help.

"Not very hospitable," Billy Bob grumbled.

The door at the next floor up was open and led to what appeared to be the communications center of the ship. In one large room was a wall of radio receivers. In another there were video screens. Computers filled a third. Men and women in uniform were busy with the equipment.

"They got an awful lotta fancy looking stuff, don't they?"

This time the cowboy's observation was right on. It was an "awful lotta stuff," especially for an icebreaker, Ray thought. And the way it was being attended to . . . It didn't look like a ship stuck in the floes off of TaggaQ. It looked like a military—

"Shto vwee dyeleeatee?!" a scolding voice demanded.

Ray turned and saw a woman approaching, her heeled shoes attacking the tile. Before Ray could respond, the woman's face, which had been quite severe, changed abruptly and took on a quasifriendly appearance.

"Ah . . . you must be the policemen from America."

"We must be," Ray said, still amazed by her ability to switch gears.

"It is a privilege to have you aboard our vessel."

Ray nodded, thinking that they had a funny way of showing it.

"I am Dr. Svetlana Denisovich of the Russian Oceanic Research Institute." She put her hand out to Ray. Her dark eyes matched her dark hair, and though she had a certain European beauty, she also gave off a sense of urgency and intensity that made Ray uncomfortable.

"Officer Ray Attla," Ray said. He shook her hand.

"Officer Cleaver," Billy Bob chimed, struggling to produce his ID.

"Very good," the woman said. She smiled at Willy. "And this is a policeman too?"

"I'm Willy," he said. "I'm kind of their deputy."

"Ah . . ." She nodded. "It is always good to have a deputy." She paused and offered them a forced smile. "Gentlemen, on behalf of the captain, I welcome you aboard the *Arctic Star*."

ELEVEN

"ALLOW ME TO show you around the ship," the woman said. She was being so cordial now it was almost indecent. "As you can see, this is our communications center." She turned and gestured at the video room. "The *Arctic Star* is a nuclear icebreaker equipped with the most advanced communications technology in the world."

"Did you say 'nuclear'?" Ray asked.

"Yes. The ship is powered by a nuclear reactor." She urged them to follow her farther up the hall. "Here we have the computer room." Instead of a collection of PC screens, this room held a gray, cratelike box the size of a minivan. "This is Bolshoi Sobaka: Big Dog."

"It sure is big all right," Billy Bob said.

"What is it?" Willy asked.

"It is a powerful supercomputer that allows us to access great amounts of information."

"And why do you need access to great amounts of information?" Ray asked. He was growing impatient with this tour.

She shrugged. "Why does anyone need access to great amounts of information?"

"What I'm trying to ask is, what are you doing out here?"

"The *Arketchyeski Zvyezda* is on a research expedition."

When she failed to elaborate on this, Ray asked, "Researching what?"

"We are conducting a series of environmental studies on the condition of the ice in the Arctic Ocean."

Ray nodded. "And why, exactly, do you have to do that within spitting distance of Alaska? What's wrong with the floes off of Siberia?"

"RORI has ships fanned out from here to Murmansk, collecting similar data."

"I assume this has all been okayed by the State Department or the Coast Guard or whoever it is that needs to give their approval."

"Of course. All diplomatic red tape has been taken care of."

"Of course." Ray wasn't sure why, but he was having a hard time buying anything this woman said. "Are you *wintering* out here?"

"Yes. We were preparing to finish up for the season when the ice trapped us. We even tried blasting our way out with explosives. But it was impossible. So we are making the most of it, carrying on with our studies and experiments. Now, if you'll step this way, we can take the elevator and I'll show you around the bridge." She started down the corridor.

"Actually, Dr. Denisovich, we're here on official business."

"Yes, I know. You are checking to make sure that we are not up to something . . . uh . . . illegal out here in your bay. But I assure you that we have all of the proper documents and releases."

"That's not exactly it," Ray said.

"The captain has most of them. I'm sure that he will let you look them over and even supply copies, if necessary. The other, the environment forms, are being duplicated as we speak. I will have them compiled into a folder for your convenience."

This was all a little too convenient, Ray thought.

They reached the elevator and the doctor pressed the up arrow.

"We're here to see the body," Ray finally said.

"What body?" Willy wanted to know.

"The body of the other man who was killed out on the floes," Ray said.

Denisovich shook her head, feigning ignorance, but Ray could tell she knew what he meant by the look in her eyes.

"Two men died out on the ice," he said. "One was American. A teenager from Barrow. The other was Russian."

The elevator arrived, opened, and the doctor started to get in.

"It's like I said on the radio," Ray explained, following her inside. "This is our jurisdiction. Your ship is in American waters. We need to see the body."

"What if I told you it isn't here?"

Ray smiled at this. Whether she intended to or not, the doctor had just admitted that the body existed and that she knew about it. That was progress. "I'd want to know where it is."

"Perhaps it is unavailable," Denisovich said vaguely.

"It had better get available in a big hurry," Ray told her. It was time to push. "Listen, if you let us take a look, we can be out of your hair in an hour. We just need to verify cause of death. That's it. But if you won't let us see it, then I'll have to call my captain. He'll contact the FBI. In a couple of hours they'll be all over your ship like ants, checking every nook and cranny. They'll not only go over your paperwork with a fine-tooth comb, they'll bust you for any safety and code violations, scrutinize your sanitation methods, your food, the living conditions of the crew . . . It'll be a mess, I guarantee it."

"They can do all that?" Billy Bob wondered.

Ray glared at him. He had no idea. The FBI would, however, be interested in this. They would at the very least send a couple of agents to give the ship the once-over.

"You think they got a helicopter?" Willy asked.

Ray nodded. "They'll fly in on one."

The elevator dinged and the door slid open. Denisovich said, "This is the bridge," but made no move to get off. Instead, she reached out to the panel and pressed S2. The door lurched shut again and they began to go down.

"This is highly unorthodox," she complained. "Our own officials haven't even had an opportunity to view the remains."

"Are they flying out here for that?"

"Probably not. Unless there is a problem. If there is no problem, we will have a funeral aboard ship and bury the man at sea."

"Who determines whether there's a 'problem'?" Ray asked.

"Our captain. But he has placed someone else in charge of investigating the death."

"We'll need to talk to him as well," Ray said.

"You are presently talking to *him*, and *he* was hoping to look into the matter more fully before facing U.S. authorities. But apparently American policemen cannot be distracted as easily as *he* expected."

Billy Bob laughed and Willy laughed with him.

"You find this humorous?"

"Trying to distract this here American po-liceman," Billy Bob said, patting Ray's shoulder, "is about as easy as trying to get a pit bull off yer leg after he's already set his teeth into the bone."

Denisovich blinked at him, confused.

Billy Bob was about to launch into an explanation when Ray interrupted with, "You're in charge of the investigation?"

"Such as it is."

"What do you mean?"

"I am a senior researcher, not a detective. My area of expertise is oceanography."

"What have you got so far?"

Denisovich shrugged. "The man was found in the water. He froze to death."

"The body shows no signs of any other cause of death?"

"I have yet to see the body."

"Isn't it on board?"

"Yes. But we only recovered it from your people this afternoon. I have been working and unable to devote any time to it. We will be here until at least March, possibly April. There is no great hurry."

The elevator opened and she led them into a poorly lit section of the ship.

Willy shivered. "Man, it's cold down here."

"Yes," Denisovich agreed. She took a parka from a hook on the wall and pulled it on. "We are now under the ice. This part of the ship is what we call the *mogeela*, which means 'the tomb.' "

"Good name," Ray said, following her through a mazelike series of turns. They went through a hatch. Another. Another. They kept passing other hatches that were closed.

"What's in all of these?"

"They are holds," Denisovich explained. "Supplies are kept in them. By the way, my captain will require a copy of your report."

"Fine," Ray said.

"This is cool," Willy said, trailing his fingers along the steel bulkhead.

"Kinda gives me the creeps," Billy Bob said.

Ray tended to agree. It was like a dungeon, and the complete absence of any sign of life made it that much more disturbing. It wasn't the sort of place you wanted to navigate alone. That was saying you could navigate it at all. It seemed to him that they were going in circles, and he figured that even with a map, it would take a while to find the elevator again.

They stepped through another open hatch, went down a narrow corridor that looked exactly like all the rest, turned, went through a hatch that was standing open, met a Y, went to the right, went left at another Y . . .

"How do find your way down here?" Ray wondered.

"I've been assigned to this ship for three years," Denisovich said. "All of the subdecks are arranged in the same pattern. Looked at from above, the hallways form a pattern, with every arm eventually leading back to the center."

"Was the elevator at the center?"

"No. It is at the point of an arm."

Ray was about to ask which arm and also what was at the center when a shadow emerged from an open hatch. Willy screamed, Billy Bob clutched Ray's arm, and Ray sucked in air. Denisovich said casually, "*Strostveecha*, comrade."

The man, who was carrying a sack of potatoes under one arm and an elongated box under the other, nodded obsequiously, grunted, "*Strostveecha*, Vrach Denisovich," and pressed himself against the wall so they could pass.

"It thought it was . . ." Willy said, unwilling or possibly unable to complete the thought.

Ray was pretty sure he knew what Willy meant.

He had expected the man to be the tupilak. And down here, in this dingy, rather ghastly hold, Ray was about half ready to agree with him. Though he didn't suffer from claustrophobia, that he knew of, he was getting weary of the narrow corridors, the darkness, the low ceiling . . .

"Here," Denisovich said. She stopped at a hatch door and spun the wheel. It clinked, and when she pushed against the door with her shoulder, there was a hiss of air as the seal was broken.

Ray thought he detected the scent of formaldehyde.

Denisovich switched on a light, and they found themselves in a small laboratory. Tables had been set up along one wall and were lashed to a rail that ran around the room. The tabletops had ledges—to keep things from sliding off in rough seas, Ray assumed. Books, file folders, and computer printouts were stacked along the ledge. On the opposite wall there was a refrigerator, a small freezer, an industrial sink, and a crate of glassware, carefully packed in cardboard.

At the center of the room was another table. This one was more substantial, with thick steel legs that had been bolted to the floor. A blanket was spread out over the table, and beneath the blanket was the unmistakable shape of a supine human body.

TWELVE

DENISOVICH DREW BACK THE BLANKET.

Ray, Billy Bob, and Willy stared at the face she had revealed. Like Tommy's, it was blue, the skin rubberlike in appearance.

"Oh, boy . . ." Billy Bob said, backing away.

"His paperwork is here somewhere," Denisovich said, seemingly disaffected.

"Looks like a Halloween mask," Willy said. "Is it a real guy?" He reached out to touch the cheek, but Ray caught the boy's hand and shook his head at him.

"Here we go," Denisovich said, collecting a file from the table. "Name is . . . Mikhail Chekorov. Been with the *Zvyezda* since June. *Raboocheeye odeen*: level one laborer."

Willy stood on tiptoes. "I wanna see his eyes."

"Why don't you wait outside?" Ray said.

"In the hall, by myself?"

"Then come over here," Ray directed. There was a stool near the tables. "Sit down."

Willy climbed up on the stool. "Are you gonna open his eyes?"

"I don't know."

"If you do, can I see 'em?"

"Yeah, sure," Ray answered, mostly just to keep the kid quiet. He returned to the body. Denisovich handed him a pair of surgical gloves and put some on herself.

"The skin around the neck is wrinkled," Denisovich observed, poking it with a finger.

"From bein' in the water," Billy Bob said from over by Willy. His face was pale. "What's that smell?"

"Preservatives," Denisovich said. "For maintaining specimens."

Billy Bob turned away, one hand over his mouth.

"The body hasn't been altered in any way?" Ray asked.

"Not that I know of," Denisovich said.

Ray leaned over the body. "I'm not a medical examiner," he stipulated. Denisovich watched closely as he used the penlight to look into Chekerov's ears, his nose, then, with some effort, pulled the jaw down to examine the mouth. He felt like a mechanically illiterate man whose car had quit running for no apparent reason. What was it he expected to find? Or not find?

Slipping the blanket down, he saw that the body had been stripped. "Who took off his clothes?"

"I don't know," Denisovich admitted. "Maybe he did, in the water. That's what we train our people to do: get the boots and coat off to keep from being pulled down."

"Boots and parka I can see, even pants," Ray said.

"But gloves, shirt, underwear, socks . . ." He lifted the blanket and shined the light at the man's bare feet.

"Perhaps the men who brought him aboard took his clothes in preparation for burial."

"I thought you said it would be months before you buried him," Ray countered.

"It probably will be. But he will be sealed in a *grob*—a coffin—as soon as we are finished here."

Ray didn't like the rushing that was going on. Eddie was in a big hurry to get his son into the ground, and now the Russians were pushing to "seal" this fellow up. Granted, the People and, obviously, these naluaqmiut had an aversion to death and it was therefore natural to try and dispense with the bodies as quickly as possible. But was that all it was?

As Ray continued his blundering "autopsy," he discovered a snake tattoo on the man's chest. Other than that, there was nothing of interest or note on the front of the body. The anterior, Ray remembered it being called. The skin was blue and looked as though it had recently been in the water. Big surprise there. There were no gashes or wounds.

"Help me turn him over," Ray said.

He and Denisovich clumsily flipped the man onto his stomach. With the blanket having fallen to the floor, the body lay there, sprawled, stiff, naked, and bearing a golf-ball-sized hole between the shoulder blades.

"Oh, man!" Willy exclaimed.

Denisovich recoiled.

"It's from the harpoon," Ray explained, answering the question that everyone was silently asking. "That's how the bodies were found. A guy was out hunting for seal. He thought he had one, used his harpoon . . . Turned out to be a man instead of an animal."

He shined the light into the gouge. It was neat and clean. The harpoon had been very sharp and had also been inserted with great force. Ray was actually surprised it hadn't gone all the way through the man.

Retrieving the blanket, he covered the body to the armpits. With the wound no longer visible, all eyes went to the tattoo on his shoulder: a tremendously endowed woman sans clothing.

"Wow!" Willy said, slipping down from his stool for a better look.

"Sit back down," Ray instructed.

Ray inched the blanket up over the shoulders. Though not afraid of death, per se, Ray felt compelled to preserve as much of the man's dignity as possible.

"Are you gonna open his eyes?" Willy again wanted to know.

Ignoring this, Ray shined the penlight along the neck, behind the ears . . . In order to do this right, they needed to transport the body to Barrow, a nagging inner voice kept reminding him. But unless he found a compelling reason to do so, he doubted he could get consent for that. Which left them where?

He was on the verge of flipping off the light and confessing that, as far as he was concerned, the man had frozen to death in the Chukchi, when he noticed a dark spot in the hair. Pressing the hair back like blades of grass, he saw a bulge in the scalp. It was an even darker purple and there was a short but ragged line at the center. A cut.

"Find something?" Denisovich asked, leaning to look.

"I don't know." Ray turned out the light. "Let's get him back the other way." They turned the body over and Ray covered it up, all the way over the head.

Stepping away from the table, he took out his cell phone. He had flipped it open and was in the process of dialing when Denisovich said, "You won't get out from down here."

Ray hit Send anyway, but was rewarded with a No Service signal. He flipped it shut.

"You can use the ship's radio line," Denisovich offered. She showed him an old-fashioned rotary phone hooked to the wall by a coiling cord. Picking up the receiver, she said something in Russian, then asked, "Who would you like to contact?"

"Dr. Melissa Bradshaw at the hospital in Barrow." He opened his cell phone again and read her the number from the display log.

In a moment Denisovich handed him the phone.

"I don't suppose you could have everyone wait outside," Ray said, looking at Billy Bob. When the cowboy didn't move, Ray nodded at the door.

"Oh, uh . . . okay." Billy Bob ushered Denisovich and Willy into the corridor.

The line was full of static and for several seconds

didn't do anything. Finally, it rang. As it did, Ray thought that having Denisovich leave was pointless. He wanted to have a private conversation, but the radio man upstairs was no doubt listening in.

A woman answered the line and directed his call to Bradshaw's office.

"Hello?"

"Melissa? This is Ray."

"Ray?" she asked through the static.

"I'm glad I caught you. I've got a question for you."

"Where are you? Sounds like you're calling from Siberia."

"Just about," Ray shot back. "Listen, I've got a corpse here that I need help with."

"I won't be able to get away for at least four or five hours," Melissa said. "Things are hopping here. It's the post-Christmas rush."

"Actually, I was hoping you could do it by phone."

"Do what?"

"Give me your medical opinion."

"I guess I can try. What's up?"

"Got a guy here who was recovered from the Chukchi."

"Bummer."

"Big-time. He's a foreigner—Russian—and was found with a local kid."

"Anybody I know?" she asked.

"Tommy Reed."

"Oh, no . . . you're kidding!"

"He was up here visiting his father, I guess. Went

seal hunting. Anyway, they pulled these two out of the water. I'm wondering what I should be finding."

"Well . . . signs of hypothermia, discolored skin, uh . . . there would be some water in the lungs, but unless they went down like rocks, not enough to cause drowning."

Ray nodded. He hadn't though of that. "Short of cutting the body open, which I am not going to do, is there a way to check the condition of the lungs?"

"Uh . . . you could put a tube down there. See what comes out."

"What should come out?"

"Water."

"How much, I mean?"

"If they froze first, then . . . probably not that much."

"Probably?"

"Dying at sea is not an exact science, Ray. Maybe they were good swimmers. Maybe they sucked water from the start. Who knows?"

"What about a puncture wound?"

"A what?"

Ray explained about the harpoon.

"Oh . . . that's horrible."

"There's no blood or anything around the wound."

"No, there wouldn't be. For starters, he was most likely already dead. Blood flow had ceased. And for another thing, he was basically frozen."

That made sense to Ray. "What about a head trauma?" He described the lump on the man's head.

"He could have hit his head on the ice on the way

into the water," she speculated. "Or even while scrambling to climb back out."

"Could the hunter have done it with the harpoon? Or maybe the recovery team?"

"I suppose . . . but . . ."

"But what?"

"I think I know what you're getting at."

"And . . . ?" he prodded.

"And I can't make any guesses about cause of death on a long distance line. I'm sorry I can't be more helpful, Ray. But without examining the body . . ."

"I understand."

"Anything else?" she asked.

"Not at the moment."

"Then I better go. I've got patients waiting. Listen, what you ought to do is bring the bodies back here. Then we can give them the full treatment."

"I don't think that'll work."

"All right. Well, call if you need anything else."

"Don't worry, I will."

"Good luck, Ray."

She hung up, and Ray replaced the phone receiver. He didn't like the sentiment she had expressed: good luck. As though he would need it to get through this thing.

He stood staring at the body. Blue skin, harpoon wound, gash on the back of the head . . . It would sure be nice to know how much water was in the guy's lungs. Did he drown? Did he freeze to death? Or—

There was a knock at the door and it creaked

open. Denisovich led Billy Bob and Willy back inside the laboratory.

"What would it take to get permission to have the body sent to Barrow for an autopsy?" Ray asked.

Denisovich blew air at this. "The *Artketchyeski Zvyezda* is under the captain's command while at sea."

"So he could okay it?"

"I assume so. He would have to contact the authorities back in Moscow and probably need to gain the approval of the RORI, the Ministry of Science, the Ministry of Foreign Affairs . . ."

Ray sagged. "That could take forever."

"Yes."

"Doesn't it make a difference that he died in American waters?"

"I don't know," Denisovich confessed. "That would have to be settled by our respective State Departments."

Ray stood looking at the body but not seeing it. There had to be some way to confirm cause of death—to rule out foul play. That was what was eating at him, he admitted silently. The bang on the back of the guy's head. What if it hadn't been an accident? What if someone had whacked him on purpose, then pushed him into the drink and left him out there to die?

Except, the other body . . . Tommy. That would make it a double murder. Unless . . . no. That was ridiculous. Tommy was good kid. Ray couldn't imagine him committing murder. There was no motive.

No, in all likelihood both men had succumbed to the elements. The blow to the back of this man's head had probably occurred as he fell in, as Melissa had suggested. Sure. He slipped, hit his head, went into the water. Tommy jumps in to try and save him. They both perish. Why not?

A smart man, Ray thought, would file a report and go home. Why not write off the two corpses as the result of accidental death and be done with it? Why? Because while he was ninety-eight percent sure that Tommy and the Russian had fallen victim to the cruel Arctic environment, that last two percent wouldn't let him quit yet.

"Are you finished in here?" Denisovich asked.

"For now," Ray said. "Do you have a doctor aboard ship?"

"Everyone on the senior staff has a Ph.D."

"I meant a medical doctor. An M.D."

"Yes, but . . ." She paused to examine her watch. "He is not on duty, except for emergencies, until seven."

"This could qualify for an emergency, couldn't it?"

"I wouldn't recommend bothering him until his shift starts." She made a motion with her hand, tipping an imaginary glass.

"He's a drunk?"

"Not a drunk. He simply enjoys his vodka. Like many of the rest of the crew. You have to understand that this is a rather dull posting. We have nothing to do but work, eat, sleep . . ."

"And drink," Ray added.

Denisovich continued to defend her shipmates. "Our only entertainment consists of games, cards, a collection of video programs—"

"But you can apparently get off the ship," Ray pointed out. Here he was thinking of the Russian's excursion with Tommy.

"Yes. But where are we to go? There is ice in every direction."

"There's always TaggaQ."

She nodded. "Please take no offense, but . . . when you are used to Moscow, or even Leningrad, this little town of yours is less than exciting."

"It's not *my* town," Ray countered. He tended to agree with her though. TaggaQ was a spot in the road that didn't have anything approaching a night life. "Do very many crew members go into town?"

She shook her head. "Not anymore. At first, some did. But there is simply nothing to do there."

"What about hunting?"

"What about it?"

"Do crew members hunt?"

"A few."

"Which is how he," Ray said, gesturing at the corpse, "and Tommy got together?"

"Clearly. Many of the locals have offered their services as hunting guides, cooks, laborers, etcetera."

"And some of them have been hired on?"

"Yes."

Ray considered this, then turned his attention back to the body.

"You sure we can't call the doctor down?"

"I would advise against it," Denisovich answered. "He can be very ugly when he is disturbed before his shift."

There was a long pause.

"What're we gonna do now?" Billy Bob asked.

Ray sighed. He needed a doctor to look this guy over. Short of that . . . He needed to take a look at the back of Tommy Reed's head. If there was a matching wound . . . "One of us needs to go back to TaggaQ and convince Eddie to let us examine his son."

"Be careful out on that ice," Billy Bob said.

"What do you mean, be careful? Why does it have to be me?"

" 'Cause he's yer people. He'll do better with you."

While coming off as slightly bigoted—"yer people"—the cowboy was right. Ray knew he would have a better chance of getting Eddie's approval to work with the body.

"I'll need you to lead me across the ice," Ray said to Willy.

"Cool!"

"What'll I do?" Billy Bob asked.

"Sit tight. Keep an eye on this guy," Ray said, pointing at the body with a thumb.

"That really isn't necessary," Denisovich said. "We can secure the deck."

"If you don't mind, I'd like my partner here to see to that personally."

"So yer sayin' I get to babysit Mr. Checker-off?"

"Plus I want you in the room when the doctor

does the examination. I'll try to be back before then. But just in case . . ."

"I gotta stay down here all by my lonesome?" Billy Bob said. "With . . . with a dead body?"

"Unless you want to go see Eddie."

"What a choice," the cowboy grumbled.

"I'll be back," Ray told him.

"You better be."

THIRTEEN

As they followed Denisovich into the corridor, Ray couldn't help feeling sorry for Billy Bob. Staking out a dead body in the dungeonlike bowels of a Russian icebreaker wasn't his idea of fun either. But somebody had to do it. Ray wanted to get this thing wrapped up, and to do that he knew he had to make sure the bodies didn't run off on him. He had made that mistake once before, and wouldn't again. Tommy's body was safely stowed in the cemetery shed, under lock and the watchful eye of his father. But Chekerov was just lying there, on a big ship, full of people Ray did not know and therefore could not trust.

They reached the elevator, which in Ray's mind shouldn't have been where it was, and got in.

Out of the blue Denisovich asked, "Are you suggesting that the two men did not die by accident?"

He looked at her. "Did I say that?"

"You're thinking that. Aren't you?"

"Not exactly."

"Then why do you require the doctor? And why

are you going back to examine the other body again?"

"I'm just trying to be thorough," Ray said. He could tell from the look in the woman's eyes that she didn't buy this. "It might have been an accident."

"And it might not have been?"

Ray shrugged. Since she had breached the subject, he asked, "What about this Chekerov? Did he have a problem with anyone on the ship?"

"I was not familiar with him. We have 137 on board. I know most by face, some by name. Others I would not recognize on the street."

Ray nodded, then thought to ask, "How is it that you speak such good English?"

She offered her first genuine smile. "I was educated in your country."

"Where?"

"UCLA."

"Go Bears . . ."

"Yes," she said, the smile lingering. "Los Angeles is an incredible place. America is an incredible place."

"But you went back to Russia?"

She nodded solemnly. "It is my home."

Ray understood this. It was the same reason that, after attending college in Anchorage, he had chosen to return to Barrow. Home was a powerful thing.

"Do you have family?"

"Parents, three brothers, four uncles, two aunts, a grandmother . . ."

"Quite a clan."

"Do you have family as well?"

"All I've got is my anaaluk," Willy interjected. "My uncle. It's just him and me. I don't got no brother or sisters. My mom and dad run off when I was little." He shared this with a remarkable lack of emotion. "I used to have a grandfather, but he died."

"That's very sad," Denisovich consoled.

"It's not so bad," Willy said cheerfully. "Me and Anaaluk get along good. He's my buddy and I'm his."

"I thought you said you had an uncle who owned the hardware store," Ray said. "And another who owned the snow machine shop."

"Oh, them. They're not real anaaluks. They just let me call 'em that."

The elevator opened and they exited onto the communications deck. There was a small knot of men in one of the doorways.

"Here's the captain," Denisovich said. "I'll introduce you."

She led them to the door and waited as the men discussed something. The captain, wearing a uniform, was tall and distinguished looking. Not as old as Ray had expected, but with silver hair and a beard. He was frowning, shaking his head every so often and occasionally muttering *"Nyet."*

The conversation stretched, and it soon became apparent that it was escalating into an argument. The main proponent for the opposing side, whatever it might have been, was a stocky man with a dark mustache and very bushy eyebrows. He was making a case for something, growing more passionate with every *"Nyet"* the captain emitted.

Finally, the captain waved his hands at the man and turned away. His face softened as he saw Dr. Denisovich, becoming almost tender. Ray thought he detected a hint of chemistry running between the two.

"Captain," Denisovich said in a professional tone.

"Vrach," the captain responded.

Denisovich rattled off a long sentence of Russian. Ray recognized the words "Barrow" and "TaggaQ."

The captain turned his attention to Ray and Willy, his bearded face now smiling. "*Strastveecha.* Gree-teens, Amar-i-can freens." He offered his hand to Ray. When Ray had shook it, the captain bent and extended his hand to Willy.

"You are both Ezkeemo, no?"

Ray nodded and braced himself for the usual questions.

The captain spoke excitedly to Denisovich. When he finished, she translated, "He wants to know if you live in ice houses."

Ray and Willy both shook their heads.

The captain said something else. "He asks if you have a dog sled."

"No," Ray said, trying to mask his irritation. It was bad enough to endure stereotypes in English.

"We used to have a dog," Willy said. "But it got run over by a truck."

Denisovich relayed this to the captain, who issued an "Oh . . ." of pity and patted Willy on the head. More Russian followed.

"He says that he has a dog at home in Moscow."

"Great . . ." Ray said.

"What kind?" Willy wanted to know.

Denisovich conferred with the captain. Then: "A Siberian husky."

The captain laughed as though this was quite a joke. When he was finished, he asked another question. "He wishes to know if you eat raw whale meat."

Ray nodded, almost wishing it wasn't true. "Yes, but we also eat regular food."

"My favorite thing is cheeseburgers."

There was a lag as Denisovich translated this, then the captain burst out laughing. He patted Willy affectionately. He said something else to Denisovich, bowed slightly, and strode down the hall away from them, chuckling.

"What was that last part?" Ray wondered.

"He bids you farewell, good luck, and hopes that you do not meet a polar bear unless you are looking for one."

"Funny guy," Ray said.

"He is a good captain," Denisovich said.

"I was sort of hoping I could talk to him about Chekerov."

"He would not know about that."

"What do you mean? He knows he's dead, right?"

"He knows a worker is dead. But it is not a member of his crew."

"I'm not following you."

"There are really two separate groups aboard ship. One is the crew that is responsible for travel—for making the ship go and keeping it safe. The other is the scientific team. Chekerov was part of the scientific team."

"I thought you said he was a common laborer."

"Yes. A 'grunt' as you say here in America."

"So he was working under your supervision?"

"Well, in a way. I am the assistant in charge of research. The head of the team, the man who oversees operations, is Dr. Igor Radikoff."

"Igor . . . ?" Ray asked. The name brought to mind images of Dr. Frankenstein.

"He was the man speaking to the captain when we arrived."

"Maybe I should have a talk with him," Ray thought aloud.

"For what purpose?" Denisovich asked, tensing.

"He might be able to tell me something about Chekerov."

"Perhaps. But what do you hope to learn?"

Ray shrugged. "Just about anything would be helpful. So far we haven't been able to talk with the hunter who found the bodies, the police officer who recovered them . . . The father of the Inupiat victim couldn't tell us much . . . We don't have a doctor here to do an examination of the bodies . . ."

"As I told you, the doctor will be on shift later."

"Exactly. We're spinning our wheels waiting on folks to show up. I'd really like to get this matter settled, file the case and go home."

Denisovich nodded, and Ray thought she seemed relieved, as though glad to hear that he wanted to finish and leave.

"I cannot guarantee that Dr. Radikoff will agree to meet with you."

"Doesn't hurt to ask," Ray said. He was growing weary of the direction the investigation was taking. Thus far they had no clear answers to anything. The most frustrating thing was that it appeared to be so simple. And probably was: the result of bad luck. An accident. If only he could confirm that with facts.

Denisovich directed them to a lounge area where several crew members were sprawled on couches and across chairs, some napping, others watching a big screen television. "Please wait here while I request a meeting."

Ray slumped into a chair. He was tired and his ankle was bothering him. He took a small plastic bottle of ibuprofen out of his jacket pocket and swallowed a pair of tablets before noticing Willy. The boy was watching him closely from the next chair.

"What're you taking?" he wanted to know.

"Aspirin," Ray said.

Willy shook his head. "Those weren't aspirin. Aspirin are white. I know cause Anaaluk has to take 'em every day."

"Is that right?" Ray put the bottle back into his jacket.

"Yeah. Every day. The doctor told 'im to."

"Does he have arthritis or something?"

"No. He's got a sick uumman." Willy tapped the left side of his chest.

"Oh." Ray recalled hearing that aspirin was often prescribed for heart patients. Something about its blood-thinning properties.

"So what was that you took?"

"Ibuprofen. It's like aspirin."

"Really?"

"Really." Ray found the boy's interest odd.

" 'Cause one of my anaaluks—not a real anaaluk, but he lets me call him that—he takes pills kinda like those, except they're blue. They make him have more energy."

Ray nodded. What good old Anaaluk was downing sounded a whole lot like amphetamines. It wasn't enough that the kid was nearly an orphan—his uncle had heart problems and his quasiuncle was a doper. What a life.

"Hey!" Willy said. He pointed at the big screen TV. *"Baywatch!"*

Ray realized that the kid was right. Young women in high-cut bathing suits were running across a beach in slow motion, their ample, unsupported breasts rising and falling to the delight of the small Russian audience. One of the men pointed excitedly and said something indecipherable. Others clapped and hooted.

"I always watch this at my anaaluk's house. Not my real anaaluk 'cause we don't got power, but over at the anaaluk that owns the hardware store."

"I get you," Ray assured him.

The women on the screen, all of whom were very tan and had long slender legs, reached the water and leapt in. From back at the lifeguard tower a young man, also very tan and with a washboard stomach, spoke into a radio. His lips didn't match the audio, which had been translated into Russian. The crew members booed whatever it was he said. Perhaps, Ray thought, he had ordered the women to put on some clothes.

"It's a good show," Willy said, watching as the women swam in slow motion. "They always save people. That's what I'm gonna do when I grow up."

Ray found the boy's innocence refreshing. Instead of slobbering over the female bodies being displayed, he was thinking of the job they were supposedly doing and wanted to do likewise. Ray decided that he liked Willy. He was more than just another kid. He was a boy who, despite a strange and dysfunctional living situation, had somehow maintained his ability to trust, believe, dream . . .

On the screen, the swimming women reached the drowning victim: a dog that had been pulled out by the receding tide.

Some of the men laughed at this. Willy's expression changed to one of concern. "I hope they save him."

"Me too," Ray said.

Thankfully, they pulled the dog ashore. Laying him out on the sand, the three women knelt provocatively, leaning over the animal to check his vital signs. Again the crew members showed their appreciation for the views being offered.

Willy clapped too, but not for the cleavage. He was applauding the resuscitation of the dog.

The animal had just made it back to all fours and

was shaking when a voice said, "He will meet with you briefly."

Ray turned and saw Denisovich. She had a serious look on her face, as though she had just arranged Middle East peace talks that were not expected to go well.

"How would you like to stay and watch TV?" Ray asked Willy. *Baywatch* wasn't exactly his idea of appropriate adolescent entertainment, but the kid was obviously already an avid fan, and he wanted to talk to Radikoff without a tagalong.

"Okay," Willy agreed happily.

"I'll be back in a few minutes." Ray got up and followed Denisovich into the hallway and over to the elevator.

When it opened, Denisovich reached in and pushed the button marked 5. "Floor five. Dr. Radikoff's office and quarters occupy the entire level."

"Aren't you coming?"

She shook her head. "I'll keep an eye on Willy for you." Her expression and tone were almost grim.

"But I'll need an interpreter."

Another head shake. "Dr. Radikoff speaks fluent English." She reached out and held the elevator doors to keep them from shutting. "And if I might make a suggestion?" She waited for his consent.

"Go ahead."

"Be careful not to make him angry."

"I wasn't planning on it."

"He is not a patient man and angers quite easily."

"Thanks for the tip."

"Also, if he does lose his temper, do not back down. Simply do as the captain did and stand your ground. Don't apologize. That implies weakness. Dr. Radikoff despises weakness."

She let the doors go and they closed on Ray. As the elevator began to rise, his stomach growled. It wasn't an expression of hunger, he realized, but nerves. For some reason, he felt like a twelve-year-old being sent to see the school principal.

FOURTEEN

WHEN THE ELEVATOR doors opened on floor 5, Ray found himself face-to-face with a very large man. In his opinion, the guy was qualified to be governor of Minnesota: a wide, almost square body, no neck to speak of, arms that were almost as big around as Ray's waist, and a gleaming bald head. The only thing Ray had on this guy was an inch or so of height.

"Shto?" the man grunted.

Ray could tell by the inflection that this was a question. He could also tell from the man's face that it was something of a challenge.

"I'm here to see Dr. Radikoff."

"Shto?" He took a step forward, hands balled into fists.

"Dr. Denisovich sent me up to see Dr. Radikoff . . ." Ray said slowly, enunciating carefully. He had his back up against the wall of the elevator. There was nowhere to run.

The man rattled off something in Russian.

"Pardon me?"

The man repeated it, teeth clinched.

"Uh . . . No comprendo Russian. Except *'zveyzda.'* I can say 'star.' And *'strastveecha'* . . . hello." Ray smiled, but it was not returned.

"Name . . . *manyekyen.*"

Ray wasn't sure what *manyekyen* meant, but it didn't sound like a compliment. "I'm Officer Ray Attla." He moved to extract his ID, but was suddenly being pressed against the elevator wall, a thick forearm across his neck. This was not only uncomfortable, his breath effectively cut off, but it perturbed him. In the instant before he reacted, Ray thought that someone visiting the United States ought to have more respect for the local law enforcement agencies.

In order to ensure that this respect be given, Ray used a move he had learned from Billy Bob. The cowboy had been training in karate for nearly three years now, and while he wasn't too proficient with all the kicks and punches, he had mastered a technique known simply as the groin strike and had passed it along to Ray.

Ray brought his knee up hard between the brute's legs. This produced a groan, but the forearm remained fixed at his Adam's apple. He repeated the maneuver. The third time, the man finally sank to his knees. Gasping for air, Ray stepped around him and onto the fifth floor.

There was a door to the right, another to the left. Straight ahead was a third. None of them were marked and all were closed. He was about to try the door to his left, his strategy being to work in a clockwise fashion until he found Radikoff, when the door to the right swung open. Out stepped a man who rivaled the Jesse Ventura look-alike in size and attitude.

This guy, who actually looked a little like Hulk Hogan because of a wild shock of blond hair and a closely cropped goatee, said something in Russian that sounded a whole lot like a threat.

"Hold on," Ray responded, fishing for his ID. He flashed the badge at the man, with little effect.

Ray glanced around for a stairway, but didn't see one and was about to retreat to the elevator when the door ahead of him opened and another man came out. It was Radikoff.

He spoke to the security man in a demanding, questioning voice, his bushy eyebrows hiding his eyes.

The second security man explained.

Radikoff glared at the man, shook his head, then proceeded to chew him out.

The man nodded apologetically, and this seemed to enrage Radikoff. He chased the man down the hall, swiping at him with a sheaf of papers.

When the guard had escaped through the door, Radikoff returned. "Attla?" he said in clear English.

"Yes."

"I told them you were coming. But they are imbeciles." He was still fuming and, Ray noticed, didn't offer an apology. "Why must they all be such *ee-dy-oots*?"

Ray shrugged.

Radikoff looked past him into the still open elevator where the man continued to kneel, his legs keeping the doors from closing. The doctor muttered something that could well have been profane, then strode toward the door he had emerged from. "Come," he said with an edge of irritation.

Ray followed him into a spacious office. It was well-decorated with art and attractive furniture and effectively made you forget you were aboard a ship.

Radikoff went to his desk—a large, gleaming plank of oak that held a gold pen and pencil set and a small crystal globe containing a winter scene with a snowman. He sat down in his high-backed leather chair and leaned back, waiting impatiently for Ray to take the chair in front of the desk.

As Ray did, he noticed an array of diplomas on the back wall: Harvard Business School, Harvard Medical School, MIT College of Science.

Radikoff caught him looking at the diplomas and smiled. "I am a product of the West," he said proudly. His countenance then shifted radically and he was tight-lipped and sober. "How may I help you, Officer?"

"I'm investigating two deaths that—"

"Yes, yes—I know this. Please dispense with the nonessentials. What, specifically, do you require from me?"

"Well . . ." Ray was taken aback by this. "Uh . . ."

"Speak!"

"Did you know Mikhail Chekerov?"

"He was a common worker. I believe he was hired by one of my assistants. I would not know him if he came up and kissed me on the cheek."

"You missed your chance on that one," Ray said without thinking. He immediately regretted this.

"What was that?"

"Nothing."

"Are you mocking me?"

"No . . . sir." He threw in the "sir" in hopes of placating the man. Denisovich had said don't get him angry.

"I don't have time to be treated with disrespect by a man who thinks of education as reading the back of a cereal box."

Ray smiled. Radikoff was a jerk, just as Denisovich had implied. Her other advice rang in his ears: don't back down.

"Is there something you find humorous, *Officer*?"

Ray stood up and got out his ID again. He flipped it open at Radikoff.

"So? Am I supposed to be impressed? I am a very busy man and I have no time for—"

"Do you have time to be dragged ashore and placed in front of a judge?"

Radikoff drew back as though Ray had just slapped him. "You have no right to—"

"I have every right to. You are currently in American waters. I am an American police officer. If I so choose, I can shut you down, drag the entire crew to, say . . . Fairbanks. Put you on trial . . ."

"For what? What offense have I committed?"

"Try, interfering with a police investigation."

Radikoff dismissed this with a wave of his hand. "That will never fly."

"I think it will. But even if it doesn't, you'll be

ashore for weeks, perhaps months, depending on how full the court schedule is. You and your team will be calling the Fairbanks city jail home for however long it takes to get a trial date. And in the meantime, you'll be dead in the water—literally. We're talking money down the toilet."

The mention of money caught Radikoff's attention. He sniffed, but didn't have a comeback.

"All I need is a few minutes of your time to ask some simple questions. Then I'll be out of your hair." Ray was still standing, looking down on Radikoff with what he hoped was an imposing expression.

"Very well," Radikoff said. He grinned as though Ray's response had pleased him.

Though he had only just met the man, Radikoff struck Ray as a head case: someone who was arrogant, pompous, and thrived on making others cringe before him. Those who didn't buckle apparently intrigued him.

"Back to Chekerov," Ray said. "Why was he off the ship?"

"We let the crew do as they wish when they are not on shift."

"Including go ashore?"

"Some of them."

"Which?"

Radikoff shrugged. "I'm not up on crew benefits."

"Who is?"

"Dr. Denisovich can tell you that."

"What about fraternizing with the locals?"

"What about it?"

"Is it permitted?"

"Again, I have no idea. These are trivial matters. I am concerned with the project. It consumes my time and energy. I have little interest in who goes where, only in whether or not they do their job."

"Did Chekerov?"

"Did he what?"

"Do his job?"

"I don't know!" Radikoff said tersely.

"But you just said that—"

"Do you have a hearing problem, Officer? The daily goings on of our workers is not my affair. I oversee the entire project. I am the project manager."

"Okay . . . then . . . tell me about the project."

"I was given to understand that Dr. Denisovich had explained it to you."

"She did. But it was pretty vague. Maybe you could give it a shot." Ray was feeling more confident and even a little cocky now that Radikoff had backed off a little.

"We are researching the polar ice cap and its interaction with the environment."

"That's kind of what she said. Could you be a little more specific? What does this research involve?"

"It is very complicated and you would not understand."

"Try me."

"It has to do with the widening gaps in the ozone,

global warming, the slow increase in the temperature of the seas, the possibility that another ice age may be approaching."

"Okay. But what are you doing? I mean, why is the *Arctic Star* sitting in the ice off the coast of Alaska?"

Radikoff sniffed and repositioned himself in the chair. With the fingertips of one hand tapping against those of the other, he began, "What we are trying to accomplish is the first full-year record of the movement and temperature variation of ice plates in the region of—"

He broke off when the phone behind him rang. Swiveling in the chair, he donned a headset with a mike. *"Shto?"*

As he began a conversation in Russian, Ray sat back and eyed the diplomas again. It was obvious that Radikoff was a smart guy. Anyone who could pull down an MBA and an M.D. from Harvard, as well as a Ph.D. from MIT, had to have some major brainpower. But thus far he was also proving to be quite clever. The man wasn't about to tell him what he wanted to know. Not in plain language, at least. For whatever reason, Radikoff seemed content to continue the scientific doubletalk until he either ran out of time or interest. And now this phone call. Maybe it was part of the plan too—a stall tactic.

Ray found all of this curious. What was it about the *Arctic Star* project that required this runaround? It wasn't like it was top secret or anything. They were sitting out here in plain view of the coast. Doing what? Checking the ice? Was it that simple?

If so, why not say as much? Why not explain how the technicians went out and did core samples or whatever it was they did to test the floes? Why not give him a rundown on the actual operation and offer to show him the crew in action? Chances were, a police officer looking into two apparent accidental deaths would turn down such an offer and go away satisfied. Why aggravate him with this "movement and temperature variation" baloney?

While Radikoff barked foreign phrases into the phone, Ray tried to think. He was ready to be done and call it a day, but couldn't get rid of the nagging suspicion that there was more to this than anyone wanted to admit. Why he thought this, he had no idea. It was just a gut instinct. A hunch. Sometimes these hunches paid off and helped him break a case. Other times they were the result of fatigue and turned out to be totally bogus. Unfortunately, he couldn't always tell the difference. Like right now. Was he being hypercritical of the events and individuals involved, looking for evil intent where there simply wasn't any?

Grandfather often accused him of trying too hard and getting himself worked up over the wrong things. The old man liked to compare Ray to a ptarmigan caught in a snare. Instead of using its eyes and mind to discover the answer to its plight, the bird flailed its wings and fought until it was exhausted and easily claimed by the hunter. Ray's propensity to make mountains out of molehills—and vice versa—had earned him the nickname "kinnaq tinmiaq," which meant, literally, crazy bird.

Grandfather tended to chuckle when calling him this.

Ray glanced at his watch impatiently. Noticing this, Radikoff held up a finger to indicate just a minute.

Feeling increasingly restless, Ray rose and began to wander the office. There was nothing "scientific" about it. Everything spoke of success and luxury: a wet bar in the corner, an entertainment center with three TV screens and a bank of speakers, a leather couch, two overstuffed leather chairs, a coffee table with an attractive stone sculpture and a splay of magazines, the top issue bearing a picture of a woman on a fashion runway. It was more like the office of a company president or a CEO. There were six clocks arranged next to the entertainment center. They all showed different times and, Ray realized as he approached, were labeled: Moscow, Tokyo, Los Angeles, New York, London, Paris.

Why, he wondered disapprovingly, would a Russian researcher need to know what time it was in L.A.? The whole thing seemed pretentious. The same for the guards outside. Who did Radikoff think he was?

While none of this felt right, it did not constitute just cause for further investigation. It didn't constitute anything. Just because some guy on a ship had money and chose to live like a rock star didn't make him a multiple murdering tupilak.

Ray stopped in the middle of the room. *Multiple murdering tupilak*? He rubbed his eyes and decided that he was, in fact, too tired to be here. His mind was beginning to marry fact with fiction. That even in his own imagination he would accuse a man, a virtual stranger, of a crime, when it was not yet apparent that a crime had even been committed, was ridiculous. Unprofessional. But to allow terms like tupilak to bubble up and attach themselves to people he was interviewing . . . He needed to get some sleep. Or maybe eat. Get a cup of coffee to clear his head.

Radikoff finished his call, held up another finger, and placed another.

Ray sat back down and waited. Thankfully, this call took only a matter of seconds.

When he finished, Radikoff said, "I've arranged for you to speak with Comrade Chekerov's *kojeetyel*—his roommate."

"Oh . . . ?"

"I have a conference call in two minutes," Radikoff said, standing to offer his hand. "I'm sorry I couldn't be more help."

Ray shook his hand.

"Dr. Denisovich will meet you in the elevator."

"What about the . . . the brute squad?"

"They will not be a problem for you."

"You sure?"

"You have my word."

Ray nodded and went to the door, wondering if Radikoff's word was worth anything.

FIFTEEN

TO RAY'S RELIEF, the hallway was free of would-be professional wrestlers. He went straight to the elevator and pushed the down arrow.

As he waited for the elevator to arrive, he admitted to himself that he didn't have a handle on Radikoff. The guy was something of an enigma. First, he acted hostile and defensive, then he blew smoke, then he suddenly changed tack and agreed to let him talk to Chekerov's roommate. That was the trouble with men of authority, Ray thought: you couldn't tell when they were being difficult because they had something to hide, and when they were simply being egocentric jerks.

The doors opened, and there was Denisovich.

"We meet again," Ray deadpanned.

"I left your Willy in the company of the men in the lounge. I hope that meets with your approval."

At first Ray thought she was developing a sense of humor. Willy wasn't "his." As for leaving him with a group of Russian sailors stuck on a ship in the Arctic Ocean . . .

"They were watching a program called *Pol v-Gorod.*"

"Sounds exciting," Ray joked.

"Actually, it is American show: *Sex in the City.*"

"Oh, well, that's appropriate for a thirteen-year-old."

She nodded, as though in agreement, and Ray had to laugh.

"What's funny?" she wanted to know.

"As far as I can tell, nothing," Ray said.

Sniffing, she explained, "You will be speaking to a man on level one." She consulted a note she had in her hand. "A Stephen Kilga. He was Chekerov's roommate."

The elevator door opened and they exited onto the first floor. The smell of fried meat hit them, and Ray was suddenly starving.

"Kilga's crew is in the mess hall," Denisovich explained.

Ray followed her to a gated door that required a credit card key to gain entrance. As Denisovich produced her card, Ray asked, "Why the lock?"

"A safety precaution," she replied, working the card through the slot.

This didn't satisfy him, but he decided not to push it. "What's with Radikoff?"

"What do you mean?" she asked, pushing the door open.

"I mean, he's . . . an interesting guy."

"Yes. He is eccentric, but also brilliant."

"Well-off too, from the looks of his office."

"He has been compensated for his achievements."

"What achievements would those be?"

"He is responsible for many breakthroughs in the field of geophysical engineering."

"Such as?"

"He is the father of modern alluvial and sea floor penetrative technology."

"Translation, please." Denisovich was starting to sound almost as bad as Radikoff.

She blinked at him curiously. "Dr. Radikoff is nearly single-handedly responsible for the present revolution in subterranean and suboceanic pathways." Ray was about to confess that this made no sense when she added: "Tunnels."

"Tunnels?"

"Yes. His equations and theories have led to numerous breakthroughs in the construction and maintenance of safe, erosion-resistant tunnels. Especially under bodies of water."

Ray nodded. Finally, something that made sense. "So you're here studying the ice to figure out how to tunnel under it?"

"Exactly. In the near future there will be a passageway connecting Siberia with Alaska, bridging the gap between Asia and North America."

"Are you serious?" Ray found this difficult to believe.

"The Arctic Ocean is shallow, as oceans go. And with Dr. Radikoff's radical advances in engineering, we can construct such a tunnel, making railroad and even automobile traffic between Asia and North America possible."

Ray was dumbfounded by this. He had heard talk

of a connective railroad from Russia to America before. But that was all it had amounted to: talk. It was far too expensive, not to mention impractical, to attempt.

"This is for real?" he asked. "I mean, your government and our government are behind the project?"

Denisovich nodded.

If that was true, Ray realized, it would explain why the ship was being allowed to sit off the coast here. It would also shed light on the security guards, the two separate crews—sailors and scientists . . . It even put Radikoff into perspective. If he was some kind of super genius engineer, a cross between Bill Gates and Einstein, changing the way man interacted with his environment . . . No wonder he was in the money.

Ray's mind raced at the potential impact of a trans-Arctic railroad. It would be greater than the discovery of oil on the North Slope. Alaska would be . . . what? The Ellis Island of the twenty-first century? He shuddered at the idea.

"Here we are," Denisovich said, leading Ray into the mess hall. She gestured at a young man in a chair next to the wall, near the entrance to the kitchen. "That's him." He was about twenty, wearing oil-stained coveralls and a knit cap. Seemingly banished from the array of tables, he was sitting by himself, balancing a plate of food in his lap, forking in bites at an almost manic pace.

"How do you know that's Chekerov's roommate?" Ray thought to ask. "If you didn't know Chekerov—"

"I was told that he would be waiting by the

kitchen," she shot back, apparently catching the insinuation.

"Ah . . ."

When they reached the man, Denisovich said, "Comrade Kilga."

The man looked up from his plate, mouth full, eyes wide. He quickly wiped his lips on the sleeve of his coveralls and struggled to stand.

Denisovich waved him back down. "At ease, comrade." She pulled two chairs over from the closest table, gave one to Ray, then began speaking to the man in Russian.

Ray sat watching, trying to read the man's face. He wasn't sure what Denisovich was saying, but whatever it was, the man was not thrilled to hear it. Ray caught the name Chekerov several times and then Attla. The man's eyes shifted to Ray for a brief moment, then went back to Denisovich. He had completely forgotten his plate, which still contained a small mountain of mashed potatoes and a slab of bread slathered with butter.

When Denisovich finally paused, giving the man the opportunity to speak, he just sat there, eyes looking up at her nervously. Denisovich launched into another paragraph of Russian. Thirty seconds later she asked something that had Chekerov's name in it. This time the man hesitated, then shook his head.

More Russian followed. The man shook his head again.

"What are you asking him?" Ray wondered.

"If he knows the whereabouts of his roommate. He says he does not."

"He doesn't know Chekerov is dead?"

"Dead?" the man asked, eyes flashing.

Denisovich admonished Ray with a glare. "It is not common knowledge aboard the *Arctic Star* that a crew member has died."

"Dead?" the man said again. He had obviously recognized this word.

Denisovich waved her hand and pacified him with more Russian.

"What are you telling him now?"

Ignoring this, she continued to question the man, each time drawing a shake of the head.

Finally, Denisovich turned to Ray. "He has never been off the ship with Chekerov. They do not work on the same shift."

"Ask him how long he's known Chekerov." Ray waited as Denisovich relayed the question, nodded at the answer, then translated it for him.

"Only since coming aboard ship. They were assigned to the same room. Other than that, they have little in common. He seldom sees him, except in the communal lavatory. You have to realize," Denisovich explained, "that there is a night and day to life on the *Arctic Star*. One shift is always at work while the other sleeps. We have only half as many beds as there are crew members."

"Which was Chekerov? Night or day?"

Denisovich consulted the man. "Night. Which I would suppose allowed him the freedom to go hunting during the day."

"When did he sleep?" Ray wanted to know.

Denisovich shrugged and didn't bother relaying this.

"So this guy wouldn't know if Chekerov was popular, unpopular, an experienced hunter, a thrill seeker, proficient in cross stitch . . . ?" When Denisovich squinted at this, Ray added, "Never mind. Ask him if he knew about Chekerov going ashore."

Denisovich did this. Or maybe she talked sports with him. Ray couldn't tell.

After more head shaking and a few grunted responses, Denisovich told Ray, "No. He has no idea how Chekerov spent his free time."

"Ask him if he's ever been off the ship."

She did, and at last the man's face grew animated. He rattled off something, then, balancing his plate on his knee, pulled a card from the pocket of his overalls. It was a photograph that had been laminated like a driver's license. He showed it to them proudly and said, "Sonya."

"She's pretty," Ray said, smiling and nodding. "Is that his wife?"

"Girlfriend. He promised her he would be faithful while he was away, which is why he doesn't go ashore."

"A man of principle," Ray said approvingly. "Too bad Chekerov didn't stick to the ship." This caused him to wonder, for the first time, about Chekerov's family. "Was he married?"

"This is his girlfriend," Denisovich repeated.

"No. I mean Chekerov."

"I don't know."

"Can you check?"

"I suppose. What importance is it?"

Ray didn't have an answer for this. He wasn't sure that anything he and Billy Bob had done thus far was of any importance whatsoever. "I'd just be interested to know."

"We can pull his file in the communications center."

The man was looking at the photo card now, probably dreaming of going back home to Russia, Ray thought. "Can we look at Chekerov's room?"

Denisovich nodded. She said something to the man, then, "*Spaseeba*, comrade."

"*Spaseeba*," Ray said, using up nearly half of his Russian.

The man nodded and returned his attention to his plate, suddenly ravenous again.

Ray followed Denisovich through a hatchway at the rear of the mess hall and into a narrow corridor. The click-clack of Denisovich's shoes and the swish of her skirt were amplified in the tight, metallic space.

"Are there many women on the ship?" Ray asked.

"I am the only one."

"That must be tough."

She shrugged without looking back at him. "It is annoying to be with so many men. But I have gotten used to it."

"They don't give you any trouble?"

"Trouble?"

"You know . . . sailors away from port for too long."

She laughed. "They are not so foolish as to make that mistake."

Ray wasn't sure what she meant by this. Maybe her rank made that sort of thing unthinkable. Or maybe she was a black belt in Russian self-defense and would wipe the floor with anyone who made that "mistake."

They went down a set of metal stairs to another hatch that led to another corridor, this one even more dimly lit. Ray was having the same sensation he'd had when they ventured into the bowels of the ship to view the body: a tinge of claustrophobia and a swelling desire to go back to the main deck for a breath of real air and a look at the sky. He marveled at the crew's ability to live under such conditions.

They came to a row of doors, each with a number inscribed above the frame. *"Oden . . . dva . . . tree . . ."* Denisovich stopped at the third door. "This should be it." She knocked, waited, then pushed the door open. It was pitch-black inside, dark enough to have been a portal into space or the depths of the ocean. Denisovich flipped a wall switch and two bare bulbs protected by steel cages blinked to life. There was a slight flickering, as though the current was not quite constant. It bothered Ray and made him a little dizzy.

The room was tiny, only five or so feet wide, perhaps eight feet long. A spacious sepulcher, Ray thought, the claustrophobia becoming more pronounced. It had a bunk built into one side, a narrow metal cabinet crowded into the other. There was hardly enough room to turn around, much less live.

As if reading his thoughts, Denisovich said, "The men work twelve hour shifts. When they are not eating or recreating in the upper lounges, they sleep. So the accommodations need not be luxurious."

That made sense to Ray. Still, the room was like a sardine can. He began to look around in hopes of finishing up before the walls closed in on him.

"What is it we are looking for?"

Ray caught her use of the plural pronoun and also the interest in her voice. She either was anxious to help, anxious to get him out of her hair, or . . . or what? "I'm not sure."

He glanced at the crisply made sheets on the cot and the blanket that had been folded neatly and placed on the pillow. These guys got points for housekeeping.

Ray bent and looked under the bunk. There were two fat duffel bags stuffed under it. Both had the same Russian word written on the side in magic marker. Ray pulled one out and showed the marking to Denisovich.

"Chekerov," she translated.

He loosened the drawstring and the stench of dirty socks hit him. It was full of laundry. He pushed it back and pulled out the other. Same thing. So much for good housekeeping. Chekerov hadn't done his wash in quite some time.

"They do have laundry facilities aboard, don't they?" he asked, half joking.

"Of course. Laundry is picked up every other day."

Rising, Ray went to the cabinet. It had a latch and a padlock, which was hanging unfastened. He slid the lock off and opened the doors. Inside was a split level compartment. The upper section was filled with personal hygiene items: shaving cream, toothpaste, a dingy comb, deodorant . . . The lower section held a carton of cigarettes, a couple of paperback books, a few tattered magazines, a half-dozen pencils, and a notebook. Ray picked up the notebook and fanned through it: handwritten Russian verse. Pages of it.

"Find something?"

"Poetry," Ray said. "I think." He handed it to Denisovich.

She looked at the page he had open. After reading for a moment, she smiled. "Love poems." She read some more. "They're actually pretty good. Or at least, this one is." She turned the page, read another, then flipped to the inside cover. "This is Kilga's."

"Must be writing about his girlfriend."

"Must be," Denisovich said.

She handed it back and Ray put it on the shelf. After closing the cabinet, he stood surveying the room. There wasn't anywhere else to hide things. To hide what? he wondered. What was he hoping to discover? A note from Chekerov stating that he was accident prone, that he couldn't swim . . . ?

"Do you keep records on who leaves the ship?"

"Yes."

"So we can look up what time Chekerov went hunting?"

"Yes. Will that be helpful?"

"I doubt it. But it won't hurt to check."

Denisovich stepped out the door, and Ray was about to follow when a thought hit him. "There's no closet in here. Where do they keep their clothes?"

"Work coveralls are issued each morning. Along with sleeping attire."

"They don't have any personal clothing?"

"No."

"Not even underwear?"

She shook her head. "It makes things much simpler."

Ray cringed at the idea of having to wear someone else's underwear, and immediately decided that he was far too American—too white—for his own good. Not long ago, an Inupiat would have considered underwear an unnecessary curiosity.

"If they don't have their own things and the laundry is every other day," he said, "then they don't have a chance to accumulate a lot of dirty clothes."

Denisovich seemed puzzled by Ray's sudden obsession with laundry.

He knelt at the bunk again and pulled out the two duffels. "So what's in these?" He opened one and began pulling out clothes: a stiff shirt, stiff socks, stiff overalls, all radiating a smell that made Ray's eyes burn.

"Comrade Chekerov was apparently less than fastidious," Ray observed. He reached over and began dumping the other bag: more ripe clothing.

"What a slob," Denisovich said in disgust.

The bag was nearly empty when a lump fell out: a

shirt wrapped around something heavy. Ray peeled the shirt away and, for the first time since the investigation had begun, felt a tinge of optimism. Maybe his instincts hadn't been wrong after all.

"I'd say he was more than a slob," Ray surmised, eyeing the thick bundles of U.S. cash. "I'd say he was some sort of crook."

SIXTEEN

"IS IT . . . IS IT REAL?"

Ray used his thumb to fan through one of the packets. They were all thousands. "I'm no counterfeit expert but . . ." He withdrew a single bill from the stack and held it up to the light. "Looks genuine to me."

Denisovich picked up a packet. "There must be . . . ten thousand dollars."

"More," Ray corrected. "In fact . . ." He counted the bundles, estimated the number of bills in each, and did the math in his head. "There's about . . . seventy-five . . . maybe a hundred thousand here."

Denisovich gave a gasp of amazement.

Ray scooted the laundry over and sat down on the cot, next to the money. "Where would a laborer get this kind of cash?" he thought aloud.

"Maybe he robbed a bank," Denisovich guessed.

"Maybe. But why would you be working on an icebreaker in the middle of nowhere if you had the money to go and to do whatever you wanted?"

She shrugged. "He could have been hiding out,

waiting for the authorities to stop looking for him?"

"Possible," Ray admitted.

"I can call Moscow and see if there have been any crimes that fit this," she said, waving at the money.

"Good idea," Ray said, only half listening. They suddenly had motive in Chekerov's death. It still could have been an accident. But . . . Ray glanced down at the stacks of money. What if someone had killed him to get the cash? It could have been as simple as that. Or they could have stumbled onto something more complex that would better explain the cache of U.S. currency: a drug deal gone bad, one criminal betraying another, revenge . . .

On the other hand, if someone had committed murder in order to obtain the money, they had obviously failed. At least, on the latter account. Here sat the dough. If you'd killed the man, why not go to his room, grab the money, and take off? But then, there was nowhere to go out here on the ice.

"The records on who leaves the ship . . . how accurate are they?"

"What do you mean?"

"Could you go ashore without anyone knowing about it?"

"I don't think so. Why?"

"I'm just wondering about Mr. Kilga. Where do you suppose he was while Chekerov was off hunting?"

"Kilga?"

"It's his room too. His roommate is dead. He's sleeping on top of a big wad of money . . ."

"Chekerov's off-duty time would have been Kilga's work shift," Denisovich pointed out.

"Is there any way you can verify that? Confirm that Kilga was where he was supposed to be?"

"I can check with his supervisor."

"Okay." Ray sat there, trying to piece things together. The discovery of a motive was good . . . and bad. It had the effect of cranking the investigation up a few levels on the seriousness scale and also of further confusing things.

He sighed at the money. "We need a place to keep this. It's evidence."

"The captain has a safe."

"That'll do." Ray began wrapping the bundles back up in the shirt.

"Should I have Comrade Kilga arrested?"

"Can you do that?"

"With the consent of the captain."

"Do you have a detention room or something?"

"We have a brig."

This surprised Ray. "Does it see much use?"

"There are fights, and occasionally a crew member is caught with contraband. That is what happened to the doctor."

"The one we're waiting for to do the exam of the body?"

She nodded.

"I though you said he was asleep . . ."

"In the brig. He is currently on detention for possession of vodka." She looked at Ray expectantly. "Would you like Kilga to be arrested?"

Ray shook his head. "Not yet. Maybe not at all. But it would be nice if he were around to talk to."

"I will have his shore privileges revoked."

Ray agreed to this, though he doubted it would be necessary. If Kilga was truly out of the loop, he would continue to keep his promise to his girlfriend. If he was involved, and learned that they had found the money, he wouldn't worry about "privileges." He would run like a rabbit. Which he might have done already. Talking to him in the mess hall could have sent him into a panic.

Ray stood up and put the bundled shirt under his arm. "Let's go back up and do a little digging."

When they arrived on the communications floor and had made their way to her office, they were met by a gruff, mouthful of Russian. It came from an overweight, raccoon-eyed man who was slouching in the chair behind her desk. He had a ring of gray hair that stood at attention around a bald scalp, making him look as though he had just stuck his finger in a light socket.

Denisovich said something to the man, then ordered him up, out of her chair. Ignoring this, he leaned back and, in a bored tone, assaulted her with Russian.

"This is Dr. Butyerki," Denisovich said with a frown. She started to introduce Ray, and he recognized his own name before Butyerki belched and muttered, *"Prokleenat polesheeya . . ."*

Denisovich tore into him like a mother after a wayward child. He reacted to this by covering his face with his hands, then rising and stumbling toward the door.

"He's drunk," Ray said, watching her manhandle him into a chair.

He muttered something, to which she replied, "Liar . . ."

"What did he say?"

"He claims he is merely tired."

"Is he too sloshed to help us with Chekerov?" Ray wondered.

"Let's do our 'digging' first," she suggested. "I'll have someone fill him up with coffee."

Ray started to point out that coffee had no effect on inebriation, other than possibly keeping the person awake, but decided it wasn't worth it.

Denisovich called a young uniformed man in and had him assist the doctor to the mess hall. Then she took her seat behind the desk and picked up the phone. While she made calls, Ray slipped out and went to the lounge to check on Willy. The kid was sprawled on one of the couches, out like a light. The men were gone now, probably on shift or maybe sawing logs of their own back in their rooms, but someone had seen fit to cover Willy with a blanket. The TV was still on, now offering up a subtitled version of *Sally Jessy Raphael.*

Ray found the remote and hit the mute button, silencing Sally just as she was revving up to discuss a man who had been having an affair with his wife's sister. He then returned to Denisovich's office.

"The Moscow police are not familiar with any

robberies involving that much money," she said as he walked in. "They are using their computers to contact other enforcement agencies."

"What about Chekerov? They have anything on him? Priors?"

"Priors?"

"Has he been arrested before? Does he have a record?"

"I gave them his name, and Kilga's, and they will let me know."

"Good. What about the shore log?"

Here she referred to her computer. "The information should all be in the system." She tapped the keyboard, waited, tapped some more. "Uh . . . let's see . . ." She leaned toward the screen. "Chekerov made a request last week to go off-ship. It was okayed by his supervisor and then . . ."

"Then what?"

She shook her head and typed something else in. "That's strange."

"What?" Ray stepped around the desk for a look at the screen. It didn't help, since everything was in Russian.

"The day he went hunting . . . the day he died . . ." She sighed and tried another key sequence. "No. It's not here."

"What do you mean?"

"The system went down that day and some of the information was lost."

"That's convenient."

"How so?"

"I was being sarcastic."

"Oh." She tried something else, then gave up. "There's no way to tell who went ashore that day."

"Does the system go down a lot?" Ray asked suspiciously.

"Not a lot. But periodically. Computers are not always reliable devices."

"What about Kilga? Can you pin him down on that day?"

She tapped on the keys. "He was . . . working."

"You're sure?"

"According to his supervisor, he reported on time and was on duty for the entire twelve hour shift. Which gives him an alibi."

"Maybe," Ray scoffed.

"How could he work and murder a man at the same time?"

"You're relying on the computer. And you just admitted it was unreliable."

"Are you suggesting that the record has been altered?"

"I'm just saying that Kilga is still on my list."

Denisovich seemed confused by this.

"Look, what if he knew about the cash and killed Chekerov for it? Or maybe he even had a part in obtaining it. He and Chekerov have a disagreement about strategy. He sets up a little 'accident' on the ice. Bingo! Goodbye partner. Hello big money."

"But he was working."

"Sure. And the computer log for the guys on leave just happens to go down. Why couldn't he arrange for that? For that matter, why couldn't he say he was sick, skip his shift, then alter that in the computer file?"

"You think he is the killer?"

"No. I'm just saying we don't know enough to eliminate him. Yet." Ray paused, then, "We don't even know if there is a killer. Accidental death is still a viable option." He shook his head at all the things they didn't know, the tangle of things they did, and at his sudden, inexplicable decision to share all of this with Denisovich. He should have been postulating and brainstorming with Billy Bob, not a Russian scientist.

"We need a cause of death," Ray said. "If Butyerki can give us that, we'll be in much better shape."

Denisovich agreed and they left the office to collect the doctor. They found him in the mess hall, a cup of coffee cradled against his chest, his mouth in overdrive as he chewed the ear off the officer who had been assigned to watch him.

The young man looked relieved to see Denisovich and Ray. He stood and nodded at Denisovich. She said something to him, and he nodded again before leaving. She then asked Butyerki a question. He sighed and held out his hand. It was a little shaky, but wasn't wavering all over the place.

"He's ready," she said.

Ray wasn't so sure, but also didn't want to wait around for the guy to sober up completely.

When Butyerki had downed the last of his coffee, they escorted him to the elevator. Willy was in the hall.

"Where are you going?" he asked sheepishly.

"Nowhere," Ray said.

"I wanna go."

Ray considered ordering him to remain in the lounge.

"Please . . ."

"Okay." Ray sighed. He was in no mood to argue.

On the trip down, the man belched loudly, cleared his throat, and began half humming, half singing, what sounded to Ray like a Russian drinking song.

The elevator doors finally opened and they linked arms with the doctor, pulling him up the dingy, dimly lit corridor, his voice echoing eerily off the metallic walls and floor.

As they approached the room where the body was being kept, a head protruded from the doorway: two bug eyes and a round-O mouth. It was Billy Bob.

"Oh, it's you!" he said.

"Who'd you think it would be?" Ray wondered. "The bogeyman?"

"I heard that singing and . . ." The cowboy shivered. "It gave me the creeps."

They went inside and stood by the table that held the corpse. The doctor seemed oblivious. He was still singing, his voice a sleepy baritone.

"Dr. Butyerki," Ray said. When this failed to get the man's attention, Ray pulled back the blanket that had been draped over the body.

Butyerki's tune stopped abruptly and his face flashed with interest, even alertness. "What do we have here?"

"He speaks English?" Ray said.

"Yes," Butyerki said. "*He* does."

"He was educated at Stanford," Denisovich said.

"Why didn't he speak English before?" Ray asked.

"English is an ugly language," Butyerki explained in a coherent tone. "And so vague. I much prefer the tongue of Mother Russia." He leaned toward the body. "I'll need more light."

Billy Bob went over and got a lamp.

"And a chair," he said.

Denisovich fetched a stool.

Butyerki grinned down at the body. "This could take a while."

SEVENTEEN

STARTING AT THE HEAD, Dr. Butyerki moved slowly and meticulously over the body, muttering to himself as he went. After the initial pass, he made another, then asked that the body be flipped over. When he came to the harpoon wound, he asked casually, "what happened here?"

Ray explained.

"I see." Butyerki went on. On his second examination of the back of Chekerov's head, he squinted at the bruise.

"We were wondering if that was what killed him," Ray said.

Butyerki didn't seem to hear him. He requested that the body be turned over again, and when it had, covered it with the blanket.

"Seegaretta?" he asked Denisovich.

She shook her head.

He asked Ray, but got the same reply.

"Don't tell me nobody's got a cigarette for me." He waited until Billy Bob had confirmed this, then said to Ray, "I thought all of you people smoked like chimneys."

Ray didn't know how to respond to this.

"My uncle smokes all the time," Willy volunteered. "But he says it'll kill you. And he says that I shouldn't ever smoke."

"Your dyadya is a smart man," Butyerki said. "I, however, must have a cigarette."

He glared at Denisovich until she finally said, "I'll go get you one."

"Get me a pack," the doctor said. "And some coffee. I'm really feeling *plohoy*."

Ray wasn't sure what *plohoy* meant, but decided it wasn't good. The doctor was pale, the rings around his eyes even more pronounced. And his hands had begun to tremble.

When Denisovich had left to attend to the doctor's demands, Ray prodded, "So what do you think?"

"About what?" The doctor was rubbing his head with a hand.

"Cause of death."

"Aspirin . . ."

"He was killed by aspirin?" Willy wondered.

"I must have aspirin," the doctor said.

Billy Bob dug in the pockets of his parka. "Will ya settle fer a couple-a Tylee-nols?"

Butyerki held out a hand without looking up, and Billy Bob gave him the tablets. The doctor downed them without water and sat massaging his temples. "Now, what was it you asked me?"

"Cause of death."

"Oh, yes . . . Uh . . ." There was a long pause, and Ray thought the doctor was going to pass out, or maybe throw up. Instead, he sat up straighter. "The man was subjected to freezing temperatures. He suffered from various levels of frostbite. He also, no doubt, was hypothermic when he died."

"So the elements killed him."

"No. And neither did the injury to his left anterior quadrant."

"Could he have drowned?"

Butyerki looked up at him and frowned. "I don't think so. But we would have to suction the lungs to find out if they contain water."

"Can you do that?"

The doctor sighed melodramatically. "Not without a cigarette." Despite this declaration, Butyerki rose stiffly and went to the cabinets lining the wall. He opened them and began rummaging around. In a minute he returned to the table with a piece of surgical tubing. "I pray to God this is clean," he said, making a face at the tubing.

"You don't want to contaminate the body?" Ray asked.

"I don't give a *prokleenot* about this cadaver. I am more concerned about poisoning myself. Who knows where this tube has been?" He sniffed the tube. "I'll need a receptacle of some sort."

Willy picked up a stainless steel tray. "How about this?"

"Fine."

"What else do you need?" Ray asked.

"A cigarette. And coffee." He began stuffing the

tube down Chekerov's throat. When it met with resistance and wouldn't go any farther, the doctor muttered something and went back to the cabinet. He returned with a piece of wire and used it to push the tubing into the body.

"How are you going to get the water out?" Ray asked.

Butyerki took no notice of this. He withdrew the wire and put his lips to the tubing. Sucking hard, he quickly removed the end from his mouth and aimed it at the tray. But nothing came out. He tried again. A third time.

"The lungs are empty," he announced, pulling the tube out of the body.

"You're sure?"

"Of course I'm sure," the doctor grumbled. "Where in *adskee-ee* are my cigarettes?!" he bellowed to no one in particular. "I could have gotten them myself in less time."

"Could the lungs have dried out since the body was recovered?" Ray asked, trying to keep the doctor on track.

"Perhaps."

"Do you think they did?"

"No."

"Why not?"

"You asked me what I thought. I think the lungs are dry and have been dry."

"Meaning . . . the man was dead when he went in the water?"

"Yes," Butyerki said tersely. "It is a cruel thing to

deny a man his vodka. But to keep cigarettes from him is a crime."

"You believe Chekerov died from the blow to the back of his head?"

"Who?"

"Chekerov. The victim."

Butyerki shrugged. "Perhaps."

"What is your medical opinion?"

"My medical opinion is that if I am not supplied with a cigarette in the next two minutes, I will begin to suffer from withdrawals."

"Your opinion as to cause of death," Ray specified.

Obviously irritated, Butyerki huffed, "He received a contusion to the skull, a probable concussion. He most likely lost consciousness, his brain tissue swelled, and he was dead when he hit the water."

"What about the frostbite?"

Butyerki sighed again. "I'd say it was suffered before the concussion."

Ray considered this. If Butyerki was right—a big *if*, since the guy didn't exactly seem reliable and wasn't giving his all for the cause—then Chekerov must have been out in the floes, exposed to the extent that he had frostbite and possibly hypothermia, before someone hit him in the head. Or before he fell and hit his own head.

"Could he have fallen and done this?"

"Perhaps," Butyerki said. His hands were trembling, and now one knee was bobbing impatiently.

Denisovich returned then with the precious cigarettes and a steaming cup of coffee. Butyerki didn't bother to thank her. Snatching the cigarettes, he shakily lit up and inhaled deeply. "Oh . . . I am saved."

"Could Chekerov have fallen and hurt himself like this?" Ray asked again.

"Who?" Butyerki asked.

"The victim."

"Oh . . . uh . . . perhaps. But it is not likely. He would have had to fall from a height onto the back of his head. And then, as you have described, rolled into the water."

"What about falling over the side of the ship and hitting the ice?"

"That could do it," Butyerki agreed, smoking hungrily. "But that would not explain how he wound up in the water."

True, Ray thought. No matter how he ran through the scenario, he couldn't get Chekerov, much less Tommy, into the water without a murderer.

"He could have been lost," Denisovich tried. "Dying from the cold. Then if his feet completely and suddenly slipped out from under him, he could have severely bashed his head on the ice near an opening in the sea."

"Very near," Ray said, thinking that it would be tough to do. "And that doesn't explain his hunting companion's death."

"He could have fallen into the water while trying to save Chekerov."

Ray nodded. It was possible. "The only way to confirm that is to examine Tommy."

"Who?" Butyerki said. He was already preparing to light a second cigarette from the butt of his first.

"We'll need to go into town to do that."

"I thought you already tended to that," Billy Bob said. There was an edge to his voice, as though he feared he was about to be left alone with the corpse again.

"I haven't been off the ship yet," Ray said. He looked to Butyerki. "We'll need you to come too."

"What about me?" Billy Bob wondered.

"Dr. Butyerki is not allowed ashore," Denisovich said defensively.

"Surely an exception can be made for this," Ray argued.

"Have they got a store there?" Butyerki asked. "They sell cigarettes? Vodka?"

"I'll have to check with Dr. Radikoff," Denisovich said.

"Tell him I'll take responsibility for seeing that the doctor doesn't wander off."

She nodded but didn't look convinced.

Ray patted Billy Bob on the shoulder. "We'll be back."

"Promise?" the cowboy asked warily.

As they made their way to the elevator, Ray reflected on the curious priorities aboard the *Arctic Star*. Dr. Radikoff had a pair of bodyguards, but no one had been assigned to guard Chekerov's body. Maybe because no one knew it was there yet. Although, considering the fact that the guy had thousands of dollars stuffed under his bed . . . Ray felt better knowing Billy Bob was babysitting the corpse.

"Does your city have vodka?" Butyerki asked Willy as they got onto the elevator.

"What is it?" the boy asked.

"Vodka? It is the salvation of Siberia, the milk of Mother Russia—"

"Booze," Ray translated. "And no. There's no vodka in TaggaQ. It's dry. The whole North Slope is dry."

"Dry?" Butyerki asked, as though he had never heard the term or possibly did not know the meaning of it.

Ray nodded. "No alcohol is allowed."

Butyerki grumbled something in Russia. "What is this North Slope of yours? The American version of the gulags?"

"My uncles make their own beer," Willy volunteer.

"Beer?" Butyerki perked up.

"Which is also illegal," Ray pointed out.

"They say it isn't illegal if you don't sell it," Willy said.

"That's not true," Ray muttered.

"But they sell it sometimes."

Ray made a mental note to look into this later. Busting a couple of small-time moonshiners wouldn't exactly change the world, but every little bit helped.

"What about cigarettes?" Butyerki asked as the

elevator doors opened and they got off on the communications floor.

"Yeah. I know where to get them," Willy said.

Butyerki smiled and put his hand on Willy's shoulder. "You are a good *malcheek.*"

"I am?"

"Yes. A very good boy."

They waited in the TV lounge while Denisovich went to get permission for their little medical expedition. There were three men in the lounge now, two of them fast asleep. The third was watching a dubbed version of *Cops*.

"Ah . . ." Butyerki said when he saw the screen. "This is a good program."

Ray shook his head, thinking that if the men on board derived their impression of the United States from television, it had to be horribly distorted.

"See look," Butyerki said, pointing at the set. "This man is about to try escaping." He and Willy watched breathlessly as a beady-eyed man who was acting erratically, probably from drugs, began to struggle, then fled the scene on foot. The police officers took up pursuit, as did the cameraman, who caught it all on tape.

"In Russia," Butyerki said, "you might get shot for running away like that."

"In America too," Ray said. "Especially if you're the wrong color and you happen to live in L.A." This was intended to be a joke, but was lost on Butyerki.

"He is a fool," the doctor said. "They never get away on this program."

"Sometimes they do," Willy said. "I've seen 'em get away sometimes."

Ray checked his watch: 6:47. For a long moment he wasn't sure whether that was A.M. or P.M. It was P.M., he finally decided. Though it didn't feel like it. It felt like he had been up all night. But it was hardly even night yet.

He was comparing his left ankle with his right, trying to tell himself that the sprain wasn't so bad, when Denisovich returned.

"Well . . . ?"

"The doctor will be allowed off the ship for two hours, provided I am with him."

"Two hours? That's not long enough."

Denisovich shrugged as if she didn't particularly care whether or not it was long enough.

Ray stood and motioned to Butyerki and Willy. "Come on, guys."

Neither of them moved or even blinked. They were enthralled in a commercial for Victoria's Secret. Ray reached over and nudged the doctor. "Let's go."

Butyerki got up slowly, eyes still on the screen. He eased toward the door, turning around only when the last lingerie model had disappeared and an ad for Dodge trucks began.

"What a country, America," he said appreciatively.

En route to the main deck, Ray tried to calculate how long it would take them to snow-machine to the village, take a look at Tommy, and snow-machine back. He gauged it at about ninety minutes. That was saying they didn't meet with any unexpected delays. That was also saying Eddie let them examine Tommy's body. If he didn't give his approval, Ray knew he would have to call back to Barrow, arrange for a court order. That would take forever. And if Eddie tried to bury his son in the interim, things could get quite ugly.

Denisovich led them from the elevator, out the door, into the night. The wind had picked up, and Ray guessed that it was well below zero with the chill factor. Butyerki and Denisovich had picked up parkas, gloves, and boots in the mudroom and they had all zipped and buttoned up and covered their faces. Still, it felt uncomfortable being back out in the elements.

"Must the boy go with us?" Denisovich asked through her mask as they crossed the deck.

"He's our guide over the floes," Ray said.

When they reached the side of the ship, Butyerki looked over and swore. "Where is the *sodeen*?"

"There isn't one," Denisovich grumbled. "We have to climb."

"No. I cannot climb."

"Yes, you can."

"No." Butyerki took a step backward. "I refuse."

"Why?"

"I am afraid of heights."

Ray had to fight the urge to force the doctor over the side. "Do it and I'll spring for a pack of cigarettes."

"A carton," Butyerki shot back, his agoraphobia suddenly in remission.

"Fine," Ray grunted. He waited for Denisovich, Willy, and Butyerki to throw their legs over the side and begin their descent of the climbing ropes before following suit. Denisovich and Willy made their way carefully but smoothly down. The doctor, however, acted as though he were completely uncoordinated, clinging to one rung of rope, wavering, finally latching on to the next.

Two hours, Ray thought. It would take them that long to get Butyerki down to the ice.

EIGHTEEN

By the time Butyerki let loose of the last rope and was standing on the frozen surface of the Chukchi Sea, Ray had been on his snow machine, with Denisovich behind him on the seat, for nearly ten minutes. He was cold and anxious to get moving.

"We won't make it in an hour," Denisovich said with a sigh as Butyerki walked stiffly to Willy's machine.

"What's Radikoff going to do about it?" Ray asked. "Keep us after school?"

"Withhold my salary," Denisovich said.

"You're kidding?"

"No. He was against allowing Butyerki ashore and would only agree if I promised to have him back in the designated time period. Every minute beyond that I will owe him a part of my pay."

"What a jerk of a boss." Ray revved the snow machine and waited as Butyerki loaded himself behind Willy. "He ought to dock Butyerki's pay." Ray advised her to hold on and, after she was firmly gripping his waist, he started forward, following Willy.

The ride to shore seemed longer than the ride out to the ship. Probably because of the wind, Ray decided. Even in his gauntlet mittens his fingers were numb. Had he known they would be touring the floes tonight, he would have brought his liners and some hand heaters. But supposedly they had been dispatched to take a quick look at a couple of accident victims. A quick look . . . Yeah, right.

They were nearly to TaggaQ before he could see the shadows of the town buildings. The place was still nearly blacked out, in deference to the rampaging tupilak. At this time of the evening, during the holidays, while under siege from a supernatural monster, it would be tough to find a carton of cancer sticks for Butyerki, much less a warm, well-lit place to do the autopsy.

Ray followed Willy's machine as it left the floes and continued, without hesitation, onto the snow and ice-encrusted mainland. Though you couldn't clearly see the demarcation, Ray could feel it. Inside. Solid ground was where he belonged, he decided. It was where human beings belonged. Period.

They rumbled into town and down the deserted streets. Willy pulled up across from Kuleak's police headquarters.

"Where are we going?" he asked Ray.

"To the cemetery."

The boy's eyes grew until they were bigger than the holes in his mask. He shook his head.

"That's where the body is," Ray explained.

"I don't wanna go there."

"We were just looking at a body on the ship," Ray said. "This is the same thing."

"No. The cemetery is different."

"We won't do the autopsy there."

Willy was shaking his head.

"We can do it here." Ray pointed at Kuleak's office. As he said this, he realized that transporting the body would be a problem. Even if Eddie agreed to the autopsy, he would probably balk at having his son moved. In Eddie's way of thinking, locking the body in the shed was a good way to keep Tommy's spirit from roaming around. Carting the corpse around would amount to disrespect and might invoke the spirit's wrath.

"Drop the doctor off at the cemetery, then come back and wait in the office. It's open," Ray told Willy. Whether they came back with or without the body, they could meet up with him at the police station.

Ray took the lead to the cemetery, and when they were still a couple of blocks away, Denisovich asked, "What's that weird light?"

"Fire," Ray told her over his shoulder. "For the grave diggers."

At the cemetery fence, Willy barely allowed the doctor time to disembark before gunning the engine. He did a tight 180 and sped back toward Kuleak's. Ray turned his machine off and ushered Denisovich and Butyerki up the hill through the graves.

Their breath was loud in the quiet of the night. So

were their steps, each boot causing the snow to groan. The torch flames whipped and hissed in the wind, and the ticking of the picks against the ice sounded like a misfiring grandfather clock.

Ray stopped at the grave, which was now nearly twice as deep at it had been. Still, it had a ways to go before being able to accommodate a coffin. "Eddie?" The men in the hole all had on hoods and masks and were hunched, their faces toward the ground. The three heads bobbed up at him, the eyes somehow admonishing, as though he had barged in on something private, even sacred.

"Eddie?" he asked again.

Two of the hooded figures returned to their tasks while the third grunted, "He ain't here."

"Where is he?"

"Don't know." The man raised his pick and began hacking at the crooked wall of the grave.

Ray nodded at the sheds and led Denisovich and Butyerki toward them. He was thinking that he might have to do a *Cops* routine and break down the locked door when they arrived at the shed. But the door was open a crack. Ray pushed it back a little more. "Eddie?"

There was no answer, so he opened it all the way. The inside was a perfectly black rectangle. "Eddie?"

Ray found his penlight and shined it into the void. The coffin was still there, waiting for them.

"How do we move it?" Denisovich asked.

Ray shook his head. "Maybe we should just do it here. It'll be a whole lot easier." He was thinking that maybe they could be finished with the exam before Eddie got back from wherever it was he had gone.

"I cannot work like this," Butyerki said, sounding like a prima donna. "A *groob . . . tyemnee . . . holodnyee* . . . My breath is turning to ice."

"The whispering of stars," Denisovich said. "To Siberians like yourself, it is a sign of good luck."

"Good luck, my eye. This is precisely why I left Seebeerski and will never go back."

"Think cigarettes," Ray said.

"I climbed the rope for cigarettes, but this . . ."

"There's another carton in it for you if you do the autopsy here."

"Three cartons," Butyerki countered.

"Two."

"Camels?"

"Deal."

Butyerki took the penlight and entered the shed. He approached the coffin as a mechanic might approach a car, flipped the top open like a hood, and went to work. After making his way down the front of the body to about the waist without comment, he paused and lit up a cigarette. Inhaling, he blew smoke and muttered something in Russian.

"He says it's cold in here."

"I said," Butyerki corrected, "it is colder than Hades in here. Do try to be more accurate with your translations, won't you please, Doctor?" He smoked for another minute, rocking slightly on his boots. "I thought it was cold in Seebeerski." He slapped his mittens together. "I am a walking *l-yed koob*."

"Ice cube," Denisovich told Ray.

Butyerki glared at her, then turned his attention to Ray. "My fingers are numb. I must leave to get warm."

"The sooner you finish," Ray said, "the sooner we can leave."

"I am finished."

"Not yet, you're not."

"Da." Butyerki flipped off the penlight. "The *jzernee dama* is singing."

"What?" Ray looked in Denisovich's direction for an explanation. He couldn't see her in the dark, but heard her mumble, "The fat lady."

Ray wanted to laugh. There was nothing quite so amusing as having Americanisms converted into another language. In a different setting, it would have been humorous. But here, in what amounted to absolute darkness, standing in a shed, a foot away from a dead body in the subzero night . . .

"Just finish the examination."

"Nyet."

Ray was in no mood for this. "Okay. Three packs."

"Four."

"Four, then! I don't care."

"Camels?"

"Yes! Just do it!"

The penlight flipped on and Butyerki flipped away the stub of his cigarette. He efficiently surveyed Tommy's waist, legs, and feet. When he raised back up, he said, "It would be much easier and infinitely more helpful to look at the cadaver with its clothing removed."

Butyerki's cold objectivity made Ray shiver. What had once been a boy—Tommy, a living breathing human being—was now a "cadaver." An "it." Ray felt a stab of sadness.

"Do the best you can," Ray told him.

"It must be turned over," Butyerki said. He stepped back and lit another cigarette, implying that this was grunt work and that he would not be participating in it.

Ray took hold of the coffin and shook, hoping that the chipping he and Billy Bob had done earlier might have jarred the body loose. But Tommy was solidly frozen to the wood sides and bottom.

"We'll have to work on breaking him out," Ray said. He looked to Denisovich, but she too had backed up. "I'll need help." He found the crowbar they had employed on their first attempt at this. "You hold the box," Ray told Denisovich. "I'll try to chip him loose."

Denisovich reluctantly stepped forward and took hold of the side as Ray began jabbing the sharp end of the bar into the ice that had formed between the body and the back of the coffin. Butyerki set the penlight on the ledge running along the wall of the shed and began bobbing, cigarette dangling from his lips, slapping his mittens together as though he were applauding their effort.

"We can't see," Ray said.

Butyerki turned the penlight to the left.

"Would it be too much trouble to ask you to hold it?"

The doctor ignored this and started pacing, whacking himself on the legs.

With the light shining directly at them, Ray had to squint to make sure he wasn't getting too close to the body. He made slow progress, creating a crack from the shoulder to the thigh and then working to deepen it. It took him nearly ten minutes to strike the bottom of the coffin. The bar hit it with a thud, and the crack extended up past the head and beyond the feet. "He might be loose now."

Denisovich helped him try to turn the body. It was still frozen underneath and a little along the other side. Ray used the bar to break the ice at the top, the bottom, the side . . . It was a little bit like trying to work a frozen casserole free from the pan.

"I think if we both turn him . . ." Ray said, setting the bar down. He waited for Denisovich to get set, then counted: "One, two, three . . ." They both pushed and pulled. There was a ripping sound and the body clanked over, facedown. The ripping had been the parka, which was now bleeding goose down.

"Okay," Ray said, out of breath from the effort. "Your turn, Dr. Butyerki." He moved back and squinted through the glare of the penlight, trying to make out Butyerki. "Doctor?" Ray snatched up the light and swung the narrow beam around the shed, then went to the door. The penlight didn't do much against the Arctic night, but it did confirm what he was already dreading: Butyerki was gone.

Ray swore.

"I was afraid of this," Denisovich said. "He has talked of defecting."

"He has? Why didn't you say anything?"

"I figured that the two of us could keep him contained. He's in bad health and in a foot race couldn't outrun a child."

"Maybe not, but this isn't a foot race," Ray grumbled, flicking off the penlight. Darkness immediately enveloped them and, aside from the torches that were popping like flags in the wind at the grave site, there was nothing to set apart sea from land, buildings from fields, civilization from wilderness.

"He could be anywhere," Denisovich said. "But . . . he couldn't have gone far."

"We'll split up," Ray said, trying to sound optimistic. Distance was not the issue. It was location. Butyerki could be ten feet away, hunched in the shadow of the shed, and they would never know it. "You go straight out of the cemetery," Ray said, pointing, "down the street. I'll circle through and meet you at the police station. Our truck's there and there are some extra flashlights."

Denisovich nodded and started off. Ray stood there, silently cursing his luck. Though Denisovich would be disciplined in some manner if they didn't locate Butyerki, it was Ray who was ultimately responsible for the AWOL doctor, and he had said as much back on the ship. This was his idea. He had promised to see that Butyerki got to and from town without incident. So much for promises.

He went back into the shed and used the penlight

to check the corners. There was a chance, however small, that they had simply overlooked him. No. He was not in the shed. Tommy was the sole resident.

Sighing, Ray quickly made a lap around the structure. He considered calling Butyerki's name. But hearing his name would only cause the doctor to run harder.

He reached the front of the shed again and then went down along the fence. He looked for tracks, but the snow was crusted to a firm sheen and, except for the occasional drift, did not allow for any. When he reached the gate, he turned around and went in the other direction, the tapping of his boots on the ice somehow matching with the pick strikes in the grave pit. He watched his shadow jerk one way then the other as the torches and the penlight struggled weakly against the darkness.

As he checked the final fifty yards of fence, he realized that what had been a messy case was now a bona fide international disaster. Chekerov's stash on the ship was probably a Russian problem, if it came down to splitting hairs. But his death had taken place on U.S. soil—or rather, ice. And now Butyerki was making a break for it. That was clearly something the FBI would be interested in. The INS as well. So the mess was not only messier, but bigger, more ungainly. Ray knew it was quickly getting away from him.

He paused at the gate to survey the street. It was so dark, he couldn't see all the way across it. The penlight was good only for a few meager feet.

Don't panic, he told himself. Maybe they would

find Butyerki. The guy could have simply stepped out to relieve himself. Or maybe he went for more cigarettes. Or what if Butyerki had decided to prove him wrong and located some vodka? That was possible, wasn't it?

He started up the street, telling himself that Denisovich was right. Butyerki couldn't have gotten far. He had to be out here somewhere, lurking next to a building or behind a parked car. If only they had a few more people and some lights . . .

Ray checked his watch. Time was working against them in so many ways. It was late enough that even those who presumably didn't fear the roving tupilak were calling it a day and extinguishing their lights. Back in the shed, Tommy was lying there, facedown, chips of ice everywhere . . . Wait till old Eddie saw that. He'd probably sue. Then there was the slim hour they had left to get Butyerki back to the ship.

If they didn't find Butyerki, however, Ray decided, the time factor would be mute.

A block later he could see the lights in Kuleak's office. As he approached, he could make out Willy's and Denisovich's faces in the office window. They had obviously not stumbled onto Butyerki.

It was time to call in the cavalry. He would phone Barrow and have Lewis, the captain, whoever else he could muster, come to TaggaQ. Because in a matter of minutes it would not only be as cold as Hades, as Butyerki had put it, but all Hades would be breaking out.

NINETEEN

RAY HUSTLED PAST the truck and up to the police office, his ankle throbbing. The stint of activity was bothering it. He could feel it swelling up, despite the air temperature, and knew that if he didn't elevate it soon, he might be immobilized.

Denisovich and Willy met him at the door. "No sign of him?" she asked as he entered.

"No." Ray went to Kuleak's chair and sat down. He gingerly put his foot up on the desk.

"We have to keep looking!" Denisovich said. She had an anxious expression on her face now.

"I need to rest for a minute," Ray said, feeling old and decrepit.

"Give me the keys to your truck," she said, holding out her hand.

"I don't think it's locked."

Denisovich nodded. "I tried the doors."

Ray shifted to pull the keys from his pocket.

"Willy and I will get the flashlights and—"

"Be careful," Ray said, extending the keys. "He

could be dangerous." As he said this, he changed his mind. "I'll go with you."

Before he could move to rise, Denisovich snatched the keys from him. "Rest for a few minutes. If we see him, we'll come back."

"And in the meantime he'll find a new hiding place."

"We have to try to find him," Denisovich said. "If we don't get him back to the ship . . ."

Ray sympathized with her position, especially since he was in it with her. Heads would roll over this. "Okay. But stay on the main street. Make a quick pass, then get back here. I'll try to figure out a search plan." He almost laughed as he said this. Search plan? With a Russian scientist, a local kid, and a gimp policeman? More like a last ditch effort.

Denisovich nodded and went out the door with Willy in tow. Picking up the phone, Ray dialed the Barrow police office and . . . got a busy signal.

"Unbelievable . . ." he muttered. He pulled out his cell phone and tried again. Another busy signal. It had to be the circuit or something. The Barrow PD had several lines and an automated answering service. He tried again, then folded the phone and put it back into his parka.

The FBI would be his next call. Or should be. He dreaded having to call the government into this. They would send someone from Fairbanks or Anchorage who would abruptly pull rank and hijack the case. Though that wouldn't be all bad. At least then he and Billy Bob could head for home.

The money on the ship and Chekerov's blow to

the head were enough to warrant a federal investigation, Ray admitted.

His adjusted his aching ankle and, in the process, knocked a pad off the table. It took a gymnastic-like maneuver to retrieve it and he almost lost his balance and fell. When he was upright again, the pad in hand, he huffed at it. Kuleak was a very enthusiastic doodler, Ray thought, frowning at the pad. Amidst the various names and numbers scrawled on the page was an elaborate design of converging lines. In fact . . . Ray held it back a little. If you looked at it the right way, it was almost a picture: a pencil representation of a tunnel with girders and . . . Were those small circles supposed to be lights? He flipped through the pad and found other drawings: more tunnels. Apparently Kuleak had a thing for tunnels.

On the last page of doodles was a cross section of a ship. The *Arctic Star*, most likely, Ray decided. It was highly detailed for a doodle sketch, with decks and connecting hallways. Kuleak had missed his calling, Ray thought. He should have been an architect or maybe a technical artist. He seemed to possess far more talent with a pencil than he did with a badge.

Setting the pad down, he lifted the phone again. He would try Barrow one more time before calling the FBI. Maybe the captain could come up with a plan of attack that didn't involve Fibbies.

At that moment the door opened and Willy yelled, "You better come here!"

"Did you find him?"

"We found somebody."

Ray removed his leg from the desk and stiffly limped to the door. Instead of helping, the short rest and elevation had caused his ankle to become nearly useless. It felt like he was walking on a big, painful stump.

"Where?" Ray asked as he closed the door behind them.

"In your truck."

"What? Where's Dr. Denisovich?"

Willy pointed at a car parked across the street.

"Why is she over there?"

"Because he's got a gun."

"Who?"

"The guy in your truck."

It suddenly registered. Someone had crawled into the truck, probably to keep warm, and was now in possession of their shotgun. Except . . . It was kept in a lockbox, and only he and Billy Bob had keys.

Ray felt in his pockets, then swore. He gestured at the parked car that Denisovich was using for cover. "Get over there and stay down."

"What are you gonna do?"

"I don't know."

He waited as Willy trotted across the street and hunched behind the car. It had to be Butyerki in the truck, Ray decided. Who else could have picked his pocket? But since when did doctors do that sort of thing? Apparently this one did and had been planning his little defection for a while. Possibly since before they left the boat.

Ray pulled his sidearm and limped toward the

truck, squinting to see into the cab. It looked empty. He inched closer, straining to make out an occupant. Did Kuleak have any guns in his office? Ray tried to think. He hadn't noticed any locked cabinets. Maybe in the desk somewhere.

He was considering turning around, going back to search for a rifle, when he noticed movement in the cab. A shadow briefly danced on the windshield. There was definitely someone in there. Butyerki. And he had a gun.

This would be fun to explain, Ray thought as he slowly made his way forward. A defector lifts his key, takes his gun, holes up in his truck . . . The only thing that could make the situation worse would be shots and, God forbid, bloodshed.

Ray tried to put that out of his mind. Surely he could negotiate a peaceful resolution to this thing, even if it meant promising Butyerki asylum.

He stopped some ten yards from the truck, at an angle that would make a potshot from the windshield or the driver's window difficult. "Dr. Butyerki?!" Ray watched for movement, but there was none. "Dr. Butyerki?! You need to put the gun back into the lockbox and get out of my truck before things get ugly."

He waited a moment, but there was no response. "I'll have to call in the FBI," Ray threatened. "You'll be taken into custody, returned to the ship, possibly prosecuted by both of our governments."

Nothing.

Ray stood there. He was just about out of ideas.

Rushing the truck would be insane. Butyerki didn't have the keys to the ignition, so unless he knew how to—

On cue, the truck's engine turned over. Ray cursed again, and as the wheels began to spin on the ice, he did what he knew to be tantamount to suicide: he ran and leapt into the pickup bed.

He heard Denisovich shouting as the truck fishtailed up the street. Ray remained flat against the bed until the driver had control. He then raised up and glared at the back of Butyerki's head. He could tell it was him.

"Stop the truck!" Ray yelled, aiming the gun at him.

Butyerki took the corner hard and went into a slide that sent Ray flying across the bed. He slammed his hip on the metal siding, lost his grip on the gun, and for several seconds his vision was obscured by an enthusiastic wall of stars. He forgot about his ankle, the truck, Butyerki, everything except the fact that fire had engulfed nearly half of his body and seemed reluctant to let go.

When his vision finally cleared and the pain began to subside, he realized that he was no longer in possession of his sidearm and that the truck had stopped. The engine was idling. He heard the door pop open and struggled to right himself. He glanced around the bed of the truck for his gun, but it was gone.

Using the side of the bed as a crutch, Ray raised up to his knees and saw the doctor standing there, a shotgun leveled at his chest.

Butyerki held a finger up to his mouth.

"When you shoot me, it's not going to be quiet," Ray said. He was angry now, about the bruised hip, the fact that this guy had run off on him, that apparently his service revolver was lying back in the street somewhere, that Butyerki had the gall to use his own shotgun against him . . .

"I'm not going to shoot you," Butyerki said in a whisper.

"What are you going to do?" Ray demanded.

The doctor shushed him. "Keep your voice down."

Ray glanced around and saw that Butyerki had parked in the mouth of an alley.

Motioning with the gun, Butyerki said, "Get in the cab."

Ray sighed and, with some effort, climbed out of the bed. When he was in the cab and had shut the door, Butyerki said, "I'm going to put the gun down now. And I want you to make me a promise."

"You want me to what?"

"Promise me you'll hear me out before you do anything."

"Whatever."

"Do you promise?"

"What choice do I have?"

"Very good." The doctor set the shotgun across his lap, a finger still on the trigger, the barrels still pointed in Ray's direction.

"What's going on?" Ray demanded.

"That is precisely what I'm about to tell you." Butyerki clumsily lit a cigarette, doing his best to keep one hand on the shotgun at all times. "You probably believe that I am defecting."

"The thought crossed my mind." Ray eyed the gun. If Butyerki so much as glanced in the other direction . . .

"I'm not."

"Oh, yeah? Then what, exactly, are you doing? Don't tell me you ditched us at the shed to go for a smoke."

"I wish that were so."

Ray waited as Butyerki smoked nervously.

"They're going to kill me."

"Who?" Ray asked skeptically.

Butyerki inhaled, exhaled, shook his head.

When he failed to elaborate, Ray prodded, "Who's going to kill you?"

"They're going to kill me," he repeated glumly.

Ray eyed Butyerki and the gun in his lap, thinking that maybe the guy was simply wacko. He seemed to be suffering from paranoia, delusions, and was possibly even suicidal. The best way to handle this, he decided, was to humor the guy.

"Maybe I can help you."

"Maybe you can."

"Why don't you give me the gun and we'll drive back to Barrow. You'll be safe there."

Butyerki turned on him. "Don't patronize me! I'm not stupid."

"I didn't say you were."

"I'm not giving you this gun." He patted it affectionately.

"Okay, then . . . how about if we just go to Barrow?"

Butyerki shook his head. "They can get me there just as easily as they can get me here."

"We can protect you."

The doctor laughed sadly at this. "I wish that were true."

"We could fly you to Anchorage or even remand you to the care of the FBI."

Butyerki worked his cigarette feverishly.

"What do you want me to do?" Ray asked.

"I don't know. I just . . . I don't know."

Since he seemed to be stalled, Ray asked, "Did you know about Chekerov? About the money?"

The doctor gave him a sideways look, clearly surprised. "Who told you about the money?"

"I found it."

Butyerki nearly dropped his cigarette. "Where?!"

"What does it matter if you're not involved?"

"Oh, I'm involved. Up to my neck in alligators, as the expression goes." He sat smoking, staring out the windshield at the darkened alley.

"I still don't understand what you want from me."

There was no answer for at least half a minute. Finally, Butyerki said, "Chekerov told me about the money. He told me where he got it. He told me all about it." He paused to smoke. Sagging a little, he explained, "He came to me with a toothache. I'm no dentist, but aboard ship I have to be a jack of all trades when it comes to medical problems. Upon examination, I determined that one of his molars required extraction. I pulled it." He fell silent again.

Growing impatient, Ray sighed, "And . . . ?"

"I used both a local anesthetic—novocaine—and, because he had a history of negative dental experiences, I also employed nitrous oxide."

"Laughing gas?"

Butyerki nodded. "It has varying effects, depending on the individual. Some become happy. Others fall asleep. Most relax. A few become talkative."

"Chekerov was a talker," Ray guessed.

"Yes. Before, during, and especially after the procedure, he told me his deepest, darkest secrets. I learned that he is married, has two children, and keeps a mistress. I learned that his journeyman laborer papers were forged. I learned that his favorite food is McDonald's hamburgers and that given a chance he would defect to the West. To the United States, of course."

"Why didn't he? He was off ship on a hunting trip."

"He was going to. But not right away. He wanted to build a history of shore leaves, then, on another hunting trip, simply disappear. I believe that he hoped to fake an accident and make it appear that he died out on the floe. That way no one would come looking for him. And he could live comfortably on the money."

Ray nodded. "Not a bad idea."

"Except he never got a chance to carry it out."

"Why?" Ray wondered, now curious about the punch line.

"Because they killed him."

"Who did?"

"For the money, that's why. And because he knew."

"Knew what?" Ray asked. Butyerki wasn't making much sense.

"He was *pyesek-borov*. And somehow they figured out that he told me about it."

"He was *what*?"

He inhaled and blew smoke. "I wish to God I'd never treated him. Why didn't I just get drunk and forget about it? I might have gotten fired, but at least I'd be alive."

"Who's after you?" Ray wanted to know. "And who killed Chekerov?"

"The funny thing is, I don't even have the money." He turned and grinned at Ray with crazed eyes. "I didn't do anything wrong. But they're still going to kill me."

Ray was about to tell him to calm down and then repeat the two basic questions—who and why—when a light glared at them from the end of the alleyway.

Butyerki swore. "Get out!"

"But—"

He had the gun in hand again. "Get out!"

"Okay . . ." Ray opened the door and slid out. "But what are you going to do?"

Ignoring this, Butyerki jammed the shifter into reverse and began skidding backward into the street. Ray saw the truck do a wild, shuddering turn at the first corner before fishtailing out of view.

He heard feet behind him and turned to see two flashlight beams coming at him.

"You let him get away?" Denisovich asked.

"He had a gun," Ray said. "I didn't have a whole lot of choice."

"I can't believe it," Denisovich panted. "We lost him! What will I tell Dr. Radikoff? What will I tell the captain?"

"I was just thinking the same thing," Ray said.

TWENTY

RAY BEGAN WALKING UP THE ALLEY.

"We'll need to contact the ship," Denisovich muttered, following him.

"Is that guy the tupilak?" Willy asked. The boy didn't sound afraid anymore. He sounded excited.

TaggaQ hadn't seen this much action in years, Ray realized, his mind scrambling to come up with a crisis management plan.

"This could well cost me my position," Denisovich huffed.

"Butyerki seemed to think that someone was after him," Ray said. He let that sink in before adding, "He claimed he was on someone's hit list."

"That's ridiculous," Denisovich said dismissively.

"Is it?" They had reached the end of the alley and could again see the torches at the cemetery. They were like stars around which the entire region revolved. Ray set out for them.

"We should go back to the police station," Denisovich said.

"I need to look at the body first," Ray said.

"But without Dr. Butyerki—"

"I know what I'm looking for now."

Denisovich said something else, but Ray didn't catch it. He was trying to lay things out in his head. If Butyerki really was tangled up in Chekerov's money problems, and if someone really was out to get him, to murder him . . . what better way to do it than send him ashore and then have him disappear? That was what had happened to Chekerov. Maybe Butyerki had done the smart thing by running. Or maybe he was a nutcase who had been on a Russian icebreaker too long and was desperate for a taste of American freedom.

It was interesting that Denisovich was omnipresent in this investigation, Ray thought as they made their way toward the flickering torches. She had stuck with him since he boarded the *Arctic Star*, accompanied him to see the body, delivered him to Radikoff, sat behind him on the snow machine en route to shore. The captain of the *Star* was obviously concerned that the matter be cleared up. Or, more accurately, Dr. Radikoff was concerned. That was who seemed to be calling the shots. But the thing that didn't jibe was why? Why assign a research scientist to shadow him? Why not put one of Radikoff's brutes on him? Or some other security type?

He eyed Denisovich suspiciously. What if she wasn't what she pretended to be? After all, Butyerki hadn't run from him. Butyerki had talked to him. He had run from Denisovich.

Ray shook his head. No. Too improbable.

Except . . . His only real reason for ruling her out was gender. So what if she was a woman? Did that mean she couldn't kill someone? What if she was Radikoff's chief of security or something and the whole Ph.D. thing was a sham? She could be former KGB for all he knew.

He took a deep breath and told himself to slow down and examine the facts. There was a great deal of conjecture and supposition and circumstantial evidence, but few facts. All he really knew was that two men had died on the ice. Another man had jumped ship and was scooting around a small Alaskan village in a Barrow PD-issue truck. That didn't exactly add up to an international conspiracy.

But then there was the money: the proverbial wrench in the works. Where would a journey laborer get that kind of cash? If only Butyerki hadn't been so nervous and tangential in his storytelling.

When they reached the cemetery, Willy balked. "I'm not going in there."

"It's okay," Ray told him. "It won't take long. And besides, I need your help."

"You do?"

Ray nodded and led Willy and Denisovich through the whalebone gate, across the slick ice path, and past the diggers, who never even looked up. They found the door of the shed hanging open, just as they had left it. Ray shined the penlight at the interior and saw the coffin, lid still up, the body still facedown.

He glanced around before entering. It wouldn't take long to find out what he needed to find out. But he didn't want Eddie around. The guy might get violent. And he wouldn't have blamed him. He could only imagine what it would be like to lose Keera or Freddie. The pain would be indescribable. Then to have some out-of-town cop manhandling the remains . . .

Ray went to the coffin and aimed the penlight at the back of Tommy's head. The hair was plastered against the skull by a sheet of ice. It would take more crowbar work to break it away and loosen the hair enough to examine the scalp.

"What should I do?" Willy asked, gawking at the body.

"Hand me that crowbar," Ray said, aiming the light at it.

Willy handed him the crowbar, and Ray positioned the penlight on the shelf along the wall.

"Can you hold him for me?" Ray asked Denisovich.

She took hold of the shoulders.

"Willy, you stay at the door and watch for Eddie."

"How come?"

"Just tell me if he's coming. Tell me if anyone comes in this direction."

"Okay."

Ray began to chip carefully at the ice on the back of Tommy's head. This was crazy, he told himself. Not only was it highly disrespectful of the deceased, but it was highly unorthodox. Wait for a doctor, a voice in his head kept saying. But there wasn't time for that. Or was there? Why didn't he just pull rank, have both of the bodies quarantined, have a doctor brought in from Barrow and do this thing right? What was all the rush about?

It was about a large sum of money, another voice in his head answered. It was about a proud father wanting to bury his son quickly and in line with tradition. It was about a Russian ship that, most likely, was a sovereign vessel and could handle its dead however it wanted to.

The ice was smooth, hard, and difficult to splinter off. Ray didn't want to apply too much pressure for fear of breaking through and harming the body. That would be just his luck. Instead of finding out how Tommy died, he would put a gouge in the boy's head and either be shot or sued by Eddie. Maybe both.

"What does *pye-sek o-brov* mean?" Ray thought to ask.

"What?"

"No, wait . . . it was . . . *pye-sek bor-ov*," he amended.

"Sandhog."

"Excuse me?" Ray paused from his task.

"It means sandhog."

Ray lowered his eyebrows. So Butyerki *had been* off his rocker.

"Why do you ask?"

"Dr. Butyerki said something about it."

"What did he say?"

"Just that Chekerov was a *pye-se* . . ."

"Pyesek-borov."

"Right."

Denisovich removed her hands from the body. In

the dim beam of the penlight she almost looked as though she were in pain.

"What's the matter?"

"What else did Butyerki tell you?"

"Not much. Mostly that a nonspecific 'they' was out to get him. He was pretty upset."

"But he said that Chekerov was a sandhog?"

Ray nodded, then shrugged. "What's a sandhog?"

"Someone who works on underwater tunnels."

"That makes sense. That's the whole purpose of the *Arctic Star* being here, right?"

Denisovich was shaking her head. "Why that liar!"

"Who? Butyerki?"

"The *Arctic Star* is here for research purposes only. The project itself—the tunnel under the ocean—has yet to be approved by our governments."

"You said that the United States and Russia were cooperating on this."

"They are. But in stages. If our research on this expedition confirms the viability of using Dr. Radikoff's techniques, then the funding will be allotted and the project will go forward."

"I'm not following you."

"If there are sandhogs aboard, there's some sort of digging going on."

Ray was about to ask something else when Willy warned, "Here comes somebody!"

"Come in and close the door," Ray instructed. He closed the lid of the coffin, then went to the penlight and extinguished it. "Get down."

Their breathing was loud in the quiet of the shed, but in a moment it was drowned out by the sound of boots approaching. The door creaked open and a light abruptly hit the coffin. In the next instant the light was off, the door closed again. The boots left. Ray waited until they could no longer hear the footsteps, then waited thirty seconds longer.

Rising, he said, "Good work, Willy."

"You want me to keep watching?"

"Yes." Ray switched the penlight back on and returned to the coffin, where Denisovich was already opening the lid.

"Let me get this straight," Ray said, crowbar in hand. "They're digging this tunnel without approval?"

Denisovich shrugged. "That's what sandhogs are for."

"How could they manage that?"

"They are trained to work in just these kinds of environments."

"No, I mean, how could they be digging without everyone knowing about it?" Without *you* knowing about it, he was thinking.

"Dr. Radikoff fitted out the *Arctic Star* with a special subdeck that opens to the water. Using the technology that he developed, it would be an easy thing to bore into the shallow sea floor."

"And they could do this without the research team's knowledge?" Again he was thinking specifically of Denisovich, of whom he was still suspicious.

"With the twelve-hour shifts and the divided crews

and the work that we are focused on performing—yes, I suppose they could."

Ray wasn't convinced. He started chipping at the ice again. "So you think maybe Chekerov was killed because . . . he threatened to tell the authorities about this unauthorized project?"

"Perhaps."

"The money could have been blackmail?"

"Possibly." She muttered something in Russian.

"My sentiments exactly."

"We must call your people."

"My people?"

"We need more policemen. And we must somehow get your partner off the ship."

"Why?"

"Because if they really are after Butyerki, they will soon be after us."

"They, who? Radikoff and his goons?"

Before Denisovich could answer, the ice on the back of Tommy's head came loose in one big chunk, taking some of the hair with it.

"Geez . . ." Ray gingerly removed the slab. "I was hoping that wouldn't happen." He handed Denisovich the crowbar. "Hold this for a second." Using the penlight, he tried to warm the hair follicles enough to move them around without snapping them off.

"You don't see Eddie out there, do you?" he asked Willy without looking up.

"Nope."

"Good." If someone did this to *his* son, he knew

he would go berserk. It was a sacrilege. But at the moment it was also a necessity.

Ray's fingers were getting numb from the cold, and in the gauntlet mittens his hands were about as useful as a pair of salad tongs. He slowly began to fold the hair back in this spot, then another, hoping to see some evidence of a scalp wound. There was no blood on the hair, as there had been with Chekerov. He inched along the upper neck to the crown, then behind the left ear. Nothing.

"Anything?" Denisovich asked, craning to look over Ray's shoulder.

"Not yet." He went to the area behind the right ear. "The coast still clear, Willy?"

"Yep. Nobody out there but the guys digging the grave."

"Good." As Ray tried to part the hair, a clump broke off in his hand. He cursed this.

"What's the matter?"

"I'm tearing this boy up, that's what's the matter." Despite his official role in the investigation and the need for this information, he felt terrible about what he was doing. How would he explain it to Eddie?

"Hang on," he said as the light hit the naked scalp where the hair had come loose. "Here we go."

"What?" Denisovich wanted to know.

There was a thumping sound, and before Ray could turn, he heard Willy shout, "Hey!"

Looking to the door, he saw the light from the torches reflected on the snowy graves.

"What's the matter?" Ray reached for the penlight, then felt himself falling. The pain and the recognition that he had just been struck on the back of the head came on the way down. He hit the cold, concretelike earth with a thud and heard the breath leaving his chest. Rolling onto his side, he looked up. The darkness of the shed had been replaced by a glorious orange sky. As he lay there, blinking at the dawn or the sunset or the end of the world, a host of meteors began to fall, prickling his body with a hot, tingling fire.

The sensation might have been pleasant, had he not known, in the inner sanctum of his being, that he was losing consciousness, and perhaps his life.

TWENTY-ONE

. . . A CLOCK TICKING, time running out, running away . . .

. . . he could hear it, feel it, and knew that he had to respond. But how? He was floating, his feet unable to reach the ground . . .

The window was covered in frost. He had to use a credit card to clear it. Inside, he could see the glow of the fire and the dim outline of the shaman, whose face was hidden by an elaborate mask. It was adorned with feathers and had eyes painted on it and a mouth. The mask was ominous and intimidating in the gray half-light.

The shaman was moving, rocking back and forth methodically, growing more and more agitated. On his hands he wore huge gloves with fingers nearly as long as a man's arm. He waved his hands and caused the flames to rise and smoke, the shadows dancing.

The garb was protection. A safeguard against the tuungak. But there was no one else in the room. No sick child in need of a cure. No fisherman seeking a blessing. The shaman was alone. Alone with the gods.

The wind blew and the tiny frame house shook.

. . . he could hear the drums playing—*thump-thump-thump*—in a clumsy rhythm that made him want to do a clumsy dance . . .

He scraped the window again because the ice was blowing, swirling in the air, clouding the glass. The shaman took no notice of him. Kneeling, the masked figure drew a pot to himself. It was large and ornately carved out of soapstone. With expressive hand motions, the shaman pulled a bone from the pot. Setting it down, he pulled out another, and another and another. Soon he had constructed a primitive stick figure on the earthen floor: two scrawny legs, a long scrawny torso, an abbreviated neck, two pencil-thin arms. It was headless and grotesque.

. . . popcorn on the stove and smell of warm oil and the popping . . .

The pot was bigger now, and when the shaman reached in, he nearly disappeared. When he reemerged, he was carrying a head. A severed human head. The face was familiar. It smiled through the window at him, and he took a step backward.

* * *

. . . the engine kept sputtering even after he switched off the ignition—dieseling—giving off blue smoke from the tailpipe that was oil-rich and made him cough . . .

The shaman carefully put the head at the top of the bone body. He then stood over it and lifted his arms to heaven. Rocking again, he began to sing, and the words were a summons to the dead spaces of the spirit world:

O Manaqtaaq Qutchigniqtaq
Listen and hear
Listen and come
O Manaqtaaq Qutchigniqtaq
Give now a uumman
Bring your suannan

O Great Dark One
Listen and hear
Listen and come
O Great Dark One
Give now a heart
Bring your power

. . . the wind and the darkness were one voice clicking with one tongue, admonishing, shaming, click, click, click . . .

O Manaqtaaq Qutchigniqtaq
Paglan, paglan
Make your aimaagvIk here

O Manaqtaaq Qutchigniqtaq
Rise and live in this timi
Rise, live, hunt

O Great Dark One
Welcome, welcome
Make your home here
O Great Dark One
Rise and live in this body
Rise, live, hunt

The shaman repeated his song, circling the bones and the head. When he had come all the way around his creation, he dropped his arms and fell to his knees. The fire erupted, flames reaching up past the ceiling, past the stars.

And from the dirt floor the bones became one.

. . . fingers on the table, drumming impatiently, how much longer . . .

There was no flesh, only bones hanging together like the joints of a marionette. The thing stood awkwardly, clumsily, puppetlike, until it towered over the penitent shaman. It stood swaying unsteadily, the head sitting crookedly on the bones, the face turned almost sideways, eyes wide and dead, mouth hanging open to show black teeth and a black tongue.

. . . the second hand of an enormous clock or boots on a big man walking or a hammer, yes, a hammer on metal in a wide, empty space where sound could run and play, beating the metal, punishing it, demanding . . .

The shaman, head still bowed, pointed at the door. The creature looked and began to shuffle in that direction, its every movement hideous.

He pressed his nose to the frozen glass. The face on the head, the eyes, the mouth . . . Yes.

When the thing disappeared, the shaman removed his mask.

He saw and understood.

And he was afraid.

TWENTY-TWO

THUNK . . . THUNK . . . PING . . . THUNK . . .

It was far away and almost musical. There was an echo, or maybe more pinging coming from an even greater distance.

He listened for what seemed like a very long time before noticing that the cadence wasn't even. And rather than notes or the beat of drums, the sound was dull and metallic.

As his mind attempted to classify the noises, he became aware of the fact that he was lying down: supine, legs splayed, head turned to one side. Something cold was pressing against his cheek and temple.

He had no desire to move, and somehow felt that if he tried, he would lack the power to do so.

Thunk . . . Thunk . . . Ping . . . Thunk . . .

It was mechanical, and yet . . . He was reminded of the shrews that tried to make their home in his attic each winter. In bed at night you could hear them scurrying around overhead and, every so often, trying to work a hole in the insulation. This was the same deliberate, purposeful sort of sound. Not random or a force of nature.

He was lying there, the nerves in his arms and legs just now beginning to send his brain messages concerning their status—mostly that they were stiff and cold—when he finally realized what he was hearing. Of course: digging. Something or, more likely, someone, digging. Yes, someone. With shovels or maybe picks.

Eyes still closed, he entertained an image of a grave pit illuminated by a set of torches. Digging a grave. For whom? It flashed to mind that perhaps it was for him.

This motivated him to roll over. He groaned at the effort, thankful that he was not dead, yet almost wishing he were. His head pounded as though it had split open. When he had reached his back, and the back of his head touched the ground, he groaned again and opened his eyes in time to see the darkness filling with bright yellow stars. He quickly rolled back to his stomach.

Panting, he reached a hand up to his head. There was a massive lump rising up from his otherwise rounded skull. It was tender to the touch and there was crusted blood on the surrounding hair.

It came to him then: looking down on Tommy's body, seeing a wound, preparing to say as much, feeling himself go down. Someone had clouted him. Oddly, it hadn't hurt as much then as it did now. Thank goodness for unconsciousness.

The pain came in waves that were synchronized with the pulse of his heart. They began at the epicenter of the lump and moved swiftly out, around his head, down over his eyes, into his jaw . . .

He wanted to get up, but felt broken. This was no bump on the head, he could tell. It was a concussion. And his confusion right now had to do with having blacked out.

Ray took several deep breaths and told himself not to panic. If he went into shock, it was all over.

He consciously tried to relax every muscle, his mind attempting to run away from the pain waves. But there was no place to go.

The clinking and thudding continued. He opened his eyes and, after the stars had subsided, saw nothing. Pitch-black. If he was outside, having a grave dug for him, then the universe had somehow been extinguished. The air had also been mysteriously warmed. Maybe he was in the shed, he thought. He reached an arm out, hoping to find a wall or a table. Nothing.

Relaxing again, willing off shock, he pieced together what had happened. He remembered the beam of the penlight illuminating a nasty laceration on the kid's head. Evidence that he hadn't just drowned or expired from exposure. Willy had been at the door. The boy had said something. He looked up, but . . .

He recalled, then, giving Denisovich the crowbar to hold. She had used it to crack open his head! Denisovich! She was the murderer! He hadn't actually seen her. But who else could have done it? She was standing right there with a weapon in hand. A lethal weapon. He was lucky he wasn't dead.

Maybe they thought he was! And they were digging a plot for his body. Even worse, maybe they knew he was still alive but were going to bury him anyway.

Ray tried to turn over again, and made it to his side before a tsunami of pain forced him to stop. He had been right about Denisovich, he realized as he tried to breathe his way to relief. No wonder she had marched him step by step through this investigation. And as soon as he saw Tommy's head and knew for a fact that this was a crime, not an accident, she had taken him out.

Lying there in the dark, listening to the picks and shovels do their work, he wondered how they would explain his disappearance to the captain, to his family. They would probably say he got lost out on the floes. Maybe they would claim not to have seen him since he left the *Arctic Star*. A search party would be organized and the floes would be scoured, to no avail, since he wouldn't be out there. He'd be in grave at the cemetery. And they would eventually call off the search, believing that he had been swallowed up by the sea.

The thought of his captain and colleagues writing him off as an accident victim made him angry. He was as good at survival as anybody. But the idea of his family having a coffinless funeral broke his heart. He could see Margaret and Keera and Freddie and Grandfather lined up, tears streaming, never having had a chance to say goodbye, never really achieving proper closure.

In one swift movement he sat up, and as his head

swam and pounded, he cursed the pain. He wasn't ready to die. He wasn't going to die, he vowed. Not without a fight.

He reached a kneeling position without fainting and waited a moment to let the new and enthusiastic fireworks show fade. When it did, he stood up. His legs were weak and shook under him. He felt strangely top heavy, as though his head were a cannonball that his shoulders couldn't quite keep balanced.

Stumbling in a direction that he hoped might lead to the door of the shed, he went only a yard or so before his boot hit something. Bending, he felt . . . flesh. At first he figured it was Willy. Denisovich had probably attacked him too. But further examination revealed it to be an arm. An arm from an adult. Too big for Willy. His hand moved up the shoulder, the neck, to the head. It was a woman, he could tell, lying facedown.

Denisovich?

He rolled her over carefully and felt for a pulse. She was alive. He put his head down close to her mouth. She was breathing.

He nudged her lightly, trying to rouse her. "Doctor? Doctor?"

"What?"

The answer came from somewhere behind him.

"Who is that?"

"Who wants to know?" The accent and the perturbed attitude were unmistakable.

"Butyerki?"

In response, there was a groan.

"Are you hurt?" Ray asked.

"Only my pride."

"Come here and help me. Dr. Denisovich has been attacked."

"How terrible." This was drenched in sarcasm.

"She's unconscious."

"Lucky her."

"What's the matter with you?"

"The same thing that is the matter with all of us: we are *myertvee*."

"We're what?"

"Dead."

Confused by this, Ray momentarily wondered if Butyerki might be right. "No. I don't think we are."

"We soon will be."

"How do you know?"

"I told you before. They wanted to kill me. Now they are going to kill you too."

"Can you at least help me with Dr. Denisovich."

"What is the point?"

"The point is, she's injured. And you're a doctor."

"It will only slow the inevitable."

"Get over here!" Ray insisted. He heard a rustling sound, labored breathing. Suddenly a light went on. It was tiny, yet blinding.

"Where'd you get the light?" Ray asked, shielding his eyes.

"I am a doctor," Butyerki said, as if this explained everything.

Ray looked down and saw that Denisovich had dried blood around her nose. He then glanced around and realized that they were not in the shed.

The floor was metal, the walls metal . . . "Where are we?"

"In Hades," Butyerki said, leaning over Denisovich. He tested her pupils with the tiny light. After checking her pulse, he ran a finger along her leg. It jerked responsively. "Good reflexes . . ." He lifted her head and examined the back of the skull. "What do you know?" he said in a joking manner. "A contusion."

"You don't sound surprised."

"Why should I be? Half the world has had their head broken. This *ee-dee-yot* has an obsession with bashing in skulls."

"What idiot?"

There was a loud clank and a door creaked open in the distance. Butyerki put out the light. "Down!" he ordered in an urgent whisper.

Ray could hear feet shuffling close by. Not in the same room. Maybe out in the corridor. They were aboard the *Arctic Star*, he decided, though he had no idea why.

When the footsteps had grown faint and then finally ceased, Butyerki flipped the light back on. It was the size of a quarter, Ray saw, attached to a key chain.

Butyerki sighed as he hunched over Denisovich again.

"Is she okay?" Ray asked.

"As okay as you can be when you are slated for execution."

"What are you talking about?"

"I'm talking about that." Butyerki aimed the light

at the corner where two sacks were lying next to each other. They were long, green, zipped shut.

It took a few seconds for Ray to realize that they were body bags. He got up, his head complaining violently, swayed for a moment, then went over to them. Unzipping the closest one, he found two eyes glaring up at him. He knew the face. It was Police Chief Kuleak.

"I saw a pad in his office," Ray thought aloud. "He figured out something was going on out here. Something illegal."

"Something deadly," Butyerki added.

Ray felt for a pulse, mostly out of instinct. It was obvious that Kuleak was dead. He then zipped the bag shut and unzipped the second one. Another face. Also Native. It wasn't familiar, but Ray was pretty sure he knew who it was. "Old William . . ."

"I don't know his name," Butyerki said wearily. "All I know is that he died like all the others."

"Let me guess," Ray said. "A blow to the back of the head."

"Da."

"How many have there been?"

"Let's see . . . Chekerov, his guide . . ."

"Tommy."

"Then these two. And the three of us. That makes six."

Ray swore softly as he came back over to Denisovich. "We're not dead yet."

"We will be."

"What about Willy?"

"The boy?" Butyerki shrugged. "Maybe they will

take him back to Russia. There is a market for American boys, you know."

Ray wanted to punch Butyerki. Not only was this statement disgusting, but it was probably true. "Shut up!"

"You asked me a question."

"Maybe instead of spouting gloom and doom, we should try to figure a way out of here."

"There is no way out."

"Have you looked?"

"I don't need to look. We are on the bottom tier of the ship. There is no elevator to this level, there are guards at the stairwells. We are, as you Americans like to say, history."

"Is the door locked?"

"Whether it is locked or not makes no difference. There is nowhere to go."

Ray went over and tried the door. It was unlocked. "It's open."

"Of course. Why lock the door on a bunch of dead people?"

"Shut up!!" Ray stood there, trying not to faint, trying to think. "What's that noise?" he asked.

"The sandhogs."

Ray listened for a moment. "Don't tell me they're tunneling by hand."

"No. They are clearing the mouth from yet another cave-in."

"Another?"

"The operation has been plagued with them. I have treated a dozen crush injuries and had to pronounce death over four workers, not including

Cheverov. It seems that Dr. Radikoff's most wonderful innovations in structural engineering are turning out to be *navoz*: so much scientific dung."

"You mean his theories don't work?"

"Ask the dead sandhogs." Butyerki gave out a little laugh. "The transcontinental railroad is a bust."

"Then why is Radikoff—"

"To quote another Americanism: image is everything. As long as the investors and our prospective governments perceive the project to be on schedule, he will continue to have billions of dollars at his disposal."

"I thought the ship was here on research in the first place."

"It was. Except Radikoff apparently was nervous about his technological theories."

"So he started digging to find out if they would work."

"Precisely."

"And they didn't," Ray said. The case was finally starting to make sense. "Chekerov knew about the failure . . ."

"All the sandhogs did. Dr. Radikoff is a brilliant scientist and engineer—but not so smart in matters of human behavior. It was only a matter of time before one of them reported what they saw."

"Or came to Radikoff demanding a payoff."

"I believe the term is 'blackmail.' "

"Which is where the money under Chekerov's bunk came from."

"Even in the shadow of death, you are a talented investigator," Butyerki said.

Ray couldn't tell if the doctor was being sarcastic or giving him a compliment. "But Radikoff isn't stupid."

"No," Butyerki agreed.

"So he had his brute squad follow Chekerov out onto the ice and murder him."

"If you are referring to the two large former Russian Olympic wrestlers who stand guard over his office . . ." Butyerki shook his head.

"No?"

"They were flown in after the first cave-in. I can only assume that Radikoff feared some sort of reprisal from the sandhogs."

"Then who—"

Denisovich gave a moan and moved her legs.

Ray went over to her and watched as her eyes blinked open. She looked at him with a vague expression that said, wordlessly: where am I and what happened?

Butyerki smiled down at her. "Dr. Denisovich? So glad you could join us. Welcome to the Voyage of the Damned."

TWENTY-THREE

I'VE GOT A HEADACHE," she complained weakly.

"Join the club," Butyerki deadpanned.

"Are you hurt anywhere else?" Ray asked.

She considered this for a moment. "I don't think so. But my head . . ." She started to reach a hand up to it, then changed her mind. "It feels like someone hit me with a baseball bat."

"Or a crowbar," Ray said.

"No," Butyerki said. "Not a crowbar. You would be dead."

"I think I'm close," Denisovich said.

Butyerki produced a bottle of pills. *"Bowl-oobeecha."* He twisted the top off. "Painkiller." After handing Denisovich and Ray each four pills, he produced a silver flask. "Also *bowl-oobeecha*." He took a swig before offering it to Ray.

"No, thanks." Ray managed to gulp the pills dry, then asked, "Why'd they let you keep that?"

"Who?"

"The *they* you keep talking about. Why didn't they confiscate it?"

Butyerki shrugged. “It is the custom to give a dying man his last wish.”

“I don’t suppose they let you keep the shotgun.”

The doctor laughed. “As far as I know, it is still in the truck.”

“And where’s the truck?”

“It does not matter now, since—”

“Where is the truck?”

“I had a slight accident,” Butyerki confessed.

“What did you do to it?”

“I merely impacted a stationary object.”

“What kind of object?”

“A building.”

“You hit a building?!”

“It did very little damage to the building.”

Ray took a deep breath. “Is the truck totaled? Can it be driven?”

“I don’t know. I tried to make it run, but the ignition would not cooperate. So I got out and started walking. Which is when I was picked up and brought here.”

“Why wasn’t *your* head bashed in?” Ray thought to ask.

This drew another shrug. “There was no need. I agreed to accompany him without a fight.”

“Him who?”

“The *koreesnee*.”

“Who?”

A door scraped the floor somewhere and Butyerki flicked off his light. They heard footsteps again, another door creaking open. The footsteps came closer . . . closer . . .

"Get down!" Butyerki urged.

Ray rolled to what he hoped was a natural looking position and closed his eyes. As he did this, he wondered if this might be a chance to escape. If he took up position by the door—wherever that was—and could jump the approaching person, then maybe—

The door groaned and a sharp sliver of light shot across the floor, falling on Denisovich and Butyerki.

"Vrach Butyerki," a voice said.

Butyerki pretended to be asleep or passed out.

"Tyepeer!" There was a long pause. Then the speaker switched to English. "I will count to three, then I will shoot you."

Still Butyerki didn't move.

"Aden . . . dva . . ."

"Da, da . . ." Butyerki said in an irritated tone. "Give an old man a chance to get up, will you?"

"Jeevo-ee!"

"What is it, another cave-in?"

"Shut up!"

"Yes, yes . . ." The doctor rose stiffly and walked in a drunken line toward the door. "I have to guess if I'll be saving a life or you will be taking mine, is that it? Or is it both: I administer first aid and then you put a *pool-ya* in my head?"

Ray squinted through the slits in his eyelids but couldn't make out who it was at the door. Backlit by a wash of glare, it could have been Kareem Abdul Jabbar or Santa Claus. There was no way to tell. Whoever it was, they were holding something long in one hand. A rope? A rifle? A broomstick?

"You stink of *al-ko-gol*!"

"It's my aftershave," Butyerki shot back.

As the door shrieked shut, Ray thought he heard the wind being knocked out of Butyerki.

"They'll be coming for one of us next," Denisovich said softly.

"Not if we can blow this popsicle stand first." Ray sat up, wishing he had Butyerki's flashlight. "Can you move?"

"If you mean, can I get up, overpower whoever's standing guard outside the door, and make a run for it . . . I doubt it."

"Do you know where we are?"

"Vaguely." She moaned as she sat up, then breathed hard from the effort. "I think . . . we are at the bottom of the ship . . ." she said, panting.

"What's that digging sound?"

"I'm not sure."

"Do you know the layout down here? Where the stairs are or the elevators?"

"If we are all the way down, in the main hold, there are no elevators. Only hydraulic lifts to move equipment to upper decks."

"Can we get out on one of the lifts?"

"Not without being seen."

Ray tried to think. "What about ventilation shafts?"

"I'm not familiar with the schematic of the ship."

"There must be some sort of ventilation system."

"I suppose."

In the quiet darkness, they could hear the pinging and chipping of picks.

"Butyerki said that they were digging a tunnel.

He said that Radikoff needed to fine-tune his devices in order to keep the investors happy. And apparently it isn't going well."

"If they have started, I no longer need to worry about losing my job. I must worry about being sent to prison."

"Not if you didn't know about it."

"That detail will not matter in the end. We will all go to prison."

"That's saying we don't die in this hole."

Ray got up and carefully scuffed his way over to the wall.

"What are you doing?" Denisovich asked.

"My impersonation of Ray Charles."

"Who?"

"Never mind." Ray felt his way along the wall. It was cold, hard, featureless. "You know what I'm wondering?"

"How we got here?"

"No. I'm wondering *why* we got here." He continued his blind survey. "I mean, I can understand Chekerov. The guy was blackmailing Radikoff. Even Butyerki, if he knew about the tunnel and the blackmail and maybe even the details of how they iced Chekerov."

"Iced?"

"Bad choice of words. Murdered." Ray finally reached a corner and started along the next wall. "But us—you and me—we didn't know enough to be a danger to them."

"Maybe they assumed we would eventually figure things out."

"Maybe." Ray came to a protrusion: a soffit. He rapped on it.

"What was that?" Denisovich asked.

"That was me." Though the soffit sounded hollow, it also sounded solidly built and felt like the same metal that covered the rest of the wall. It would take a welder to rip into it. He continued along the wall. "Or maybe we already knew too much. I found the money. We examined one of the bodies, guessed that the cause of death wasn't drowning. And we were on the verge of confirming that with the other body."

"Was there a wound on the skull?" Denisovich asked.

"Yes." He jammed a finger into the metal collar that ran around the door and cursed softly.

"Are you okay?"

"Just great," Ray grumbled. "It still doesn't make sense."

"What doesn't?"

"We didn't have any dirt on Radikoff—and still don't. Without a weapon or a motive, we would eventually have dropped the investigation, probably written the two bodies off as accidental deaths, packed up and gone home."

"Except for the money."

"That could have been drug money or . . . Chekerov could have been dealing booze on board the ship. He could have robbed a bank . . . There are any number of explanations for it."

"You would have looked into it, though."

"Sure. I already was looking into it. But what I'm

trying to say is that we didn't have any connective evidence. No prime suspects. Not even enough to prove a crime had been committed."

"So?"

"So, why knock us silly and put us down here? That's an act of desperation. Radikoff seems like a cool character. I can't imagine him panicking just because we were examining Tommy."

Ray came to the third corner and, stepping over what he knew to be two more human bodies, started down the last wall. "There's also the problem of what to do with us."

"You mean because there are so many options?"

"Huh?"

"Well . . . me—they can fire, dismiss, ruin my reputation . . . You, they can frame for some sort of crime, say . . . espionage . . ."

Ray laughed at this. "Yeah. I look like a spy."

"Or maybe theft. Say they plant that money on you or something."

"That's pretty weak. And I still don't get the why. People can do all sorts of stupid, crazy things. But they usually have a good reason." He reached the last corner and moved slowly back up the wall he had started on. "Anyway, I'm not worried about any of that."

"What are you worried about?"

"I'm worried about hunting."

"Hunting?"

"My guess is more in line with Butyerki's: they'll arrange another hunting accident for the two of us." Ray heard a sniffling sound. "You okay?"

"I'm just tired," Denisovich replied in a weak, teary voice.

"Hey, I didn't mean to . . . We're gonna be fine," he said. He didn't fully believe this, but wanted to.

Ray felt his way back to the soffit. He ran his hands along one side again, then the other. Near one end, he found what he assumed to be an access panel. Like the soffit itself, the panel was metal, held fast with screws. He tried to jiggle one loose with his fingers. That was joke. They were flush and very secure. Even with a screwdriver he might not be able to get the panel off. It would probably take a power drill with a driver attachment.

He rapped the soffit again, wondering what might be behind it: electrical wires, plumbing, an air space . . .

Ray kicked the panel with his boot. He could tell there was no way through it. The only other outlet, he thought, would be something on the ceiling—a vent or a shaft. Without light it would be difficult to find.

He had just started out from the wall, his hands touching the low ceiling, when he heard footsteps outside.

"You better get down," Denisovich warned. She was still breathing erratically, but managed to stay quiet as the footsteps approached, arrived, and the door opened.

"You're welcome," a voice said testily as a figure was pushed inside. "Such *nyeblagodarnost*."

The door slammed shut again and the footsteps left.

"Butyerki?" Ray asked.

"Present," the doctor chimed, as though responding to roll call.

"What's going on?"

"Dr. Radikoff is losing guinea pigs left and right." He expectorated, then said, "I treated two crush injuries, pronounced another poor slob dead, and what do I get? Not so much as a simple *spaseeba* or even a cigarette."

"So it was a cave-in?"

"Yes."

"The good news is," Ray thought aloud, "if they need you, they'll keep you around."

"I am not so sure." He spit again. "There is so much dirt in the air out there . . ." After coughing, he explained, "For the first time, I was taken into the tunnels."

"Tunnels . . . plural?" Denisovich asked.

"*Da*. They have a nice little catacomb going. It appears that the modifications to the *Arctic Star* that Dr. Radikoff made are the one thing that have worked. By drilling straight down for a number of meters, they have gone beneath the surface of the sea. Then the tunnels begin. They go off like spokes on a wheel. I counted six, three of which have caved in."

"A fifty percent success rate," Ray observed.

"Yes. In baseball, this is a good thing. Not in tunneling." He coughed again. "At any rate, by taking me to the victims, rather than having them brought up . . . I fear that my time is running out."

"Now that you've seen what's going on, you're expendable?"

"Something like that."

Ray stood up, prepared to continue his ceiling survey. "I don't understand how Radikoff expects all those men—those 'sandhogs'—to keep quiet. An operation this size is bound to leak information."

"Da," Butyerki agreed. "But with sufficient incentives . . ."

"Such as?"

"I would guess that the sandhogs are working on something of a commission. If the operation becomes public, they make far less money. If it stays quiet and on schedule, they get bonuses."

"It doesn't seem to be on schedule."

"No. But security can still be maintained simply enough by promising more bonuses. Money is the universal language and a most excellent motivator."

"Too bad we don't have any," Ray said. "Maybe we could buy our way out of here."

Butyerki laughed. "I have enough to bribe the man assigned to watch us. But it would do us no good."

"Why not?"

"There is nowhere to go when we get out. The lifts are in use."

"What about the tunnels?" Denisovich asked.

"What about them, comrade *vrach*?"

"Why can't we get out that way?"

"Because they probably don't go anywhere," Ray answered. "And they're unsafe."

"Yes. The officer is correct."

"Why couldn't we hide in one until a shift change or—" Denisovich tried.

"Hide beneath the floor of the Arctic Ocean?" Butyerki asked in an amused tone. "I'd rather remain here and let them kill me swiftly and efficiently."

TWENTY-FOUR

"I SAY WE CHANCE IT," Ray interjected.

"You are *jzatkee*. It is below zero under the ice and water and earth. We have no food, no water—"

"Four men are dead," Ray said.

"Actually," Butyerki corrected, "the number stands at three. Five others are in critical condition."

"I'm talking about the ones that have been murdered: Chekerov, Tommy, Kuleak, Old William . . . Then add those others in. This thing is blowing up in Radikoff's face. What's to keep him from killing us too?"

"Nothing," Denisovich answered. "I agree. We must try to escape."

"It is not that simple," Butyerki said. "The tunnels are full of workers."

"All of them?" Ray asked.

"There are only three left. Two of them are full of equipment and sandhogs."

"What about the other?"

"It's smaller, narrower."

"So?"

"So it might only have been a test hole. It probably goes a few meters at most."

"Let's find out," Ray said.

"How much money do you have?" Denisovich asked.

"Enough for our guard," Butyerki said, "but after that . . ."

"After that, all bets are off," Ray said.

"Bets?"

"Never mind. Get your money out."

There was a rustling sound, and suddenly Butyerki's little flashlight flicked on. "This is *plohoy*. I believe it will end badly." He removed a wad of cash from his boot.

"It's already ended badly for them," Ray said, gesturing at the body bags.

"True enough." Butyerki tried to hand the money to Ray.

"No. You do it. You speak the language."

"This is the only language you will need," the doctor assured him.

Ray begrudgingly accepted the cash. "Can you walk?" he asked Denisovich.

"I guess I'll have to." With Ray and Butyerki's help, she got to her feet.

"Okay?" Ray asked.

"No. I feel sick." When they hesitated, she urged, "Let's go."

They went to the door and Ray began banging on it. In a moment they heard footsteps.

"Stay back a little," Ray warned.

"*Shto?*" a voice called through the door.

"Tell him something," Ray said to Butyerki.

The doctor rattled off a paragraph of Russian, and after a brief hesitation, the door opened. Light glared in at them.

"Give it to him," Butyerki said.

Ray handed the money over. The man took it and quickly leafed through it.

"Horosha," the man grunted. He stepped aside and turned away from them.

"Go!" Butyerki prodded.

Ray helped Denisovich through the opening, into a smoky hallway. Dust, Ray realized. From the cave-ins. Glancing back, he saw that the guard was wearing a white mask over his nose and mouth, his eyes encircled with dirt.

Denisovich began to choke.

"We need to cover our mouths."

Butyerki offered Denisovich his scarf, then drew his jacket over the lower half of his face. Ray pulled his turtleneck up to his nose.

When they reached the end of the hallway, Ray asked, "Which way?"

Butyerki gestured to the left. "I would move as quickly as possible," he advised. "The money was enough for an open door and perhaps a five minute head start."

As they proceeded through the mazelike corridors, the air became more and more clouded. It stung Ray's eyes and made his throat burn, even through the fabric of the turtleneck.

"Maybe this isn't such a good idea," Denisovich admitted as Ray pulled her along.

"What did I tell you?" Butyerki said. *"Plohoy."*

They came to a set of metal stairs that seemed to descend into nothingness. The noise of the picks and shovels was much louder now and the dust was swirling, mixed with ice crystals.

"Down," Butyerki ordered.

Ray assisted Denisovich down the steps. There were at least two flights of them, and by the time they reached the bottom, it was markedly colder. There was a glow of diffused light straight ahead that shifted and faded with the breeze.

"Where's the wind coming from?" Ray asked.

Ignoring this, Butyerki led them into the brown fog. The pick and shovel work seemed to be all around them now, and a steady mechanical hum was rising in intensity.

Butyerki abruptly stopped and looked around.

"Which way?" Ray asked.

Butyerki shrugged.

Shivering as the wind actually gusted at them, Ray had an idea. "This way." He started directly into the wind, pulling Denisovich along with him.

"What? How can you see?"

"I can't," Ray replied. "But the air is coming from someplace. Let's follow it."

In another minute visibility improved slightly and they could see a tunnel mouth.

"That's the tiny one," Butyerki said.

"A ventilation shaft," Ray guessed. "We might be able to get out that way."

"And we might not," Butyerki shot back.

"Got a better idea?"

Butyerki said something in Russian that didn't sound optimistic or complimentary.

Ray pulled Denisovich into the tunnel. The ceiling was low and they both had to hunch. "You doing okay?"

"Great," she deadpanned. "Nothing like an underground hike on a beautiful brown day like this."

Ray laughed. He was beginning to like this woman. She was almost as sarcastic as he was.

The tunnel quickly became little more than a hole in the ground. It shrunk to five feet in diameter, then to four, finally to three.

"We'll have to crawl," Ray said, nearly bent in half. He had Denisovich go first, then followed, with Butyerki bringing up the rear.

"This is fit only for worms," the doctor complained.

"Should we keep going?" Denisovich asked.

"We have to," Ray said.

The tunnel went on and on and on until even Ray began to doubt the strategy. His knees were aching and he was now thoroughly cold. If they wound up having to go back, they might not make it. For starters, there was no way to turn around. The tunnel was too narrow.

"This might go all the way to Mother Russia," Butyerki muttered.

"Hold on," Ray said. Butyerki's comment had reminded him that he had his GPS with him. Or at least, it had been there before the incident in the cemetery shed. He struggled to check his pockets.

"What are you doing?" Butyerki asked.

"I've got something that can help us."

"You have vodka?"

Ignoring this, Ray finally found the device. It was the size of a wallet and flipped open to reveal an electronic digital display.

"What is it?" Butyerki asked from behind Ray.

"It's a global positioning system," Denisovich said. Pointed away from Ray, she couldn't see it, but had somehow guessed.

"Right." Ray turned it on and began pressing buttons.

"Will it work down here?" Denisovich asked.

Ray hadn't thought of that. "I'm not sure."

"The walls of the tunnel may not allow the signal to reach the satellite," she said.

"It's fading in and out," Ray said, watching the numbers change. "But . . . if it's accurate at all . . . we're heading south."

"How does that help us?" Butyerki asked.

"It tells us that we're moving toward land, not away from it."

"If it's working properly," Denisovich stipulated.

"I'd rather have vodka," Butyerki mumbled. "A good bottle of Stolka and we wouldn't care which direction was which."

Ray put the GPS back into his pocket. "I've got two words for you, Doctor: A-A."

"*Shto?* What do you mean by that?"

"If we get out of here—*when* we get out—I'll be glad to explain it to you."

Denisovich began to move again, and as Ray

crawled behind her, he toggled the light on his watch. If they didn't reach an end, an opening, something in the next thirty minutes, then he would admit defeat and sound the retreat.

They slid along for several minutes without speaking. Then Butyerki groaned, "My body is *l-yed*."

"I assume that *l-yed* translates as either tired or cold," Ray said.

"Ice," Butyerki said. "Solid ice. In a matter of a few short minutes we will all begin to suffer from frostbite, as well as hypothermia. After which we will become confused, unable to continue, and will die in this hole."

Though Ray wasn't about to admit it, Butyerki was right. Unless they got out in the near future, they might never get out. He could feel the cold moving up his limbs, into his midsection. He could also tell that his brain was slowing down. He was no longer in a hurry, no longer anxious about getting out of the tunnel. That was a bad sign.

Soon, Denisovich's pace began to lag.

"Come on," Ray prodded. "It can't be much further."

"What can't be?" Butyerki asked incredulously. "Death?"

"We can't stop. If we stop we really are in trouble."

"I'm not sure I can go much more," Denisovich said. She sounded not only fatigued but discouraged, ready to give up.

"Feel that breeze?" Ray asked, trying to come up with a motivational argument. "It has to come from somewhere above ground."

"We must be miles from the ship," Denisovich said, crawling again.

Miles was an exaggeration, Ray thought. Maybe a single mile. Maybe not that far. How long did it take to crawl a mile?

He checked his watch again and saw that they had reached the thirty-minute limit. But he didn't have the heart or the will to suggest going back.

"I always expected to die in a drunken stupor," Butyerki said, as though a drunken stupor was a good thing.

"You still might get your chance," Ray shot back.

"It's getting windier," Denisovich reported.

"That's good," Ray said. "Maybe we're almost to the mouth."

They went on for another few minutes before Denisovich said, "Uh-oh."

"Uh-oh, what?"

"It ends here."

"That's impossible. There has to be a ventilation shaft or—"

"There is," Denisovich said. "It goes straight up."

"Can we climb it?"

"It's only about six inches wide and it feels like . . . like metal or something."

Butyerki said something in Russian that had to be a curse.

They lay there in single file, their breathing loud in the confined space, the only other sound that of the wind howling. Then Ray thought he heard something else.

"Listen."

"To what?" Butyerki said angrily. "Our last breaths?"

"Shh . . ."

They listened as the wind whistled down the tiny shaft.

"I don't hear anything," Denisovich said.

"Wait for the breeze to stop. When it lets up, you can hear it."

They waited. And there, in between gusts, was the ticking.

"The sandhogs!" Butyerki said. "We have made a big circle!"

"No. That's not the sandhogs," Ray said. "There's no mechanical whine. And not enough diggers."

"Then what is it?" Denisovich wondered.

"See if you can shine the flashlight up the hole."

"Why?"

"Just try it."

"Okay . . . now what?"

"Now we yell."

"Yell what?" Butyerki asked skeptically.

"Help would be good." Ray counted to three and they began yelling. After about ten seconds he called for quiet. In between whistles of wind, they heard the picks and shovels. "Again," he said, and they yelled again.

This time when they quit shouting there was silence. "One more time," Ray ordered. They hollered until they heard a metallic thud. There was a scraping noise, and then the darkness was invaded by a yellow glow.

"They opened it," Denisovich said. "They opened it!"

Ray saw her slide forward, then up. When her feet were gone, two pair of hands reached for him. He was dragged up the shaft, which was now a gaping manhole, and into the street. They were on the main drag in TaggaQ, just beyond the bone fence of the cemetery.

The men pulled Butyerki out before one of them asked, "What're you doing in the sewer?"

"Un-jels!" Butyerki exclaimed, embracing one of the men.

As Ray had suspected, and hoped, they were the grave diggers. They had obviously heard them calling, maybe seen the beam of the tiny flashlight, and come to their rescue by pulling off the manhole cover.

Denisovich hugged them each in turn, while Ray shook their hands and thanked them. The men were dumbfounded. And Ray didn't blame them. How often did three people pop up from under the street? Ray glanced down and realized he was filthy. So were Denisovich and Butyerki. They looked as though they had just crawled on hands and knees through an earthen tunnel.

"You oughta stay out of the sewer," one of men counseled as they returned to the cemetery to continue their work.

"Words to live by," Ray agreed. He took hold of

Denisovich and began assisting her up the street, toward police headquarters.

"Where are we going now?" she asked.

"To do what we should have done a long time ago."

"Procure some vodka?" Butyerki asked hopefully.

"No. Call the cavalry and put and end to this whole sordid mess."

TWENTY-FIVE

"Do you remember what happened in the shed?" Ray asked Denisovich as they approached the door of the police station.

"Not really. I heard something, and then . . ."

"Yeah. Me too."

"Why?"

"I'm just wondering what happened to Willy. I mean, did he get attacked too? And if so, why didn't they dump him in the bottom of the ship with us?"

"I don't know."

They went inside the office, and after Ray had deposited Denisovich in a chair, he picked up the phone.

"Are there any cigarettes around here?" Butyerki asked.

Ray shrugged and dialed the Barrow PD. As he waited for the line to ring, he glanced at the desk and saw the pad of doodles. Now the random lines made sense. It was a sketch of the *Arctic Star*: the ship, doors on the bottom, a tunnel trailing away from it. "Kuleak figured it out," he thought aloud.

"Figured what out?"

"That they were tunneling."

He handed Denisovich the pad. The line rang twice before he got switched over to the answering service. Ray asked the woman to page the captain for him, gave her Kuleak's number, then hung up.

"This is why they killed him?" Denisovich asked.

"I assume so. He might have gone out there to confront Radikoff about the operation."

"Dr. Radikoff would not kill anyone," Denisovich said. "He can be controlling and overbearing. But he is a brilliant man."

"Some of the most successful murderers are brilliant," Butyerki threw in.

"You believe he killed these men?" Denisovich asked.

"I didn't say that, Doctor. Only that he, like every other human being, is quite capable of these acts."

"Old William, on the other hand," Ray continued, "found the bodies. Something which wasn't supposed to happen. And he was going around getting the town up in arms about a supposed 'tupilak.' Radikoff must have panicked and—"

"Dr. Radikoff does not panic," Denisovich said.

"Okay, maybe he was just being thorough, taking care of all the loose ends. It had to be tough running an operation that large without having the lid blow off."

"Which is exactly what happened," Butyerki said. He was rifling the drawers in Kuleak's desk.

Ray was about to tell him to quit when the phone rang. He answered it.

"Hello?"

"Attla? What the heck's going on up there?"

An excellent question, Ray thought, which he was wholly incapable of answering. "We've got a couple more casualties," he finally reported. He went on to explain his theory about why the men had been killed, told of the money under the cot, getting attacked in the shed, and, without mentioning the tunnel expedition or the tupilak sidebar, emphasized the urgent need for backup.

"Where's Billy Bob? Was he attacked too?"

"I don't know. He was on the ship, guarding Chekerov—the Russian who was with Tommy—the last time I saw him. There's also a boy that I can't account for."

"A boy?"

"He's the nephew of the man who discovered the bodies under the ice."

"The one who's now dead?"

"Yes, sir."

"And the boy's missing?"

Ray retold the part about the attack in the shed, including Willy this time.

"Sounds like a manniliqun . . ." the captain muttered. The word meant "egg beater," and he used it whenever things got chaotic.

"Yes, sir," Ray agreed.

"I'll get on the horn to the Feds. They need to be in on this. Then Lewis, Jackson, and I will hop up there by helicopter. You sit tight until we get there."

"Yes, sir." Ray wanted to head for the ship, make sure Billy Bob was okay, arrest Radikoff and have him in custody when the Fibbies arrived. But without backup . . .

"I'm serious, Attla. Sit tight. Got me?"

"Yes, sir."

"You can't lone ranger this one, understand?"

"Fine."

"We'll be up there inside of an hour."

"Okay."

"We'll meet you at the police station. Be there."

"Or be square."

"What was that?"

"Yes, sir. I'll be here."

He hung up and looked at Denisovich. "We're supposed to hang out here until the troops arrive." He glanced out the window.

"How long will that take?" Butyerki wanted to know.

"Not long. Maybe forty-five minutes."

"Long enough to seek out a kiosk and purchase some American cigarettes?"

"No." Ray shook his head. "For one thing, there's not a 'kiosk' in TaggaQ. And if there was, it would be closed by now." He checked his watch and was amazed to see that it was nearly midnight.

"Perhaps there is an all-night grocery," Butyerki said.

"You want to go out there and maybe get clobbered?"

Butyerki frowned. "A convincing argument."

Ray went to the desk and began checking the drawers.

"Don't waste your time," Butyerki said. "I already looked."

In the bottom right drawer, under a crossword puzzle book, Ray found what he was after: a gun. It was a tiny .22 with a decorative ivory handle. A nice collector's item, but not much in the power department. Since his own gun was gone, this miniature would have to do.

He found bullets loose in the bottom of the drawer. After loading it, he handed the gun to Denisovich.

"What's this for?"

"Just in case."

"Just in case, what?"

"I don't think they'll have the audacity to raid the police office . . ."

"They killed the police officer," Butyerki said.

"Good point." He asked Denisovich, "Do you know how to use it?"

"Aim and pull the trigger?"

"That's pretty much it. Take your time, try to relax and focus when you shoot. The shells are kind of small so it might take a few rounds to slow a big guy down."

"I'd rather not have to slow a big guy down."

"I'm with you. But you might not have any choice."

"Why don't you keep it and you slow the big guy down?"

"I have something I need to do."

"I thought you were supposed to stay here," Butyerki said.

"Well . . . It's sort of a judgment call."

"Where are you going?"

"Out to the ship. I have to check on my partner."

Butyerki laughed. "You have a death wish."

"No. I have a responsibility."

"Why don't you just wait until your friends arrive? They'll be here in the time it takes you to reach the ship."

"Maybe. Maybe not."

"If you manage to get aboard without dying," Butyerki said, "go by my cabin and look under the bunk. There is a new bottle of Stolka and a carton of cigarettes."

"Yeah. That'll be the first thing I do: look for booze and smokes." He went to the door. "I'll be back." He delivered this line with a thick accent, hoping to lighten the mood a little. He waited for a response, a chuckle, something. "It's from *Terminator* . . . the movie. Arnold Schwarzenegger?"

"Very funny," Butyerki said with a straight face. "You are quite the comedian."

"Thanks." Tough crowd, Ray thought as he left the office. He was tired and nervous. Mostly for Billy Bob. He had all but forgotten about him, basically forsaking his partner aboard the ship. What had he been thinking? If the cowboy was already—He couldn't bring himself to entertain the worst. Breaking into a ragged trot that reminded him of how much his ankle hurt, Ray went to the snow-machine shop.

It bothered him too that he had not located Willy,

or even tried to locate him. Of course, he had been a little busy being knocked unconscious and then escaping on his belly through an undersea air vent.

He quickly found a good machine, made sure it had enough gas, and took off through town. There were very few lights on, no movement, no sound, except for the blaring engine of the snowmobile. As he passed by the last few houses and was about to descend to the floes, he saw the blinds jerk in one of the windows. The people, while not visible, were still there. Scared out of their wits, he assumed, about the roving tupilak. In fact, they probably thought that he was it, zipping around town on a snow machine at midnight. He was lucky to get by them without having someone take a potshot at him.

As he roared over the ice, he realized that he had no guide. He wasn't about to slow down and check every section that looked iffy. There wasn't time. Instead, he went as straight as possible, as quickly as possible. With the throttle wide open, his main challenge was avoiding the larger ice lumps and cracks.

The ship was directly ahead, about half a mile away. Behind him the torches in the cemetery were the brightest points of light.

It was no wonder the People feared the floes and the night and made up stories about bizarre monsters, he thought. The Land they called home was a brutal, unmerciful environment that had no regard for man. Dying was an easy thing out here.

Pushing this out of his mind, he slowed to make his approach to the ship. The ice around it was heaped into large chunks that were impenetrable by a snow machine. He would have to go around to the other side, as they had before.

What if the climbing net wasn't down? he wondered. That would be the end of his mission. Of his misguided mission, he decided. The captain was right about having him wait. Without backup, this was almost suicidal. But he knew he would never forgive himself if something happened to Billy Bob.

Thankfully, the net was there. Ray throttled down and made a slow, cautious approach. Cutting the engine, he slid to a stop and watched for movement along the edge of the deck. He didn't see anyone. Maybe the security goons were asleep.

He climbed off the snow machine and trotted to the net. Still no heads looking down at him. Good. He began to climb, grimacing each time his injured ankle had to bear his weight on the rope.

When he reached the top, he peered over the edge and found the deck empty. As Butyerki had explained, the main threat to Radikoff and the operation came from the sandhogs themselves. The good doctor feared a revolt, not an assault from the mainland. Especially not a one-man assault.

That was good news for him, Ray thought.

He made it up and over the side, then hunched and ran for the door to the bridge structure. The mudroom was deserted, boots and jackets still littering the floor and benches. He went to the elevator and, when it arrived unoccupied, took it down to the deck where Chekerov's body was being kept. The doors opened and he exited into the dungeonlike corridor.

Shivering, he started off, trying to remember where Denisovich had turned, how far she had gone.

Ray walked for what he judged to be too long, stopped, went back. Retracing his path, he made his way to the elevator. Except . . . it wasn't there. Which meant that he had gotten turned around. He stood still, listening, hoping to hear something that would orient him. The walls all looked the same. Every hallway was identical.

He started out again, the captain's words ringing in his head: sit tight. Why couldn't he have listened?

After a few minutes, he stumbled onto the elevator. He was tempted to take it back up, climb over the side of the ship, snow-machine back to TaggaQ. But he had to find Billy Bob.

Moving more slowly, he turned, walked, turned, in what he was sure were Denisovich's footsteps. Time passed. He failed to reach the room. Or maybe he had simply passed it.

In frustration, he called, "Billy Bob?" His own voice echoed back at him. He made the next turn and tried again: "Billy Bob?" No response. After calling his partner's name several more times to no avail, he decided to give up and was about to attempt to locate the elevator again when he heard something. It was eerie, like a dog howling somewhere in the distance. He followed the sound, turning, turning back when it faded, until finally he was certain he was in the same hallway with it. There was a hatch. He went to it, pressed his ear against it. The dog had to be on the other side. It was making a mournful sound, and as Ray listened, he realized that it wasn't a dog, but a person. Singing. He made out the words "silent night."

Ray tried the arm of the hatch, but it wouldn't move. So he beat on the metal with his fist.

"Who is it?" a voice called. Ray recognized the twang.

"It's me."

"Me who?"

"It's Ray. Let me in."

"How do I know it's Ray?"

"Because I just told you it was. Open the door!"

There was a screeching sound and the hatch creaked open.

"Boy, are you a sight for sore eyes," the cowboy gushed. "I was beginnin' to think that you wasn't never comin' back." He closed the door.

"Yeah, well . . . I kind of got sidetracked."

"Is the captain here? Can we flange this here case up and go home?"

"Not quite. But almost."

"I was gettin' kinda nervous, down here by my lonesome. Just me and Mr. Dead Guy over there." He shuddered. "I tell ya, this ship makes all kinds-a noises. It's enough to get you started thinking about ghosts and goblins and bogeymen. Which is what started me singing Christmas carols."

"I heard you." Ray refrained from telling him that he had mistaken the "singing" for the howl of a dog.

"It's tough to be scared when yer singing 'Silent Night,' " Billy Bob said. "Anyway, I'm just right glad to see you, partner."

"Me too." Ray briefly explained the gist of what

had gone on and their need to leave quickly and quietly.

When he finished, Billy Bob asked, "Why don't we arrest this Radikoff fella?"

"Eventually we will," Ray said. "But I think we'd better wait for backup."

"Why? This here ship is in American waters. This is our jurisdiction. I say we march right up there and read him his rights."

"There are a few problems with that," Ray said, gesturing at the hatch. As Billy Bob cranked the bar, Ray said, "For one thing, a ship is like its own country. It'll take the FBI to arrest Radikoff. Or maybe even Immigration and Naturalization. The Coast Guard. I'm not sure."

"I don't rightly understand that, but . . . I suppose rules are rules." Billy Bob pushed on the hatch. "What're the other problems?"

Before Ray could reply, he found himself staring at the answer.

"Well, here's one of them," he said.

It was half of Radikoff's security team: the football lineman with no neck and a decidedly bad attitude. And he was barring their exit.

TWENTY-SIX

THE MAN SMILED AT THEM. It wasn't a look of hostility, though there was a certain threat implicit in his eyes. It was a look of supreme pleasure, as though his one desire in life had just been met.

"How's it going?" Ray said as casually as he could. He glanced at Billy Bob, wondering if together they could overcome the man. It was two against one, and the cowboy was now a green belt in karate. Surely they could . . .

The smile grew. "I wouldn't, if I were you." He actually seemed eager for Ray to try something. When he didn't, the man said, "Good decision." He waved them out of the room and up the corridor.

"Where are you taking us?" Ray asked.

"You've got a meeting."

"With who?"

"With *whom*," the man corrected. "Sometimes I think that you butcher your first language worst of all."

"Whom you takin' us to see?" Billy Bob asked.

The man laughed at this. "That's funny."

"You know we're po-lice officers," Billy Bob warned. "You know that, don'tcha?"

"All I know is two things: first, that I have orders to escort you to the bridge."

"Whose orders?" Ray asked.

The man either didn't know or didn't feel like answering.

"What's the other thang?" Billy Bob asked.

"The other what?"

"The other thang . . . that you know."

"Oh . . . if you give me any trouble, I have permission to take whatever steps I deem necessary to 'encourage' you to accompany me."

Ray had never met such a polite, articulate brute. "Your English is really quite good."

"Thank you."

"Were you educated here?"

"Now that you mention it, yes. I went to the University of Washington."

"Good school," Ray observed. They were approaching the elevator, and he was desperately searching for a means of escape.

"The best. We won the Rose Bowl in my senior year."

"Lineman?" Ray guessed.

"Right tackle. My brother played left. We made all-conference two years in a row. We were known as the Tasmanian Devils."

"Are you originally from Tasmania?" He was stalling now, trying to distract the guy.

"What? No. It was just our nickname, because we were fast and mean."

The elevator arrived and they got on. The former all-conference right tackle stood in front of the door, hands folded in front of him.

"How long have you worked for Radikoff?"

"I've been on the *Star* for three tours."

"It's against the law to kidnap people," Billy Bob said suddenly. "And we're not just people. We're law enforcement officers."

Unimpressed and unmoved, the man blinked sleepily at them.

"What yer doin' is against the law."

Ray tried to wave the cowboy off, but the man said, "No. It's okay. I understand. I'd be upset too if I got called upstairs. But the bottom line is that this is not kidnapping."

"Yer takin' us somewhere's against our will. We have rights."

The man shook his head. "No. That's where you're wrong. The *Star* is a sovereign vessel of the Russian Republic. When you come aboard, you leave the United States and forsake the canopy of American rights guaranteed to you in the Constitution."

Ray looked at him, impressed.

"And if you come aboard without being invited . . ." Here he raised his eyebrows at Ray. ". . . you are violating various trespass laws, not to mention putting yourself under the jurisdiction of the ship's captain and other officers."

"Don't tell me," Ray said, "you studied law at U-Dub?"

The man nodded. "Graduated at the top of my class."

"A scholar *and* an athlete," Ray said. "So why are you working as a glorified bouncer on an icebreaker in the Arctic Ocean?"

"Pays better than being a lawyer," he answered. "And it's more fulfilling."

Ray almost laughed at this.

When the elevator doors opened, the man herded them out and along another corridor. They weren't on the communications deck or on the top floor where Radikoff's office and lab were. It didn't look to Ray like the bridge either. It was a small lounge with several doors in the surrounding walls.

The man told them to stop, then knocked on a door with a Russian word emblazoned on it: K-A-something like the symbol for pi-a backwards N-T-A-H.

Ray was still trying to decipher this when a voice called through the door, *"Pree-hodeet!"*

The man opened the door and urged Ray and Billy Bob into a space about the size of a motel room. It had an efficiency kitchen with a small refrigerator, a sink and a hot plate, a twin bed, and a nook along the outside wall with a bookcase, a free-standing lamp, and a comfortable chair. The captain was seated in the chair, a book open on his lap, a pipe jutting from his teeth. He looked distinguished and quite seaworthy, Ray thought.

"Horoshee-e," the captain said, rising. He set the book aside, took the pipe from his mouth and began speaking rapidly to the U-Dub alum.

The man nodded, then, at the captain's gesturing

insistence, translated: "The captain thanks you for coming . . ."

"We didn't exactly have any choice," Ray muttered.

". . . and for being so diligent at doing your job, but he would like to, uh . . ." The man paused, searching for the right words. "He would like to assure you that he has everything under control."

"Under control?!" Ray nearly shouted. "There are three dead bodies on this ship. There's another in town. What part of that is he in control of?"

The man attempted to translate this to the captain. Ray watched as the captain's face contorted and he argued his position. Ray didn't recognize any of the words, except "Ameer-ee-ca."

"He knows nothing of three bodies on the ship, only that two men died while hunting on the ice. One was under his command, the other was from America."

The captain was glaring at Ray, red-faced.

"He's either lying or he's terribly ill-informed," Ray said.

The man didn't translate this, but simply stood there, like the captain, glaring.

"Why did he drag us up here?"

This was apparently worthy of being passed along. Ray waited, trying to read the captain's expression. It wasn't hard to see that he was upset. But Ray couldn't tell if he was being purposefully deceitful or not. Surely he knew about the bodies down in the lower deck.

After the captain's response, which Ray took to be delivered in frustration rather than an attempt to lie, the man said, "He has asked you here to impress upon you the need to allow him to handle Dr. Radikoff."

"What does he mean by 'handle'?" Ray asked.

This was relayed and came back as, "He is aware of Dr. Radikoff's failure in the *Arctic Star* project. He is also aware that the doctor has begun to tunnel without the proper approval. This is a matter that will be taken up with Dr. Radikoff's investors and with the Russian government. For the time being, the captain has seen fit only to quarantine the doctor."

"You mean he's under ship arrest?"

"Basically," the man said without consulting the captain. "Without realizing it. That's why my brother and I were assigned to guard him."

"I thought you were there because the sandhogs were threatening to revolt?"

"There was that element too. And it's what the captain wants Radikoff to think. Since the captain is not in a place to order Dr. Radikoff to cease and desist from what he is engaged in, he has taken other steps to ensure that he will not evade the law."

The captain said something else, which was translated as: "Radikoff will be prosecuted when we return home. Until then, he is something of a rogue who the captain can only corral, not tame."

It was an interesting analogy, Ray thought. "So he won't allow us to arrest Radikoff?"

The man shook his head.

"Even though the man has committed murder several times on American soil and in American waters?"

This was translated to the captain, who came back with: "Dr. Radikoff is an egomaniac and hopes to secure a place in history as one of the world's greatest scientists. But he is not stupid. Murder would only call attention to the fiasco that his great tunnel project is becoming."

"He doesn't think Radikoff is capable of murder?"

After consultation, the man said, "He believes every man is capable, but that Radikoff is too disciplined and driven—even obsessed—to do something as careless and frivolous as to clutter the area with dead bodies."

Ray considered this, unable to buy the fact that Radikoff wasn't the killer. "Just who does he think is going around bashing in people's skulls then?"

The man talked to the captain, the captain talked back. Then, "As he has already told you, the captain is aware of only one body aboard ship—that of a crew member who died in a hunting accident."

"That sounds like a lawyer talking," Ray observed.

The man smiled, as though this was a compliment.

"Can we at least question Radikoff?"

As the man asked the captain this, Billy Bob whispered to Ray, "I think they-er full of it. Why don't we read them their rights and arrest the both of 'em?"

It wasn't a bad idea, except that arresting the captain could open up a major international can of worms and, in the end, result in both he and Billy Bob losing their jobs. Also, trying to take the former-tackle-turned-lawyer-turned-security-guard into custody would be more than a little tricky.

"He will allow you to interrogate Dr. Radikoff on the condition that you do not divulge anything that would put the captain or the ship in danger."

"Namely?"

"You'll have to ask to speak with him, and do so with the understanding that if he refuses . . ." The man shrugged.

"Let me get this straight," Ray said. "We can talk to him and ask him about the murders, but we can't let on that he's already been caught and is basically waiting to be tried in a court of law."

The captain apparently read the tone of Ray's question. "*Da.*"

"That'll be a little . . . awkward," Billy Bob said. "Won't it?"

It would be ridiculous, Ray thought. "Okay, we agree." He said this mainly to gain access to Radikoff. When the FBI arrived, they could sort this mess out. Until then, he would continue to pursue the person responsible for ending the lives of three Inupiats and one Russian sandhog.

The captain's countenance shifted radically. He was suddenly jovial. After shaking hands with both of them, he said, "Have . . . a . . . nice . . . day."

The guard showed them out, then accompanied them to the elevator. "Dr. Radikoff is on the top floor. My brother will meet you there," he told them as the elevator arrived. He stood there until the doors were closed.

"Is it just me," Billy Bob wondered, "or is this case downright confusing?"

"Confusing is an understatement," Ray said. Though it made sense in a backward kind of way that the captain had Radikoff contained but had not formally made an arrest, it just didn't feel right. What if the captain was in on this too? What if he and Radikoff had put their heads together and figured out a way to fool the small town cops: admit to some administrational wrongdoing—starting the tunnel without approval—but deny not only the fact that several men had been killed, but all knowledge of any criminal misdoing. It wasn't a bad strategy. If they could sell it to the Feds, they might return home in the spring having gotten away with multiple murder.

On the other hand, if the captain really was on the level . . . why drag this out? Why didn't he just arrest Radikoff, throw him in the brig, have the Russian authorities come out and take him into custody? Was he afraid the crew members—the sandhogs, especially—might revolt if the operation were shut down? Being isolated on a ship that was trapped in the ice was a precarious thing.

The elevator doors opened and, as promised, they were met by the former Husky left tackle. The man was standing directly in front of Radikoff's door, arms folded over his impressive chest.

"Your brother sent us up," Ray tried. They got off

the elevator, but the man just stood there. "So you played for U-Dub, huh?"

He blinked, sniffed, then turned and opened Radikoff's door.

This was the quiet half of the brotherhood, Ray decided. The strong, silent type.

They went into Radikoff's spacious office.

"Wow-wee!" the cowboy gushed as the door shut behind them. "This here is what I call style. Texas style."

"It's big," Ray agreed. They sat down in the chairs in front of Radikoff's desk.

"Where do you suppose he is?" Billy Bob asked, still eyeing the furnishings.

"With our luck," Ray answered, "he's in Mazatlan by now."

"Where?"

The side door opened and Radikoff emerged. He seemed genuinely surprised to see them. "Gentlemen . . . I wish you'd given me a little advance notice." After settling in his chair, Radikoff asked, "So what was the result of the examination of the deceased crew member?"

"He didn't die in no accident," Billy Bob said.

"Then just how did he expire?"

"That's what we're here to talk about," Ray said.

"Oh?"

"We've discovered others. Other bodies, that is."

Radikoff's jaw actually fell open.

"That brings us to a total of four people who died of something other than natural causes."

"Oh . . . you must be referring to the casualties of our, uh . . . industrial mishaps."

"Industrial mishaps?" Ray couldn't believe this guy. According to Butyerki, a number of men had died in cave-ins, and yet Radikoff couldn't even bring himself to speak honestly about the tragedies. "No. These people weren't killed on the job. Not unless their job was to get bashed on the back of the head."

"I don't understand."

"They were murdered."

"Murdered?!"

Ray examined the man's face, trying to determine whether he was shocked at the news or shocked at being found out.

"Four men have been killed. Purposefully," Ray explained.

"And you have verified this?"

Ray nodded, though they hadn't actually verified it, per se.

Radikoff sighed. "Dear God, what else can possibly go wrong?"

TWENTY-SEVEN

"WHAT, EXACTLY, has gone wrong, Doctor?" Ray asked.

Radikoff had a faraway, almost defeated look on his face now.

"Doctor?"

"Everything."

"Could you elaborate?"

"It will work," he said, nodding. "My theories are sound. It's the implementation that is to blame."

"For what?"

"For the fact that after tunneling for months, we have made almost no noticeable progress."

"About the tunneling," Ray said. "It sounds to me like it's being done without the approval of our governments."

This clearly offended him. "I'll have you know that every bit of necessary paperwork has been completed. All the red tape has been taken care of. I am operating this project under a mandate from the Ministry of Industrial Science and the U.S. Department of the Interior."

"That's not what the captain said," Billy Bob blurted out.

Ray shook his head at the cowboy. So much for keeping the captain's little secret.

"The captain?" Radikoff scoffed. "The captain is a buffoon. I cannot help it if every peon between here and Moscow has not been informed as to the nature and extent of my authority. If the captain would worry about running the ship instead of pretending to be my chaperone, then I could better do my job."

"I take it you and the captain don't get along that well," Ray said.

"We get along wonderfully when he chooses to mind his own business."

"We can check into your 'mandate,' you know," Ray told him. "A few phone calls and we'll know the truth."

"That is the truth!" Radikoff shot back indignantly. "I am in total charge of the first stage of the Russian-American railway project. Whatever I say or decide, goes."

"Okay," Ray said, "back to the murders."

"I know absolutely nothing about them."

Interesting, Ray thought: a denial before so much as a backhanded accusation.

"That's what you're wondering, isn't it?" Radikoff asked. "You want to find out if I was involved. Well, I wasn't."

Ray sighed. This was going to be difficult. "Look at it from our angle, Doctor. If you are, as you say, the supreme leader of this project," Ray said sarcastically, "then you would know everything that's going on."

"What the men do on their own time is their affair."

"You also have motive." Ray paused for effect. "You want this thing to fly. Your reputation is at stake. It's not going so well. Along comes a sandhog threatening to go public with the whole story of how you're drilling without authorization—"

"I told you," Radikoff said angrily, "I *am* authorized!"

"Still, this guy, Chekerov, shows up saying he'll blow the lid and tell the press or maybe your Ministry of Industrial Science that the project is a bust, that the tunnels are caving in, that the whole thing is a tremendous waste of money."

"All great achievements take time," Radikoff argued. "Time and money."

"So you pay the guy off, to ensure his silence."

Radikoff made a sour face. "What?"

"You paid Chekerov to keep quiet about the project delays, about the setbacks . . ."

"I did no such thing!"

". . . and when he wanted more money, you killed him."

"That is outrageous!"

"And you also killed Kuleak, because he figured out what was going on out here."

"Who?"

"The police officer from TaggaQ. Tommy and

Old William were 'collateral damage.' They just happened to be in the wrong place at the wrong time and were disposed of along with the others."

"I have no idea what you're talking about!"

Ray studied the man, hoping to detect fear and possibly deceit. But all he could see was exasperation.

"I will admit that we have experienced our share of problems on this project. That is to be expected when laboratory research is taken into the field. As for the rest . . . You seem desperate to be served with a lawsuit for libel."

"It would be a whole lot easier for everyone if you would drop the act and tell us what happened." Ray was pushing in a last ditch effort to get the man to talk. When Radikoff laughed at him, he knew it hadn't worked.

"You must be out of your mind."

Ray agreed with this assessment. He had to be out of his mind to think that Radikoff would buckle and spill his guts.

"Now, if that is all, I have a great deal of work to do," the doctor said dismissively.

"Actually, that isn't all." Ray stood and waited for Radikoff to look up from his desk. "The FBI will be here in a matter of moments." This was another fib. Or rather, an uncertainty. He hoped the captain would bring an FBI rep and also hoped they would arrive soon. But if the helicopter was still off on assignment . . .

For the first time, Radikoff seemed rattled. His

eyes darted around the room, as though searching for a means of escape.

"You can tell your story to them." Ray was about to nod for Billy Bob to follow him out when Radikoff leapt from his chair and darted to the side door. He swung it open and was stopped dead by a looming presence: one of the guards.

"Move!" he ordered.

The man just stood there, blocking the exit.

"Get out of my way!"

"I can't do that, sir."

"Why not?!" Radikoff screeched.

"Captain's orders."

"The captain? You don't take orders from him. You take them from me, you imbecile!" Turning, Radikoff bolted for the main door that led to the elevator. But the other guard was behind it. "You'll both be fired!" he ranted, stepping back. "I'll see that you are assigned to a hellish post in Siberia. You will regret crossing me."

"Like Chekerov did?" Ray asked.

"I told you!" he raged. "I didn't do it!"

"Then just who do you suppose did?" Billy Bob asked.

"How do I know?"

"You'd better think up a scapegoat before the Feds get here," Ray warned. Radikoff was finally bowing to the stress and seemed poised either to let something slip or maybe to break down and confess.

"I will not be held responsible for a crime I didn't commit!"

"*Crimes,*" Ray said, emphasizing their plurality.

"I did nothing wrong!"

They heard a rumbling noise then. At first Ray thought the captain had started up the engines. Then he realized what it was.

"They're here," he said. "That's the FBI helicopter."

Radikoff was terror stricken.

"I guarantee they won't be as patient and understanding as we've been, Doctor." He paused to let this sink in, hoping this abbreviated variation of the old good cop/bad cop routine would get Radikoff to talk. "So if you have something to tell us . . ."

"Okay, okay . . ." He was breathing hard, perspiring. "I didn't exactly have authorization to dig. I mean, I'm supposed to test the equipment and drill sample tunnels, but . . ."

"But not the real thing," Ray guessed.

"Exactly."

"So you're in violation of international treaties, U.S. laws, and you've overstepped the boundaries set forth by your investors," Ray summed up.

"No one has to know."

"What about the families of the men who died in the cave-ins?" Ray asked.

Radikoff didn't have an answer for this.

"What about the families of the men you murdered?" Billy Bob said.

"I didn't murder anyone."

The rumbling sound died away. "They've landed," Ray said. "Your time is running out."

"I didn't murder anyone! I didn't dig the tunnels! I'm only an administrator!"

"Meaning you ordered the murders?"

"No!" He shook his head emphatically. "I delegated authority. I had no knowledge of what was going on."

Ray was reminded of Richard Nixon. "Who did you delegate to?"

"My staff."

"Names. We need names."

Radikoff rattled off a list. Ray didn't recognize any of them, except the last one: Denisovich.

"Dr. Denisovich is in charge of research, right?"

"Yes. She is also overseeing security for the operation."

Something in Ray's mind clicked into place. Something else hit an impasse.

"Yes?"

"Would she have been the one who paid off Chekerov," he thought aloud, "and killed the men? Except . . . why was she attacked in the shed?"

"Maybe she attacked herself," Billy Bob said. "To make it look like she was on the up and up."

Ray shook his head. "What would be the point? If she was disposing of me and Dr. Butyerki anyway, why include herself?" He looked to Radikoff. "I think you're full of it." This wasn't really what he thought, but he had to be sure that in Radikoff's panic about the FBI, the man was telling the truth. "I think you're lying."

"I'm not lying!" Radikoff insisted. "I don't know anything about the murders!"

"Maybe the Feds brought one of their new lie detectors," Ray told Billy Bob.

Catching his meaning, the cowboy said, "Yeah. Those things are somethin' else. They know if you so much as hiccup on an answer. White lies, tall tales, big ol' whoppers—they can ferret 'em all out."

"Really, you have to believe me," Radikoff pleaded. "I didn't do anything. I didn't."

The elevator door opened out in the hall and footsteps approached. The big security man turned and a voice announced, "Barrow PD."

In came Lewis and Ray's captain.

"What do you got, Attla?" the captain asked.

"This is Dr. Radikoff," Ray said. "Dr. Radikoff, this is the captain of the Barrow Police Department." He then gestured to Lewis. "And this is Officer Lewis Fletcher. He's a . . . he's a special liaison with the Federal Bureau of Investigation."

Radikoff swore.

Lewis's face curdled. "Huh?"

Ray winked at Lewis, but the confused expression remained.

"Dr. Radikoff here denies any involvement with the murders we are investigating," Ray explained. "Is that right, Doctor?" It was a last ditch effort to get a confession.

"Yes! That's right!"

"But he is in violation of a number of federal and international laws. So you'll need to read him his rights and take him into custody. I'd advise coordinating that with the captain of the ship. He may have something to say about extradition."

The captain nodded, indicating that he was on the same page.

"What you gonna do?" Lewis asked, already producing a set of handcuffs.

"I'm going into town to question another suspect," Ray said.

Ray indicated to Billy Bob that it was time to leave. They went to the elevator, and once it arrived and they were getting on, the cowboy asked, "Who we gonna talk to?"

"Well, Denisovich for sure. But . . ."

"But what?"

"It makes sense and it doesn't. I mean, I had a hunch about her when she was dogging me, keeping an eye on the investigation. But there are too many things that don't add up."

"Like what?"

"Well, besides the attack in the shed, there's the fact that she had Butyerki do an autopsy on Chekerov. She didn't have to do that. If she was trying to cover up a murder . . ." Ray's voice trailed off. "Unless . . . unless she didn't know it had been murder."

"What?"

"Listen to this. What if Radikoff didn't kill anyone, like he says. Okay? But the money under Chekerov's bunk—that had to come from him. He's the only one who could swing that kind of cash."

"Yeah . . . ?"

"Yeah. And the murders . . . What if Denisovich delegated her authority too? She has the security men take care of Chekerov, on Radikoff's order. No . . ."

"No?"

The elevator doors opened and they got off and walked through the mudroom, toward the deck.

Ray rubbed his head, which was pounding now from lack of food and sleep. "Okay . . . What if Denisovich paid off Chekerov . . ."

"I thought you said—"

". . . under orders from Radikoff. Which means we might be able to trace the money back to him. Anyway . . . she pays him. Then . . . then he wants more. So she tells the security guys to take care of him."

"Except them security fellas is supposed to be workin' fer the captain of this here boat."

Ignoring this, Ray continued his brainstorming. "Radikoff is out of the loop. Not beyond responsibility or even liability, mind you. Just out of the loop in terms of hands-on involvement."

"I think I'm outta the loop, partner. You lost me in there somewheres."

"That's okay. I think I lost myself." It was frustrating, Ray thought, to have all of these facts and events and individuals and motives and not be able to connect them. They went together somehow, but getting them into their proper places was virtually impossible.

On the deck, they saw the helicopter. It wasn't from the Bureau, as Ray had implied to Radikoff. It was the hospital's chopper and had a big red cross on the side. When he realized the pilot was still inside, Ray started for it.

"Come on," he told Billy Bob.

He went up to the glass windshield and rapped on it with his knuckle.

The pilot, who was writing something on a clipboard, glanced up at him.

"We need a ride," Ray said.

"What?" the man mouthed.

Ray pointed at himself and Billy Bob, then at the shore, which was hidden in the darkness. "We need a ride," he shouted.

The man shook his head and returned his attention to the clipboard.

Ray fished out his badge and tapped it on the glass. "Police business."

The man sagged a little, frowned, then switched on the engine. Ray and Billy Bob went to the hatch and climbed in as the rotor began to turn

"I really appreciate this," Ray told the pilot.

"I'm signed out for two hours," the man said grumpily, eyeing his watch. "If I go over that limit, which I can almost guarantee—with all this hopping back and forth to TaggaQ—the department will have to recoup the hospital for my fuel and time."

"Fair enough," Ray said, not at all sure the captain would agree to that. Although he knew the captain would if his hunch was right. If it turned out to be a goose chase, there might be trouble.

"How much is fuel?" Ray asked.

The man shrugged. "Depends."

"How much is your time, then?"

"Two fifty per hour."

"Ouch!" Billy Bob said.

"I don't suppose you could cut us some slack, maybe give us a deal, on account of this being an urgent flight—part of a murder investigation."

"I don't suppose," the pilot said, grinning as he prepared for takeoff.

TWENTY-EIGHT

THE HELICOPTER LIFTED off from the deck of the *Arctic Star*, and when it was clear of the ship, the nose dropped and they accelerated into the darkness.

"I don't much like this," Billy Bob complained, his voice barely audible over the roar of the engines. His face was a pale green in the glow of the helicopter's instrumentation.

Ray nodded. He didn't enjoy hurtling into nothingness either. Which is what they were doing. It was impossible to make out where the sky stopped and the ground began, much less direction. The disorientation immediately began to effect his stomach.

Next to him, Billy Bob moaned.

"Hang on, guys," the pilot said, apparently sensing their distress. "We'll be there in about one minute."

Ray was glad to hear this. Though he could tell from the angle of the nose, the sound of the rotor blades, and the engine that they were moving forward, it seemed they were hovering motionless in space. He couldn't make out any of the lights of the village. For starters there were only a few, and because of the glare of the instruments against the glass, it was hard to tell what was inside and what was outside. This added to the vertigo. He craned his neck and tried to catch a glimpse of the ship, but the seats blocked his view.

"Take a few deep breaths while I look for a spot to land," the pilot said.

Ray inhaled through his nose, exhaled through his mouth, then glanced over at Billy Bob. The cowboy had his head between his legs and was panting like a dog.

"If you lose it," Ray said, "lose it in that direction." He pointed toward the window.

Suddenly they were dropping. Ray clutched the armrest of the seat while Billy Bob emitted pathetic noises and suffered from dry heaves. Ray was grateful that they hadn't eaten anytime in the recent past.

"All out for TaggaQ!" the pilot said.

Ray hadn't even felt the pontoon feet of the helicopter touch down. Popping the door, he helped Billy Bob out, then thanked the pilot.

"You want me to wait?"

Ray shook his head. Even if the guy hadn't charged an arm and a leg for his makeshift taxi service, he wasn't up to another ride. And there was no way Billy Bob would agree to it.

The pilot gave him a thumbs-up. "Have a good one."

"Oh, you bet," Ray replied sarcastically.

"Stand clear!"

Hunching against the threat of the still beating rotors, Ray and Billy Bob trotted out of range. The helicopter had landed in the middle of the main street, between the police station and the cemetery.

They were running in circles, Ray thought as the chopper lifted off and fled into the darkness, back toward the lights of the ship. How many times had they been in the police station, traipsed over to the cemetery, gone out to the ship? It was late and the whole investigation was beginning to blur in his tired mind.

"Well . . . ?" Billy Bob asked, waiting for instructions.

Ray started toward the police station. "We need to talk to Denisovich. If my hunch is right, which at this point isn't even close to a sure thing, she's caught up in all of this."

"How?"

"I'm not sure. She may have killed the men. She may have ordered the killings." He shrugged.

From the street, there were no lights on in the police station. "Great . . ." Ray muttered.

They went up, opened the door. Ray flipped the light switch.

"Nobody here," Billy Bob observed astutely.

"I shouldn't have left them alone," Ray said.

They stood there for a minute, staring at the vacant desk.

"What now?" Billy Bob asked.

"Exactly." It was an excellent question. If Butyerki hadn't hijacked their truck, Ray would have been tempted to head for home and let the captain and Lewis handle the case from here.

"Where do you suppose they went?"

"No idea."

"Maybe they got hungry and decided to catch a bite."

Ray laughed wearily. "And where would they do that in TaggaQ in the wee hours of the morning?" He went back out the door, disgusted with himself for leaving Denisovich and Butyerki alone, and also frustrated at his inability to fashion a smooth, cohesive whole from the available facts.

Outside, Billy Bob asked, "Where we goin'?"

Ray didn't answer. He started for the cemetery. Maybe the diggers had seen something—someone wandering around. This caused him to think of Willy. What had become of the boy? Though he seemed pretty self-sufficient, Ray was worried about him.

For a flickering instant he considered the boy as a suspect. Could the kid have beaten them on the head? Aside from having no motivation for the act, Willy couldn't have transported them to the ship.

Ray shook his head, trying to clear his mind. His thinking was getting muddled.

They could hear the grave diggers picking away at the frozen ground from a block away. The torches soon came into view, steam reaching up from the shimmering orange flames in lazy fingers.

Ray wondered if Tommy's body was still in the shed. The diggers might have been working in vain.

The corpse might have been transported to the ship or . . .

"If Chekerov was blackmailing Radikoff," Ray brainstormed aloud, trying to make the pieces fit, "then maybe . . . say Radikoff decided to kill him. Or . . . say Radikoff told Denisovich to 'take care of it,' and she killed him. Tommy was with Chekerov when the . . . the 'hit,' for lack of a better word, went down."

"Makes sense to me," Billy Bob said.

This was no consolation to Ray. The cowboy was loyal, conscientious, dependable, ready and willing to lay down his life for his friends and colleagues, but piecing together messy cases was not exactly his forte.

"That's saying Radikoff isn't lying through his teeth."

"You think he was fibbin'?"

"Insert stock answer here: 'I don't know,' " Ray said, irritated with himself for failing to see what he had a hunch was obvious. What was he missing?

They reached the bone fence of the cemetery and could see the grave site. The diggers were hidden inside the ever deepening rectangular hole.

Ray stopped and listened. Aside from the hacking of shovels and picks against the rock-solid permafrost, and the hiss of the torches, the town was quiet. No automobiles, no snow machines, no voices . . . nothing. But then, that was to be expected at this time of night. Wasn't it? Or was the silence unnatural, he wondered, the result of fear?

"This here place shorely is dead tonight," Billy Bob observed.

It was a bad choice of words, Ray thought. Uncannily accurate, though.

"Are we going in?" Billy Bob asked.

Ray was about to say yes when he saw something out of the corner of his eye: a glimmer of light. When he looked in that direction, toward the western edge of town, it was gone. Maybe it had been his imagination. Except, when he took hold of the bone gate and began to open it, he saw it again. And like before, it was gone when he turned his head.

He watched the west for a full minute.

"Whatcha looking at?" Billy Bob asked, peering in the same direction.

"You see any lights out there?"

Billy Bob waited a few seconds. "Nope. Nary a one."

Ray shook his head. He'd heard about brain disorders that caused you to see lights where there weren't any. He turned away again, and again something flashed at the edge of his vision. He watched without looking in that direction and saw it again. It wasn't a pulse or a rhythmic light, like a beacon. It was random, sporadic, varying in intensity.

Then it hit him: Willy's house. That was where Willy's house was. "That's him."

"Who?"

"Willy. He went back home." Ray felt a sense of relief wash over him. "He's out there with a flashlight, hiding in his uncle's house."

"Ya think?" Billy Bob squinted toward the western horizon. "I still don't see nothin'."

"That's because it's so faint," Ray explained, already walking up the street. "You can't see it straight on. You can only see it with the cones of your eyes. Or is it the rods? I can't remember which is which."

"Cones and rods?" the cowboy asked. "I never heard of such a thing."

"Anyway, I bet that's him. And if it is, I say we turn this case over to the captain and the FBI, let them hunt for Denisovich while we go home and get some rest."

"How we gonna get home?"

Ray made a growling sound as he recalled the state of the department's new pickup.

"I tell ya one thing, partner, I ain't getting on no helicopter again."

"That's okay," Ray muttered, "we couldn't afford it anyway."

They walked for a while without talking. Finally Billy Bob observed, "It's farther out here than I remembered."

"Yeah." They had come maybe half a mile and still hadn't reached the Christmas tree turnoff sign. Ray's ankle was reminding him that it was injured and did not appreciate this much walking.

"My fingers are gettin' stiff," Billy Bob said.

"We'll build a fire at Willy's," Ray said. "In fact, we can spend the night there if we have to. At least, get a couple hours of sleep."

"Now yer talkin'."

Without a light it was difficult to stay on the road. The snowpacked tire tracks merged with the windblown expanse on each side without much change in grade.

After another ten minutes Billy Bob asked, "What if we wander off onto the floes?"

"We're not on the floes," Ray said. He didn't know exactly where they were, just that they hadn't veered out onto the ice.

"Are we lost?"

Ray was about to admit that he wasn't sure when a shadow that was somehow darker than the surrounding night loomed directly in front of them. They were upon it before he could tell that it was the Christmas tree.

"This way," he said, making the turn.

In another minute he could see the light that had originally drawn his attention. It was erratic and, occasionally, seemed to flicker on and off.

"That's Willy?"

"There aren't any other houses out here," Ray said. "It has to be."

But fifty yards later Ray could tell that the light was on the wrong side of the road.

"It's comin' from that church," Billy Bob said. " 'Member?"

"I think you're right."

As they approached, the squat steeple and the stilted walls slowly materialized, blacker than the black sky and somehow more solid in appearance.

"Who'd be worshippin' at this hour?"

"Let's find out."

They went up to the door and Ray tried to open it. "It's locked up."

"I don't know 'bout you, but this gives me the creeps."

They slowly made their way to the side. There wasn't a door, just a high window with the glass partially missing. A beam from what looked like a flashlight trembled through. Ray stretched but couldn't reach the sill.

On the back side, facing the ocean, they found another door. This one was not only unlocked, but open a crack. Ray pushed it back.

"What's that noise?" Billy Bob asked.

It was the same sort of noise that the diggers at the gravesite had been making, the same kind of sound they had heard the sandhogs generating: a steel blade hammering at the frozen earth.

Ray was suddenly reminded of his dream and of the constant clinking and clanking and ticking . . .

The first room they entered had been gutted, and all that remained were studs and torn pieces of Sheetrock. It emptied into a hallway in which the floorboards were rotting and creaked loudly under their boots.

"Watch your step in here."

At that same moment, the cowboy tripped and fell hard. The picking stopped and the dim glow of the flashlight that had been enabling them to proceed was extinguished.

Ray stopped and listened, but there was nothing, except the wind whistling through the drafty old structure.

"You okay?" he asked, trying to help Billy Bob up.

"I don't much like this place," Billy Bob whispered.

"Join the club," Ray said.

The light came back on and the picking started again.

As Ray crept forward, feeling along the wall and reaching his feet out one at a time, to make sure there was something to walk on, he realized they were approaching another door. The frantic beam of light was coming at them in spurts through a window above it.

At the door, Ray twisted the knob slowly, careful not to make any noise. He wasn't sure why he was being so secretive. The owner of the flashlight was probably Willy. Maybe the kid had decided that the church would ward off the evil power of the tupilak. Or maybe it was another of the worried residents, there to invoke the protection of the white man's God. There had to be a logical explanation. It wasn't like the place was haunted or anything.

As if to prove him wrong, a mournful wail arose.

"Did you hear that?" Billy Bob asked, eyes wide enough to catch some of the errant light.

"It's the wind," Ray said, though he was pretty sure it wasn't.

The wail came at them again, louder and somehow more tragic sounding this time.

"Why don't we come back in the daytime?" Billy Bob suggested.

Ignoring this, Ray eased the door open.

It took several moments for his eyes to adjust to the glaring, bouncing beam. When they finally did, he couldn't believe what they were telling him.

TWENTY-NINE

EDDIE WAS STANDING knee-deep in a pit. He had a pickax in hand and was wearing a baseball cap, to which he had duct-taped a flashlight. As he hacked away at the ground, which had once been a wooden floor, the beam of light went into the pit and bounced off the walls, jiggling radically with each swing of the pick.

Before he noticed them, Ray realized that there were three shadows sitting in one of the few remaining pews in what had once been the main sanctuary. When Eddie's head jerked toward the door, the light briefly illuminated the shadows, revealing their identities: Willy, Denisovich, Butyerki . . . They were bound with rope and had duct tape over their mouths.

Eddie swore when he saw Ray and Billy Bob.

"What in the world . . . ?" Billy Bob said.

It was like something out of a dream—a surreal nightmare.

"What are you doing?" Ray asked, not sure he wanted to know the answer.

"My job," Eddie said, turning back to the hole. Even in the poor lighting, his eyes looked strange: insane.

"What job?" Ray asked.

"I'm on the security team for the *Arketchyeski Zvyezda*."

Ray watched him dig for a moment. "This isn't the *Arctic Star*."

"I'm not stupid!"

"I didn't say you were."

He took several swings before saying, "You can either have a seat with the others or you can grab a shovel and help me."

"Help you what, Eddie?"

"It takes forever to dig a grave at this time of year."

"How about if you take a break? Put the pick down, let us work for a while."

"I'm not stupid!" he shouted.

"He's crazy," Billy Bob whispered.

"Were you planning to bury these people . . . alive?"

"It's my job. I was hired to work security and I'm gonna do it good."

"You killed them, didn't you?" Ray asked.

"Who?"

"You know who."

"I was just doing my job." He continued to swing the pick.

"And it was your job to kill your son?"

He looked up, enraged. Dropping his pick, he took up a snow beater.

Ray had the feeling he was looking at the murderer, as well as the murder weapon. The snow beater was the perfect blunt instrument to crack a person's skull: sturdy handle, long dull blade fashioned out of bone.

"I didn't know it was Tommy!" Eddie yelled, lifting the snow beater. "I loved him. He was my boy. I'd never hurt him." Here he aimed the snow beater at Ray. "And I'm gonna make sure he's buried right. I'm gonna make sure they all get buried right."

"Even the ones on the ship?"

"They're gonna go in the tunnels. That's underground. So it's okay." He put the snow beater down and picked up the pickax again. "It'll take care of the tarrak problems. All the inyusuq gonna be happy."

"What is he babblin' about?" Billy Bob asked.

"Tarrak are spirits of the dead that hang around, usually seeking revenge. Inyusuq are the spirits that are free to go to the next life."

"I'm doing what's right," Eddie explained between downstrokes.

"Of course you are, Eddie," Ray said, hoping to humor him.

"The heck he is!" Billy Bob objected. "He's goin' 'round killing folks and—"

Ray shut the cowboy up with an elbow.

"He's doing his job," Ray said, "and he's satisfying the traditions of the Inupiat."

"The Real People," Eddie chimed in nodding. "You're one of us. So you understand."

"You bet," Ray said, inching forward.

"Even when your work is difficult, you must do your best."

"I agree." Ray took another step.

"You must also be true to your heritage."

"Exactly." He managed two steps this time.

"I'm not stupid," Eddie said.

Ray stopped.

"I know the white man's ways are bad for the People."

Nodding, Ray inched closer. He wasn't at all sure what he was going to do, but something had to be done.

"But you gotta make a living, right?"

"Right."

Ray was at the edge of the pit, poised to leap away in the event that Eddie saw fit to swing the pick in his direction.

"A man has to be a man, no matter what."

"My grandfather says that to be Inupiat in our time is to have one foot in the past and the other in the future." Actually, Grandfather had never said this and was dead set against all forms of "progress."

Eddie stopped picking. "Your grandfather is wise in the ways of the People."

"The Real People," Ray answered. He reached out his hand. "Why don't you let me dig for a while."

Eddie hesitated, then handed the pick to him. "I'm very tired."

"I can see why. You've been working so hard."

"I do a good job," Eddie said, climbing out of the

pit. He went to a pew and stretched out on it. "I work real hard. And I keep the ways of the elders."

"I know you do."

"I loved my boy," he said in a quiet whimper.

"I'm sure you did." Ray handed the pick to Billy Bob, took possession of the snow beater, and then went over to the pew where Willy, Denisovich, and Butyerki were seated. After placing a finger to his lips, he removed the tape from Willy's mouth.

"You okay?"

"I think so."

He removed the tape from Denisovich's mouth.

"I didn't know!" she told him in an urgent whisper.

"Didn't know what?"

"That he was killing people. I hired him to make sure nobody strayed into the area where we were tunneling. We'd had cave-ins and we didn't want people out on the floes . . . for safety reasons. I thought he was just chasing off hunters. I didn't know . . . I—I didn't know."

Somehow, Ray believed her. For whatever reason, Eddie had taken his job as a temporary security guard far too seriously. He was obviously mentally ill and didn't seem to comprehend the consequences of his actions.

Billy Bob lifted a pair of handcuffs and Ray nodded. "Go easy."

He watched as the cowboy slipped them on. Eddie didn't even flinch. He was fast asleep. Knocking off four people in a zealous effort to "do his job" and then frantically attempting to satisfy all the traditions by burying the bodies as quickly as possible in the dead of winter had to be exhausting.

Butyerki made a muffled plea, demanding that his tape be removed. Ray pulled it off and the doctor immediately began complaining.

Ray shushed him, then said to Denisovich, "So Radikoff put you in charge of security. You hired Eddie to police the area from the village end of things. And . . . he just . . . he took matters into his own hands?"

She nodded.

"And you expect me to believe that this is all his fault? That you had no knowledge of the murders, that you didn't order them?"

"You have to believe it."

"Why's that?"

"Because it is *pravda*."

Butyerki helpfully translated: "The truth."

THIRTY

". . . AND I AM proud to present this medal to James Peterson for first place in the knuckle hop competition."

The crowd applauded and a group of high school girls at the top of the bleachers screamed as only high school girls can. Out on the gym floor, James Peterson, a lanky kid with long black hair, blushed as the judge placed a medal around his neck.

Ray glanced over and saw an expression on his daughter Keera's face that he had never seen before. It was more than mere admiration. She was looking at this Peterson boy with moon eyes, as if he was Prince Charming.

"He's so cute . . ." he heard her murmur.

Ray was about to say something, to remind her that this James Peterson was several years older than she was and that she was several years away from dating, keeping company with or even ogling boys, when Margaret nudged him. She was smiling that smile that told him to back off, that he was being overly protective.

"That kid's like . . . sixteen!" Ray objected.

"She's right though," Margaret countered. "He is cute."

A vision flashed through Ray's mind: this "cute" kid or some other "cute" kid, showing up at their front door. In the vision, he answered it wearing his badge and sidearm and told the "cute" kid in no uncertain terms to take a hike and stay the heck away from his daughter.

"It won't be long," Margaret said. She seemed amused by the fact that Keera was quickly approaching puberty.

The whole issue made Ray extremely nervous.

"Hey, partner," Billy Bob greeted Ray as he slid onto the bench seat next to him. "I'm surprised to see you here."

"Why's that?"

"I figured you'd be sacked out all day."

"I wanted to see the finals," Ray said, though this wasn't the complete truth. He was interested in the competition, but mostly he was there because he hadn't been able to sleep. The case in TaggaQ had effected him like drinking too much coffee. He was exceedingly tired, but still bothered by Eddie Reed's actions and mental state.

"They took old Eddie off to Anchorage to be looked at by some shrinks."

"That's good."

"I'm not much for all them criminals who use 'insanity' as an excuse to do awful things. But Eddie . . . I think he was plumb loony tunes."

"Yeah. If he wasn't when he committed the first two murders," Ray said, "he was afterward."

"I cain't imagine whacking any of my kin on the head and then dumpin' them in the drink."

Ray shuddered and put an arm around Freddie, who was fidgeting in Margaret's lap. "Between the grief of that mistake and the sleep deprivation . . ." Ray shook his head. Though Eddie's explanation had been incomplete, not to mention nearly incomprehensible, he had implied that killing Tommy had been an accident—that he didn't know who was with Chekerov or who he was cracking in the head. Ray shivered again. It was horrible to think about.

After a pause, Billy Bob said, "The FBI got ahold of Radikoff. Accordin' to the cap'n, they're wrangling with the Russians over who gets to prosecute him. One way or the other, he's gonna get his."

"So his digging operation wasn't totally on the level, like he kept claiming?"

"Doesn't sound like it."

"What about Denisovich?"

"They're talkin' to her too. But I don't think she done nothin' wrong."

"Me either."

"I think she was just hangin' with a bad crowd."

"Let's hope so."

Billy Bob began to give Ray a detailed rundown of the indigestion he had been experiencing since the helicopter ride on the *Arctic Star*.

"Shh!" Ray said. "They're about to start the finals of the high kick."

The main judge stepped up to the microphone. After tapping it, he said, "Ladies and gentlemen, we have two entrants remaining in the high kick and they will now be competing for the gold medal."

The people in the bleachers clapped, the girls on the top row once again squealing in tones that would have made dogs run for shelter.

The judge introduced the two boys, neither of whom Ray knew personally. He was familiar with their families though, and could see both clans down near the gym floor rooting for their kids.

"Before we start," the judge said, "I'd like to ask you all to stand." He waited as the crowd rose to their feet. "As you know, we lost one of our children yesterday: Tommy Reed. There will be a service for him tomorrow afternoon. But I'd just like to say what a great young man he was and that we will truly miss him. If he were here, he would undoubtedly be going for the gold medal.

"Please bow your heads and let's honor Tommy with a minute of silence."

The gym grew quiet and Ray could hear a few people sniffing back tears. What a tragedy, he thought.

"What're they doing, Daddy?" Freddie asked.

Ray held a finger to his lips and picked him up.

When the minute ended, the judge said, "Let's dedicate this finals competition to Tommy."

There were applause, then the judge said, "In fact, I'd like to ask a former gold medalist to come up and demonstrate how it's done."

The demonstration portion, Ray knew, was for

the benefit of tourists and folks who had never seen the event.

"Ray Attla, come on up."

It caught Ray off guard. He had expected the judge to call up one of the twenty-somethings that were in attendance.

People clapped and hooted their encouragement, and the girls on the top row acted as though Ray was a member of 'N Sync, Keera's favorite boy band.

The judge encouraged Ray with a wave. "Go up there, Daddy!" Keera said.

Margaret handed Ray the crutch the hospital had supplied him with and he held it up for the judge and the overzealous audience to see. Then he lifted his leg, which was now encased in a neon purple cast—the color choice having been Keera's.

"Oh . . ." The judge's face took on a concerned look. "What happened, Ray?"

"He already fall, break niu trying to do high kick," Grandfather informed in a deep, authoritative voice.

Moans of sympathy broke out across the auditorium.

"It's just a stress fracture," Ray explained.

"He too old for high kick," Grandfather teased. He was grinning and managed to draw laughter with this remark.

"Ha-ha," Ray said. "Very funny."

Thankfully, the judge went on to pick one of the twenty-somethings and the spotlight was turned away from Ray.

"You're too old to do it, Daddy?" Keera asked.

"I can do it," he said. "I just need to practice."

After the twenty-something hit the target a couple of times, wowing the crowd, the competitors squared off. As they took turns chasing the target, which was raised after each successful attempt, Ray watched Keera. She had that look again. Were these boys "cute" too?

"Don't worry," Margaret said.

"About what?"

"About being Superman."

"What? I'm not—"

"Even if your daughter isn't exclusively 'Daddy's girl' anymore, I still think you're pretty super."

"Ain't you two just the dinkdums," Billy Bob said.

"Do you mind?" Ray asked. "This is a private conversation."

When the cowboy had turned his head back toward the competition, Ray leaned over and kissed Margaret.

"I missed you while we were on that case," he said.

"Me too."

"I don't suppose we could figure out a way to . . ."

She nodded, an evil grin on her face. "Grandfather is going home with his brother-in-law's family. He'll be staying with them until Tuesday."

"What about the kids?"

"They wanted to spend the night at their aana's."

Ray wiggled his eyebrows at this.

"So it'll just be the two of us."

"The two of us and this guy," Ray said, tapping his cast.

"We'll get by. If Jimmy Stewart and Grace Kelly can do it, we can."

"I'm sold."

Ray gazed out at the high kick competitors, hoping they would reach their limit soon and that the closing ceremonies of this year's Eskimo Games would be short and sweet. He was ready to go home.

BIBLIOGRAPHY

Belt, Don. "An Arctic Breakthrough." *National Geographic*, February 1997, pp. 36–57.

MacLean, Edna Ahgeak. *Abridged Inupiaq and English Dictionary*. Alaska Native Language Center, University of Alaska Press: Fairbanks, AK, 1995.

People of Snow and Ice. Time-Life Books: Alexandria, VA, 1994.

Romanov's Russian/English, English/Russian Dictionary. Pocket Books: New York, 1973.